Born of Betrayal

A tender, passionate tale of love and destiny set amidst the turbulence of pre-Camelot Britain, centering on the compelling, and ultimately tragic union between King Arthur's parents, Ygraine and Uther Pendragon.

A unique portrayal of many of the legendary characters from the Arthurian legend, *Born of Betrayal* is far from the typical story as it has been told. It focuses on the tumultuous lives preceding the reign of Arthur, and reveals fascinating answers to so many eternal mysteries surrounding the characters and events of 5th century Britain, bringing the legend out of the realm of myth and into reality.

Born of Betrayal contributes greatly to our understanding of the divine role in, not only the rise of Camelot, but life itself. A myriad of spiritual messages are intricately woven throughout the story that touch deep places of the heart and soul. The result is a beautiful tapestry of truth.

*A haunting tale of prophecy, passion, and the
fulfillment of destiny.
But above all,
an enchanting story of eternal love.*

Prepare to embark upon a magical journey...

Born of Betrayal

~ A Spiritual Novel ~
by

Lacey Hawk

To see a world in a grain of sand,
And a heaven in a wild flower,
Hold infinity in the palm of your hand,
And eternity in an hour.

William Blake

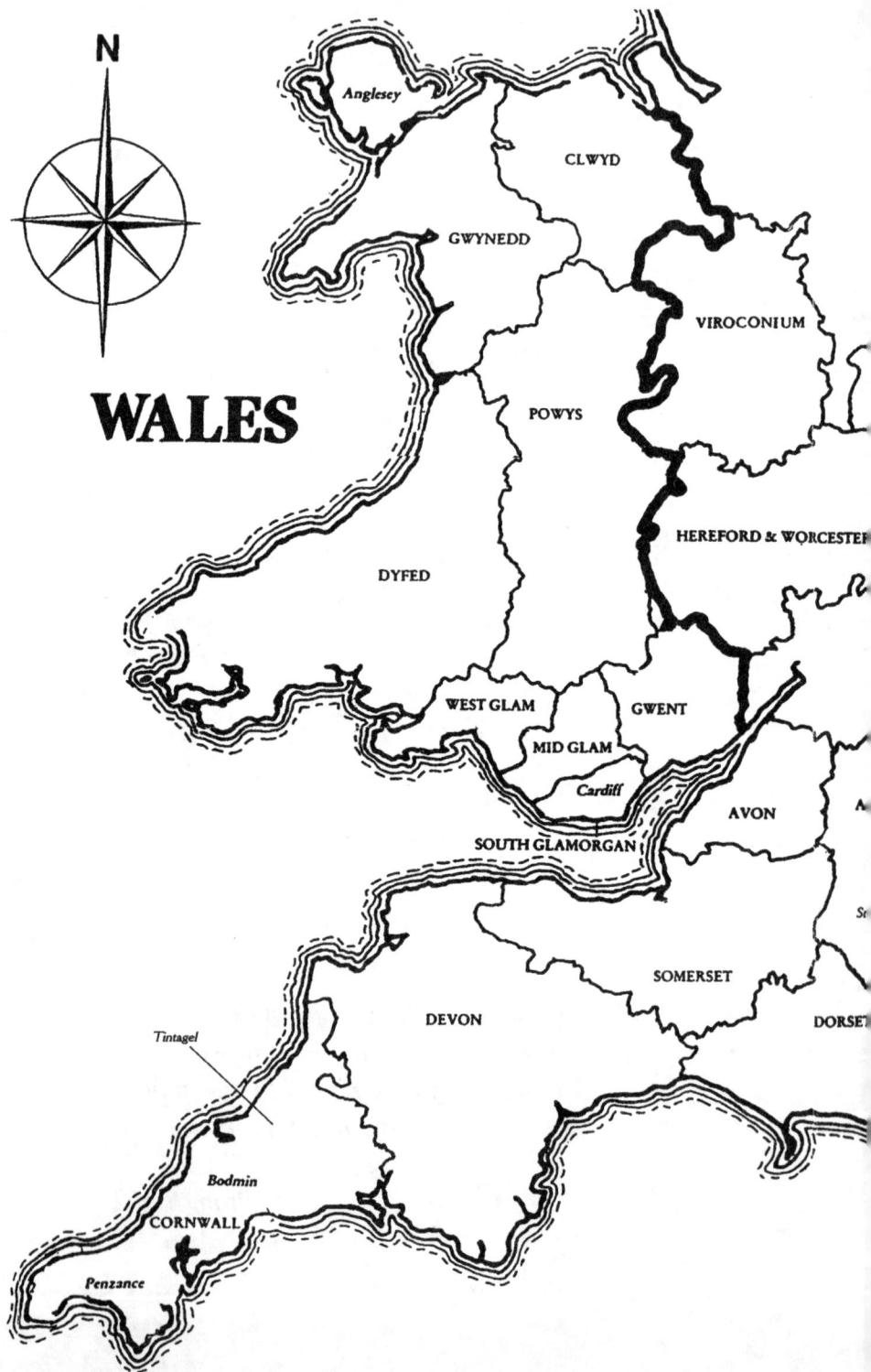

N

WALES

Anglesey

CLWYD

GWYNEDD

VIROCONIUM

POWYS

HEREFORD & WORCESTER

DYFED

WEST GLAM

GWENT

MID GLAM

Cardiff

SOUTH GLAMORGAN

AVON

SOMERSET

DORSET

DEVON

Tintagel

Bodmin

CORNWALL

Penzance

| OM | | 20 | | 40 | | 60 |
| OKm | 20 | | 40 | | 60 | | 80 |

WEST
MIDLANDS

NORFOLK

LEICS

CAMBS

NORTHANTS

SUFFOLK

WARWICKSHIRE

BEDS

GLOS

HERTS

OXON

BUCKS

ESSEX

EBURY

BERKS

LONDINIUM

WILTSHIRE

SURREY

ehenge

HAMPSHIRE

KENT

Winchester

Salisbury

W. SUSSEX

E. SUSSEX

Brighton

ENGLAND

Born of Betrayal

Published by
Blue Pearl Press
8950 West Olympic Boulevard, #416
Beverly Hills, California 90211
888 BOOKS 08

ISBN 1-891099-21-3

Cover design by Vince Anido and Christopher Hartman
Cover graphics by Vince Anido

This book is dedicated to humanity.
May peace reside within...
For that is where Camelot is born.

❧❧●❧❧

Foreward

Before you come here your divine Self (spirit) chooses a purpose... a destiny. A pre-destined course, or map, is charted out by you and imprinted within the soul. Once incarnated, if you follow the map, or path on which your divine Self leads you, 'the way' is easy. This is not to say that you will have an easy life, for that may not be what you have chosen to experience. What you will have is acceptance. You will not struggle with what is pre-chosen. With acceptance there is inner harmony and tranquility, no matter the experience.

When you incarnate you pass through the veil of forgetfulness. You forget your imprint, and it is the job of the spirit to guide the mortal Self to experience what is pre-chosen. Your spirit is always tapped in to your soul and is constantly relaying information regarding your pathway.

Every force of your nature is to live life from the guidance of the spirit so that the pathway to fulfilling your destiny unfolds with ease.

With incarnation, you are given free-will. This means that you have the power to create anew in every now moment.

You are free to make choices that may alter your pre-chosen course of destiny. The outcome of these free-will choices is known as 'fate'. You may still fulfill your destiny, but 'the way' may not be smooth. When you allow your free-will to solely take charge of your life you may have experiences that are not in your highest good, and you will feel the weight of fate.

The optimum goal is to serve Self through the merging of your free-will (materiality) and your divine-will (spirituality). This result is what is perceived as your God-will. By mortally, willingly choosing to lead your life in conjunction with your divine guidance you bring Heaven and Earth together within you. You live the heavenly life, the perfect life, of wisdom and power right here on Earth. In essence, you become Christed. You remember (re-member), becoming One within your being. You are still creating in every now moment, for you are manifesting a divine ideal into reality. You experience co-creation between your divine Self and your mortal Self, which is why you are here.

This Oneness, this communion of material and spiritual existence, in truth, already is. In order to recognize and perceive this truth, the illusion of separation that humanity resides in must transcend to a higher level of conscious awareness.

Letting go of control is the most difficult process, for the ego is powerful within the mortal mind. However, faith is more powerful, for it is the God within. When you hold in your heart a firm foundation of faith, the ego, which is the ultimate illusion, has no power. Hence, you find it easier to live and be in the moment.

You will know when you are operating from your God-will for your choices will bring inner peace. Free-will choices that are not in your highest good will bring inner turmoil. Pay attention to your feelings, your intuition, your inner voice. Be conscious of what is occurring inside of you and why. The truth is within, and it will set you free.

Jesus himself did not experience a life of grandeur. Not material grandeur, but spiritual grandeur. (Conception of the word "material" being mortal, "spiritual" meaning immortal.) Jesus held his mortal experiences within immortal thought. Thus, he emanated an aura of tranquility at all times, no matter the experience. Even with crucifixion, there was tranquility. For as much as the experience was mortal, his thoughts in relation to the experience were immortal. He accepted his destiny. He moved through it with ease and grace. He fully merged his free-will with his divine-will. He asked for, and received guidance from the God within, in all things. Thus, he lived as a Christed being, a Christed life. He said, "I am the way, the truth, and the life. Follow me."

"The way" ~ mortal life through immortal perception
"The truth" ~ claiming his divinity and living the life
"The life" ~ the living expression of God
"Follow me" ~ my example

Whatever choices you make throughout your lifetime, the most important thing to be aware of is you choose everything. Accept responsibility for your choices, for you are the only one that can ever truly be held accountable.

Born of Betrayal is an allegory of the information referred to herein, as well as of other important life issues. May you grasp the deeper meaning within these pages, for there is profound wisdom to be gained. Learning through wisdom is far superior to learning through woe.

Enjoy the journey upon which you are embarking. May it lead to a greater understanding of your own journey.

❧ *Prologue* ❧

The dark ages... the year 455...

He stood at the mouth of the cave... waiting. He knew she would come. It was destiny that would bring her to him.

She rode hard and fast, some unknown force drawing her. To where, she knew not.

The light of the full moon spilled out across the meadow, guiding her stallion, as if he knew the way.

There was a chill in the air, and even though the breath from the horse's nostrils was evident, the heat coursing through her veins made her heart pound with anticipation.

Unaware of time, she knew not how long she had ridden. But when she reached the cave, she knew her journeys' end.

There he stood, a God-like figure framing the mouth of the cave, the glow of candlelight from within surrounding him.

She slid from the horse's back, and without hesitation, climbed the mossy slope in front of the cave.

He held his hand out to her, and she placed her trembling one in his.

Through breathless lips, in her silken, French accent, she whispered, "Am I dreaming? I know not why I have come here. Only that my heart has brought me."

The moonlight reflected off of the pendant she wore... a pentacle. The silver star within the gold circle appeared radiant as it rested against the outside of her cloak.

"Evanona, you have come to fulfill your destiny," he replied warmly.

With that, he led her into the cave.

Two hours passed before the two emerged. He helped her onto her mount, his hands lingering about her waist, not wanting to let her go, but knowing he must. His heart was still pounding with the aftermath of what was shared between them.

He kissed her hand gently, and when he raised his entrancing, deep blue eyes to meet hers, there was a tear trickling down her cheek, the moistness glistening on her face in the moon-glow. His heart jolted in his chest at the sight, for she was the most enchanting creature he had ever laid eyes upon.

She whispered down to him, "I know I am not dreaming, for the love I feel is too real. I do not question the happenings this evening, for I know it was destiny that brought me here. But I have one question before I go."

She paused then asked, "What is your name, my beloved?"

He gazed into her eyes and replied, "My name is Merlin."

❧ *One* ❧

The castle was quiet and dark except for a faint glow in Corelia and Rodric's quarters.

Corelia had been nanny to Evanona, and Rodric was stable-master. They both felt as though Evanona was their own daughter, so close to their hearts she was.

Though British themselves, their service had once been in Brittany, a northwestern region of France. They had accompanied Evanona's mother there, who was British as well, when she wed Evanona's father, a French nobleman.

When Evanona was two, her mother, extremely home sick, left France with her other daughter and went back to Britain to live with relatives. Due to her father's demands, Evanona was left behind in his care.

The servants remained in Brittany, and having had no children of their own, Corelia and Rodric lovingly helped to raise the child and watched her adoringly as she grew into the beautiful woman she now was. Evanona was now Duchess of Guent, and grateful to be back in their homeland, they served her still.

Rodric stood guard outside the door, pacing as if the child

being born inside were his own. He was a thin man of medium height, and there was a fragile look to him. He ran his hands nervously through his sandy brown hair, his hazel eyes revealing his concern.

It was only fitting that Corelia should midwife this child of Evanona's, just as she had done when Evanona's daughter, Morgause was born. However, this birthing was much different.

Morgause was the Duke's daughter and was born in Evanona's own bed. This child, thought to be the Duke's, would be born in the servants' quarters, as there would be great need to be close to the outer courtyard and stables this night.

Everyone knew what part each would play concerning the special babe being born.

The Duke was gone. He had been gone for a full fortnight, and was not expected back for two more. Two-year-old Morgause was in deep slumber in the nursery, which was adjacent to Evanona's chamber. All in the castle slept except for the three bound by loyalty to the Merlin.

In the outer courtyard a dark, hooded, cloaked figure moved gracefully and without sound toward the servants' quarters. A slight rap on the antechamber door gained him entry without question. It was he... the Merlin.

"How long has she been labouring?" He inquired of Rodric as he entered.

After closing the door, Rodric turned and gazed at the handsome face of the Merlin, whose powerful form seemed to tower over him.

"Several hours sir, but it seems like days," Rodric replied anxiously as he again ran his hands through his hair.

The Merlin turned away abruptly. "I wish to be with her," he stated firmly.

Rodric shook his head and said emphatically, "But it

wouldn't be proper sir."

The Merlin sneered at Rodric's reply and rapped impatiently on the inner chamber door.

The look in Corelia's sea green eyes when she opened the door immediately alarmed him.

"She's not well sir," she said, her words breathless and ragged as her shaking fingers tucked stray strands of sable hair back into the knot at the top of her head. "I don't know what's wrong, but the babe is stuck."

A deep moan could be heard from within as another contraction tore through Evanona.

Rodric remained in the doorway as the Merlin moved past Corelia and glided across the room, accessing the situation with the eyes of one who knows all.

Evanona was very weak, her skin glistening with perspiration, having suffered an agonizing labour.

Corelia immediately returned to her side and began to dab her forehead with a cool, damp cloth as the contraction subsided.

"My beloved, you have come as you said," Evanona whispered, her words barely heard.

The Merlin knelt beside her, his eyes drinking in her beauty. Her long, dark curls were spilling over the beside, the slight tinges of red in it glinting. Her brown eyes reminded him of a doe's, as she looked upon him with complete and innocent trust.

As he continued to look upon her with adoration, he began to tenderly stroke her hair as he said lovingly, "Yes my love. I am here to make sure our child is taken to safety. The arrangements have been well laid."

The babe was to be taken by Corelia and Rodric to the sanctuary in Avebury where she would be completely protected until the time came for her to fulfill her destiny.

The Duke would be informed that the child was stillborn,

and so devastated were the two loyal servants, that they took indefinite leave.

Sadness filled Evanona's eyes, and witnessing her sorrow, the Merlin filled with compassion. He leaned closer to her, speaking from the depths of his heart. "I know this is hard for you my beloved Evanona. But I assure you, Britain's future lies in our hands, and in the hands of this child, and ultimately in the hands of the child she will bear."

Evanona weakly attempted to smile, and she wrapped her fingers around the pentacle lying over her heart. She looked deeply into his eyes as she said, "I question you not my love."

Corelia, filled with despair, took a step back as the Merlin leaned forward to place a gentle kiss on Evanona's brow. As he withdrew, Evanona exhaled her last breath, her head falling limply to the side.

Consumed with shock, the Merlin grabbed Evanona's shoulders and shook her. "Evanona!" He shouted.

Gripped with sheer panic, he looked to Corelia. "What has happened!" He barked.

Agony filled Corelia's eyes as she turned to look at Rodric, who stood wide-eyed in the open doorway. "Oh God," she cried out. "We've lost her, and the babe too."

The Merlin rose to his feet, his voice constricted with torturous pain. "Cut the babe out!"

Corelia trembled uncontrollably, and Rodric hurried to her side. He put his arm around her to comfort her as she shook her head and stammered, "But, but... sir..."

"Do it now!" He commanded.

"I cannot sir... I'm sorry," she cried out in distress.

The Merlin swiftly pulled out his dagger and did only what was rightfully his to do.

Afterward, he held the bloodied babe in his hands and gazed deeply into her eyes. As she let out a lusty yell, he held her up above his head and let out a resounding war cry.

Corelia and Rodric watched from behind in awe as the babe stopped crying and relaxed in the Merlin's grasp. The look in his eyes was almost inhuman as he turned slowly and lowered the babe into Corelia's arms, who wrapped her in warm blankets.

Her hands trembled, and tears spilled from her eyes as she, and Rodric filled with grief at the loss of their beautiful Evanona. Their grief would soon be replaced with love for the babe Corelia now held.

The Merlin turned back to Evanona. As he began to cover her up, he noticed the pentacle lying in her half-open palm. Leaning over, he took it from around her neck. Pulling the hood back from his head, he slowly sank to his knees and gazed at the star in his own palm for several moments.

"It was a gift from her sister on her wedding day sir," Corelia whispered softly, her voice quivering as tears continued to spill from her eyes.

"Carry out the plan," the Merlin said blankly, all feeling draining from his body and his heart, as though he were the one bleeding.

He rose to his feet, bringing the hood back up over his long, black hair. Then he turned slowly and made for the door.

"But sir," Corelia's voice halted him. "What shall we call her?"

Without turning, he replied numbly, "Ygraine. She is... Ygraine."

He left without looking back.

❦ *Two* ❧

The journey from Guent to the sanctuary at Avebury was a long one, and as it came into view, all that could be seen over the towering walls covered with ivy was the top of the chapel belltower.

Though somewhat formidable, a welcome sight it was to Corelia, who had been bouncing in the back of a small wagon with Ygraine for several days.

Rodric had only stopped long enough to rest two or three hours at a time, as the Merlin had made very clear the urgent need to make haste. They were instructed to keep to the road, and speak to no one.

Ygraine had barely uttered a sound the entire journey, and to Corelia's amazement, she had been 'all eyes'. She had seemed to be 'seeing things' at all times... even now.

"Following the fairies' flight, are you little one?" Corelia cooed as the wagon came to a halt.

"I tell you Rodric, this child's got the sight. She's got her mum's beauty and her papa's magic, I say."

Rodric replied, "Magic! I don't believe in magic. Seeing is believing, and I haven't seen any magic."

"Careful what you say," Corelia cautioned. "The Merlin might hear you. They say he has ways of seeing and hearing everything."

Despite his skepticism, Rodric held a deep respect for the Merlin and was honoured to be of service to him, and he paid heed to Corelia's warning. Although he did not believe in magic, he decided it better to keep quiet, and he looked over his shoulder as he climbed from the wagon.

He nervously looked around in all directions, making sure there was no one in sight that might question their arrival, then quickly walked toward the outer gate. Upon reaching it, he knocked three times on the door with the heavy iron knocker.

Soon after, the small window box slid open and a maiden asked quietly, "What is the password?"

Rodric replied, just as quietly, "Divine trinity."

The door was immediately opened.

"Leave the horse and wagon. They will be tended to," the maiden whispered.

Rodric hurried back to assist Corelia, with Ygraine, from the wagon, and the three were admitted inside.

They were quietly taken through a beautiful rose garden, which totally surrounded the inside walls of the sanctuary. The scent was heavenly, and Corelia had such a desire to pick some, but decided it best not to just yet.

Ygraine's eyes were flitting back and forth, enjoying her own scenery.

The sanctuary itself was quite large. It seemed to Corelia to be as big as the castle at Guent. She had been anticipating some horrible prison that the Merlin had sent them to, but this place was something Corelia had only dreamed of. The smell of roses and the sound of birds singing made Corelia's heart so light, she was beginning to think she was seeing Ygraine's little fairies too!

As they reached the main entry of the edifice, they were instructed to wait outside. The maiden entered, and they watched as she disappeared through another door at the far end of the room, closing it behind her.

A few moments later the door re-opened, revealing a woman of apparent authority, dark hair peeking out from under the headdress of her habit, her pale blue eyes emanating pure love.

"Come inside... please," she called out in a soothing voice as she made her way to them.

The three were welcomed into a large room furnished with a desk and several chairs, which was obviously used for receiving outsiders. The rest of this sacred place was off-limits to the outside world.

"I am the abbess, Mother Marta," she said cordially. "Please, have a seat."

Despite Mother Marta's graciousness, Corelia was still a bit ill at ease. She sat down, and holding Ygraine close, she nervously pulled the beautiful shawl that the babe was wrapped in more snugly about her as she began rocking her gently. Rodric stood near her, his head lowered respectfully.

Mother Marta sensed Corelia's discomfort and attempted to dispel it with a pleasant smile as she said, "I trust your journey was safe." She then gave them both a look of compassion. "Although you must be quite exhausted."

Corelia and Rodric looked at each other, and Corelia let out a weary sigh as they both nodded.

Mother Marta offered them a sympathetic look before saying, "It is rare that we allow those from the outside world within these walls." Her eyes filled with radiating warmth. "But I have faith in the Merlin." She glanced down at Ygraine yawning in Corelia's arms, and the affection in her eyes intensified.

After a brief pause, Mother Marta pulled her gaze away

and said, "You are welcome here, and will remain under our protection until the Merlin decides otherwise. There is a small cottage on the grounds, which has been prepared for you. I believe you will find it most comfortable. I ask only that you respect our privacy and quiet, and keep to the cottage as much as possible. Although, you may feel free to walk the gardens at your leisure. Your meals will be served to you by Leanna, who received you at the front gate, and any needs, you have only to request them."

"Thank you," Corelia responded. A genuine smile spread across her face, and she could feel herself begin to fully relax.

Mother Marta was again drawn to Ygraine. She stepped closer and gazed down at the sleeping babe. She touched her cheek tenderly and whispered, "Beautiful."

After a moment, she looked from Ygraine to the proud face of Corelia, then at Rodric and said, "Come... walk with me. I am sure you will want to rest a while. Supper will be served at dusk."

Corelia rose from her chair, and she and Rodric silently followed Mother Marta to a small stone path which led to the back of the sanctuary. As they approached the cottage some fifty feet away, the faint sound of a child giggling broke through the silence.

"Did you hear a child?" Corelia questioned as she and Rodric stopped, looking around.

Mother Marta turned and replied, "That is only Morella. One of the sisters found her by the river's edge five years ago. Abandoned she was, and the tiniest little thing. She was just a babe, no more than two moons in age. We took her in and have cared for her since."

They continued toward the cottage, Mother Marta now at Corelia's side. "She tries our patience at times though," Mother Marta said, then tilted her head slightly to the side. "Different, she is."

"How so?" Corelia asked.

"She seems to be in another world most of the time," Mother Marta replied. "We hear her talking and laughing, carrying on when there is no one there. Says she sees things too." She chuckled and shrugged her shoulders. "Quite an imagination, I suppose."

Corelia smiled knowingly and looked down at Ygraine in her arms. "Seems to me Morella and little Ygraine here may have much in common."

ುॐ•ॐಲ

The next few days were spent resting and getting familiar with their new surroundings.

Rodric was extremely weary from the long journey, and did nothing but eat and sleep for several days. In fact, he was so tired that he found eating to be a chore.

He thought of the Merlin often, wondering if he would ever forget the look of agony on his face at the loss of Evanona.

As he lay on the bed resting one afternoon, he recalled the Merlin's words when he and Corelia were given their instructions regarding Ygraine.

He had come to them a moon before her birth. He had appeared from nowhere in their quarters.

They were just finishing their evening meal when a loud crackling drew their attention to the roaring fire. A log shifted suddenly and rolled from the fire onto the brick hearth, making its way slowly toward the wool rug directly in its path.

Rodric jumped up, searching with his eyes for some tool that might be used to halt the logs progress.

"Allow me", the Merlin said, his voice nearly causing a dual case of heart failure as Corelia's "Sweet Jesus!" and

Rodric's "Good God!" rang out at the same time, both servants simultaneously clutching at their chests.

They looked upon him in total disbelief as the Merlin picked up the searing, red-hot log with his bare hands, and placed it back into the flames. As he turned, he was very aware that both were staring at him in wide-eyed amazement, Rodric's mouth gaping.

"Close your mouth man, lest a fly decides to take up residence within those walls!" The Merlin said firmly.

Rodric's mouth snapped shut, and he swallowed hard before saying, "I can't believe what my eyes have witnessed. What kind of man appears from nowhere and plays with fire without gettin' burned?"

"No man I know," the Merlin replied flatly, dusting the ashes from his hands.

"This is some kind of trickery," Rodric continued. "Forgive me sir, but I don't believe in magic, and I see no other logical explanation."

"I assume you are an intelligent man," the Merlin stated. "But you must learn to see with more than your eyes. Only then will you know the true meaning of power."

"They say knowledge is power," Rodric declared. "And besides, I'm not interested in power. I'm a simple man sir. My only cares are for my lovely Corelia, my Lady Evanona, her wee one, and that babe she's carrying."

Corelia rushed over, placing herself between the two men. She said, with enthusiasm, "I know who you are sir. My Lady said you'd be coming."

"I wasn't finished talking to the gentleman here," Rodric said impatiently, pushing her aside. "As I was saying, I care about 'em, and I'd protect them with my life. And that goes for you too, being you're directly connected to that babe my Lady's carrying." He raised his eyebrows. "If you know what I mean sir."

The Merlin's eyes twinkled with amusement at Rodric's gesture, but he remained silent.

Rodric took a deep breath before continuing, "Truth is, the real power is the power of love. So I guess I'm a powerful man all right. Real powerful."

"Indeed," the Merlin remarked, nodding his head, a smile threatening the corners of his mouth. He knew at that moment that he could completely trust the two standing before him. But he also knew that Rodric had much to learn.

Looking back now, Rodric's heart filled with sadness for the Merlin. He felt his own grief at losing Evanona, and he imagined the Merlin's to be ten times stronger.

"Love is power all right," Rodric thought to himself. "But losing it can make a man grow cold. It can harden his heart."

Rodric let out a sigh and began to reflect further upon the past events.

After the birth of Ygraine, he had returned Evanona to her own bed while Corelia made her way to the stables with the babe. Ygraine would spend the night safely tucked away in the hay in a vacant stall.

After having performed the most difficult task of his life, Rodric stepped out into the hall from Evanona's chamber, and found Corelia entering the nursery. He waited for the door to close before letting out a quivering sigh, and a tear slipped down his cheek before forcing himself to regain his composure. He then headed outside to begin the task of digging a tiny grave to substantiate the story of the babe being stillborn.

The false grave had been marked with a small wooden cross, and a priest was summoned to bless Evanona. Burial arrangements for her had been made, but the priest was extremely distraught over the fact that the babe had already been buried without receiving any kind of benediction. To appease him, he was taken to the grave sight to perform his blessing.

Word was sent to the Duke that both mother and babe had died in childbirth. He would not receive the message for at least three days, and most likely would not have returned before he had originally intended even after the news arrived. His and Evanona's was an arranged marriage, and the Duke being a brusque, heartless man, cared very little for his wife or his daughter. Morgause was to be looked after by a friend of Evanona's until his return.

It had been a long night, but Rodric had made certain that all of the aforementioned duties had been taken care of while Corelia remained in the nursery rocking the sleeping Morgause in her arms one last time.

By dawn the castle was in an upheaval. Covered with perspiration and dirt, Rodric made his way back to the nursery to retrieve Corelia.

He entered the room, only to find her gone. He walked quietly toward the sleeping child, but his emotions were so raw that he could not bear another farewell. He blew her a kiss and headed back to Evanona's chamber, knowing that he would find Corelia there.

As he opened the door, his heart wrenched at the sight of Corelia standing at the foot of the bed clinging to Evanona's favorite shawl, her body wracked with sobs.

He left the door open, and moved to Corelia's side, barely holding his own tears back. "It's time," he said quietly.

Corelia's sobs intensified as he gently put his arm around her. She resisted, still clinging to the shawl as he guided her from the room.

As they walked through the doorway, she looked over her shoulder at Evanona's peaceful face. Rodric pulled the door closed, and she fell into his arms, continuing to sob.

He did his best to console her, but her grief was deeply embedded. Then feeling a sense of urgency, he quickly led her down the corridor and back to the stables to recover the still sleeping Ygraine.

Returning from his reverie and watching Ygraine now, wrapped in Evanona's shawl, being rocked by his lovely Corelia, Rodric's heart swelled with pride. He knew this child was special, and even though he balked at Corelia's remarks of her being magical, somewhere deep inside of him he knew it was true. Even now, Ygraine was reaching up with tiny fingers to grasp at something unseen.

Thinking back again to the night the Merlin first appeared in their quarters, the Merlin's voice echoed in Rodric's memory. "Raise the child as your own. Only when the time is right will she be told the truth. For only then, will she accept the truth. Someday you will all understand the importance of what I ask of you. For now, it is better not to know."

Rodric smiled as he thought, "If the Merlin was right about seeing with more than your eyes, then this child is destined for great power." And that thought suited him just fine.

He closed his eyes, and as he drifted off to sleep, Evanona's face entered into his mind, and he held it there. A peacefulness washed over him as he realized, that no matter the outcome, Evanona had fulfilled her destiny.

❧ *Three* ❧

On the third day at the sanctuary, Corelia was sitting in the garden with Ygraine cradled in her arms. She rarely put the babe down. The love she felt for her already ran deep.

She looked at the sweet, angelic face staring up at her and said, "I'll never leave you little one. No matter what happens, I'll always be by you, watching over you. Nothing can separate us. I made that promise to your mum, and now I make it to you. Heaven help anyone who tries to take you from me."

Ygraine tilted her head slightly to one side, as if she were deeply trying to understand what was being said.

The sound of a child's laughter broke Ygraine's concentration, and she jerked at the interruption.

Corelia looked behind her, for the sound seemed to come from behind the cottage. She caught a glimpse of bright red hair just before it disappeared. Sensing that the child was waiting for the right moment to again peek out at them, she kept her focus on the back of the cottage. Sure enough, a few strands of hair preceded a pair of big blue eyes.

"Come on out Morella," Corelia called out softly. "It's all right. I won't hurt you. Come, sit here beside me." She patted the empty space on the stone bench next to her.

Morella stepped out slowly and began tiptoeing gently towards them, making a special effort to be very quiet.

"You don't have to sneak around. No one will harm you," Corelia said, reassuringly.

Morella put her index finger to her lips. "Shhh... You must be quiet," she whispered. "Or you'll scare that fairy off your lap, and I want to see it up close before it flies away."

Morella's eyes got bigger as she drew closer. There was profound amazement in her voice as she said, "That's too big to be a fairy. What is it, a dwarf?"

Corelia began to laugh, and she realized that Morella had probably never seen a baby before.

"It's not a dwarf, it's a baby," Corelia stated, smiling broadly.

Morella stared down at Ygraine in disbelief and said, "I never seen one a those before. Where'd you find it? Are you gonna keep it? I could keep it if you don't wanna keep it."

"Slow down child," Corelia said, chuckling while she reached for Morella's hand. "Come, sit down."

Morella sat on the bench, but her wide eyes were glued to Ygraine.

Corelia began to explain. "First of all, I'm going to keep her because she belongs to me. I'm her mum."

"Her mum?" Morella questioned, wrinkling up her little nose.

"Yes Morella. All of us start out looking like little Ygraine here. Then we grow up a little at a time, till we're all grown up like me."

"You sure she's not one a the little people?" Morella asked, uncertain of what she was hearing.

"I'm sure," Corelia replied. "Like I said, I'm her mum."

"What's a mum?" Morella asked, gazing up at Corelia with questioning eyes.

Corelia's heart saddened. She put her arm around Morella and pulled her closer to her. She said, "A mum is someone who loves you and protects you. She teaches you right from wrong and helps you grow up to be a good person, happy and strong."

"You gonna help that baby grow up?" Morella asked, pointing at Ygraine.

"Most certainly," Corelia replied firmly.

Morella's eyes filled with tears as she said, "Who's gonna help me grow up since I don't have no mum?"

"Don't the kind sisters here take care of you?" Corelia asked.

Morella's voice quivered as she replied, "They feed me real good, but they're always busy praying to God." She put her face in her hands and began to weep. "I'll never grow up. I got nobody to help me."

Corelia put her arm around the child, pulling her head to lean against her ample bosom. "Ah, everybody grows up," she soothed. "Some of us just have a harder time of it than others."

Corelia suddenly had a brilliant thought. "Tell you what. If you want me to, I'll help you grow up, and you can help me help little Ygraine here grow up. What do you say to that?"

Morella looked up at Corelia, tears streaking her dirty face. She puffed out her little chest as she said, "I'll help. I'm a good helper."

"I think you're going to be the best helper anyone ever had," Corelia said as she dabbed at Morella's tears with a corner of Ygraine's blanket.

"Would you like to start now?" Corelia asked.

"Yes ma'am, I would," Morella replied, straightening her back as if she were preparing to take on some brave task.

Corelia handed Ygraine to her and said, "Hold her for me. She gets heavy sometimes, and I don't trust just anybody holding her."

Morella's eyes bulged. "You want me to hold her?" She asked with apprehension.

Corelia laid Ygraine on Morella's lap and instructed her how to hold her safely. Morella wrapped her little arms around Ygraine like a child holding a doll. She looked down at Ygraine and began naturally rocking her back and forth saying, "I'm gonna take good care a you, and help you grow up. I'll never let no one hurt you."

Corelia could feel a lump forming in her throat as she watched the bonding that was occurring in front of her.

That day set the stage for the next seventeen years that would be spent at the sanctuary.

Morella was like a shadow to Corelia, and indeed the child was quite helpful. She helped to bathe Ygraine, to feed her, and kept her entertained with stories of the little people.

Ygraine slept between Corelia and Rodric, and many a night there were four in the bed, as Morella hated to leave and would pretend to fall asleep as it neared Ygraine's bedtime.

Eventually, Corelia asked to have Morella's small bed moved into the cottage, and Mother Marta gratefully agreed, saying that she had never seen the child happier.

The next five years were blissful. Corelia and Rodric's love for Ygraine grew deeper each day as they watched her grow. Neither of them spoke again of Evanona. In fact, her shawl had been safely put away shortly after their arrival, as the reminder was too painful.

Neither of them spoke of the Merlin either. Both were

secretly hoping that he would never appear again, allowing them to live out their lives forever here in peace and protection. However, on Ygraine's fifth birthday, the Merlin was to show himself, but not in a way anyone would have expected.

They had spent the day outside the sanctuary walls. This was the first time Rodric had given in to Ygraine's pleading to go out, as he had been given strict instructions to keep her within the walls at all times. But he knew that the confinement was beginning to smother Ygraine, and he too was feeling it.

Ygraine and Morella wore themselves out, running and playing like two captive butterflies set free.

Upon returning to the cottage, Corelia decided to treat the girls to a bath before bed.

Rodric started a fire and pulled the heavy wooden tub in front of it. He carried in pails of water and hung them to warm over the fire. The girls waited anxiously for him to complete the task of filling the tub. When he was through, he decided to sit outside and do a bit of whittling, giving the girls their privacy.

Corelia put a handful of fresh rose petals in the water as a special treat for the girls, then helped them into the tub. She pulled her rocker near the tub and relaxed into it, embracing the much-needed respite. She leaned her head back and closed her eyes, listening to the girls talk. Their usual conversation about the fairy kingdom had taken quite a turn.

Morella reclined dramatically and said, "When I get married I'm going to take baths in rose petals all the time."

"Me too!" Ygraine said excitedly. "For I am to be a queen, and live in a castle on a cliff."

"A queen? Yes, I think I'll be a queen too," Morella drawled out slowly, waving her hand as if she were dismissing someone.

"No, you will not be a queen, but you will live in a castle," Ygraine informed her.

"I will too be a queen," Morella demanded. "You don't know anything. You're a baby."

Corelia let out a sigh and glanced at the girls. "Now, now girls."

"I am not a baby," Ygraine argued. "And I do know many things. I see them in the fire."

Corelia bolted upright. "What do you mean you see things in the fire Ygraine?"

"I see pictures inside the flames," Ygraine explained.

Corelia rose and quickly scooped her up, wrapping her in a towel. She turned the rocker toward the fire and sat down with Ygraine on her lap. "Can you see anything in the fire now sweet child?" She questioned softly.

Intrigued, Morella moved closer, kneeling in the tub watching.

Ygraine's eyes glazed over as she gazed into the flames, her face taking on a profoundly intent look. After a few moments her body jerked suddenly, and she turned her head and buried her face in Corelia's neck.

"What's wrong child? What did you see?" Corelia asked, patting her on the back.

Awestruck, Morella repeated Corelia's question. "What did you see, what did you see?"

"I saw a man," Ygraine replied hesitantly. "I have never seen him before. I have seen another man in the fire, but not that one."

"What did he look like? Can you tell me?" Corelia prodded her gently.

Ygraine closed her eyes momentarily, then replied, "He had long dark hair, and he wore a cloak with a big hood on it." She paused, then whispered, "His eyes were powerful and he was looking right at me. I believe he wanted to speak to me."

"Look back into the fire child," Corelia urged. "Tell me what you see."

Ygraine pulled her face slowly away from the protection of Corelia's neck and looked back into the fire.

Wide-eyed, Morella also peered into the flames, desperately attempting to see something.

Again Ygraine's eyes glazed, and she became very intent as her vision formed and became clear. She spoke very slowly, as if in a state of trance. "I see him. He is looking at me."

She paused for several moments, then began responding, answering unheard questions. "Yes, I like it here... Yes, they are very good to me... No, I am not afraid of you." She sat up erect, her chin raised and stated, "I am not afraid of anything." Letting out a deep breath, she relaxed and continued, "Yes, I see many things in the fire."

She tilted her head to the side in a questioning manner and asked, "Destiny? I am not sure."

After a moment, her eyes grew wide and she said excitedly, "Oh, I think I like destiny!" She put her hand over her mouth and began to giggle.

Then she sobered and asked, "You will?"

Suddenly, her eyes lit up, and her voice held a tone of complete awe. "Yes, I see it... Oh..." She reached her little hand toward the fire, leaning forward, as if trying to retrieve something.

Corelia grabbed her hand and pulled it back with a jerk, which immediately snapped Ygraine from her trance. Ygraine and Morella both gasped.

"Sweet child, you almost burned yourself!" Corelia berated her. "What do you think you were trying to get?"

Ygraine looked at her quizzically, not understanding why

she would ask such a question. "Did you not see it?"

Morella frowned saying, "I didn't see nothing."

"No sweetness, I didn't see anything," Corelia replied. "I didn't hear anything either, but obviously you heard plenty. Can you tell me what you saw and what you heard?"

Ygraine nodded and said, "He asked me if I liked it here, and if you and papa were good to me. He asked me if I was afraid of him, and I told him that I am not afraid of anything." Again, she sat up regally. "He asked me if I saw things in the fire, and if I knew what destiny was."

"Did he tell you what destiny was Ygraine?" Corelia asked, not certain she wanted to hear the answer.

"Yes," Ygraine replied excitedly. "He told me that what I see in the fire is my destiny!" Again, she began to giggle before turning serious and stating, "He will come again to speak to me."

Then Ygraine sighed as she recalled her vision, her face taking on a look of euphoria as she said, "I saw a sword... a big sword. Oh, it was beautiful. It had red jewels on it. It was so beautiful. He said that someday that sword would have great meaning to me. Oh, I wanted it so badly."

"A sword?" Corelia asked in disbelief. "Why in the world would he be talking to you of swords child? Swords are for men, not little girls!"

Calming down, Corelia asked, "Did he say who he was Ygraine?" However, she already knew what her reply would be.

"He is Merlin," Ygraine stated firmly. "I think I like him." She tilted her head slightly, in deep thought. "Yes, I most certainly do like him."

Corelia became worried, and she called out for Rodric. He entered and walked directly over to pick Ygraine up off of Corelia's lap. He planted a big kiss on her cheek. "Are you ready for bed my sweet?" He asked, before spinning her around a couple of times.

Ygraine furrowed her brows in discontent. "Please do not spin me around like that papa. It makes my stomach feel funny. Besides, I am too big to be spun around."

"Too big!" Rodric said, laughing. "Since when are you too big?" He set her down on the bed that she and Morella now shared.

"Since I saw my destiny," Ygraine replied matter-of-factly. "I have much to prepare for," she stated, as she removed her towel and put on her sleeping gown.

Rodric looked questioningly at Corelia who was helping Morella to finish drying herself. He turned his back to allow privacy and asked, "What's this all about now?"

"Get in to bed child," Corelia said to Morella as she hurriedly assisted her into her sleeping gown. "You too Ygraine. It's been a long day."

Morella did as she was told as Rodric took what he had been whittling from his pocket and secretly handed it to Ygraine. "Maybe you'll be needing this for your preparation," he whispered.

Ygraine's eyes lit up at the sight of the wooden comb she took from Rodric. She threw her arms around Rodric's waist and squeezed him tight.

"You'll spoil that child to death!" Corelia scolded as she walked toward the bed where Morella lay, sleepy-eyed. "You get to bed now Ygraine."

Ygraine hurried into bed, and Corelia covered them both up, leaning over to kiss Morella on the forehead. To Ygraine, she said firmly, "No more talk of destiny tonight." Then her voice softened, and she smiled kindly at her. "Now go straight to sleep, and may you have a grand time playing with the fairies in your dreams." She kissed her on the cheek, and turned away as Ygraine rolled her eyes around in disgust.

Ygraine whispered to Morella, "Fairies? I will not be

dreaming of fairies. I will be dreaming about my Lord."

"Your Lord?" Morella asked. "You mean God?"

Ygraine made a face of disdain and said, "No, I do not mean God. I mean my Lord, King. The one I shall marry."

"Here we go again queenie!" Morella's voice grew louder, displaying her anger. "You talk like you're fifteen instead a five. I think I liked you better when you were a baby!"

Then she rolled away from Ygraine saying, "I'm tired, and I'm going to sleep now."

Holding the comb tightly in her hand, Ygraine fell asleep almost instantly, a huge smile on her face as she envisioned the man with bright blue eyes and a wondrous face that she had seen many times in the flames. She knew that some day he would be hers, for he was her destiny.

Unfortunately, Corelia was not as content as Ygraine as she explained the events of the evening to Rodric while they were lying in bed.

Rodric attempted to assure her that everything was all right by telling her that the Merlin was just concerned for the child's safety, but Corelia was not easily appeased.

"For someone who doesn't believe in magic, you're taking all of this a might lightly, don't you think?" Corelia asked. "And what about all that talk of destiny?"

Rodric replied, "I might not believe in magic, but I know that child is special. Gifted, I guess you might say. Listen to the way she talks. She's being raised by lowly servants, and yet she speaks like royalty. You and I both know she's destined for something great. Otherwise, there'd be no need for all this protection."

Rodric brought Corelia's hand to his lips and kissed her fingers gently, then tried to reassure her by saying, "Don't you worry about nothing Corelia. The Merlin knows we're taking good care of her, and besides, she's just a child.

Whatever her destiny is, it isn't going to happen just yet. We've both got plenty of time left with her."

He pulled Corelia closer to him and lifted her chin so that he could gaze into her eyes. He whispered lovingly, "You've got the most beautiful eyes I ever saw. They've still got the look of the sea."

He kissed her lips tenderly, then looked at her with all the love he felt for her and said, "No matter what happens, we'll always have each other."

He began nuzzling at her neck, and Corelia could feel her passion awakening from where it lay hidden for so long. She responded to his touch, but her mind was still not at ease, for she knew that she could not bear life without her Ygraine. She loved Rodric with all her heart, but the child had become her reason for living, and no matter what destiny the Merlin saw for Ygraine, she thought to herself, "It better include me, or there'll be hell to pay!"

She made the sign of the cross, silently asking forgiveness for her words, but meaning every one of them.

❧ *Four* ❧

Twelve years later...

At the sight of Ambrosius' stronghold West of Avon, temporary marching camps were being set up for the imminent invasion of the Saxons.

Torches burned inside and outside the thirty-five foot thick walls. In a tent in the center of the fortress, Ambrosius, High King of Britain, and his brother and right-arm, Uther the Pendragon*, had been laying strategies to cut off the Saxon attack.

Pieces of parchment were spread out over the large wooden, candlelit table where Ambrosius sat, his head in his hands.

Uther, agitated, was pacing back and forth behind him. He ran his fingers through his hair, shook his head in confusion and said, "Are you sure Hengist will attack here? Scouts have reported sightings of Saxon ships laying anchor South of Cornwall."

Ambrosius raised his head and turned to look at Uther.

*Pendragon: Head dragon; a title used for a supreme ruler.

He replied, "That was days ago. They will be landing any time now."

Disbelieving, Uther shook his head. Ambrosius attempted to reason with him. "Why land south? Gorlois' army is strong, and his defense of Cornwall would cause Hengist to lose too many men before reaching us here. This way he comes directly and saves his strength." Then he smiled smugly and said, "Little does Hengist know, that Gorlois is loyal, and his entire army aligns with us here."

Sobering and turning back around, there was a fire in Ambrosius' eyes as he stated, "We will be ready for the Saxon barbarians.

"Did your 'prophet' tell you this?" Uther questioned, raising a brow, a doubtful look on his face.

Ambrosius rose and turned to face his brother. "I know you do not approve of my 'prophet' Uther, but he has never steered me wrong. In spite of what men say about him being the spawn of the devil, the Merlin is honourable and wise."

He paused, entering a moment of deep thought, then said, "Men fear what they do not understand rather than respect it." He let out a sigh and said, " Besides you Uther, he is the only other man alive that I trust."

"I am sorry brother. I suppose that I do not have as much faith in your Merlin and his sight," Uther responded disapprovingly.

Ambrosius moved closer to Uther, standing just in front of him. He placed his hand on his shoulder and said with compassion, "I know it is hard for you to believe in anything you cannot see for yourself Uther, and there is strength in you because of that. But you will see in the days ahead, that had you relied upon what was seen, you would be waiting in Cornwall for Hengist, and he will attack here. I promise you that."

Uther was still not convinced, and responded flatly, "I

will believe it when I see it."

Ambrosius let out another deep sigh, turned, and walked back to the table. He sat down heavily in his chair and said, "Nevertheless, I have sent for the Merlin. Gorlois will join us when the Merlin arrives."

Uther resumed his pacing while Ambrosius sat rubbing his temples, his face strained.

Ambrosius was a tall, broad man with auburn hair and an aquiline nose, revealing his Roman ancestry. He had a thick scar running down the left side of his cheek, from his eye to his mouth, giving him to look of a seasoned warrior. But in contrast, his brown eyes held a warmth that was also felt in his heart.

Uther bore no resemblance to Ambrosius, even though they were full-blooded brothers. Ambrosius followed the Roman line from their fathers' side, while Uther took on the features of their mother, who was Welsh. He had a thick mane of light brown hair, an almost feminine, but strong face, with noticeable, penetrating blue eyes. Great strength was evident in his broad chest, and muscular arms and legs. A gold armlet encircled his right wrist. It was gifted to him by his mother on her deathbed, and he wore it always, even in battle.

When Uther was not warring, he was whoring. He had an infinite love for women of all breeds.

"You sent for me?" The voice of the Merlin broke the concentration of the two men.

Surprised, Uther spun around on his heel, his hand on the hilt of his sword. Ambrosius did not flinch, and he looked up to see the Merlin standing a few feet from the table.

"Thank you for coming," Ambrosius said cordially as he stood up, smiling. "Please sit. Be comfortable." Then turning toward Uther, he said, "Uther, please tell Gorlois we are ready for him."

Uther left the tent without a word, and the Merlin took the seat to Ambrosius' right at the table.

Ambrosius removed his crown and set it down in front of him. His face was drawn as he ran his fingers through his hair.

"You look weary Ambrosius," the Merlin commented, a worried tone in his voice.

The Merlin held a deep respect for this king, who he knew, would not live long enough to bring peace to this country that was in dire need of it.

"I am weary," Ambrosius replied. "This country is full of pagans. So full, I sometimes wonder why I fight for change." He shrugged his shoulders and sat down saying, "It would be easier to turn it over to the Saxons. My whole life has been dedicated to bringing some kind of order to this God forsaken place. And for what, I ask you. For what?"

Ambrosius stared at his crown, and sadness filled his eyes. "So that I can die a bloody, lonely death succeeded by my brother who will do the same after me?"

The Merlin laid his hand on Ambrosius' arm and said, with reassurance, "There will be reward for what you have started. Mayhaps not in your lifetime, or even in Uther's, but it will happen."

Ambrosius nodded and smiled warmly at the Merlin, then said, "I trust your words my friend. I only wish I could have had the luxury of a wife to warm my bed at night and an heir to carry on what I believe in."

The Merlin leaned closer, and he looked deeply into Ambrosius' eyes as he responded, "You have surrendered to your destiny Ambrosius, and for that I honour you, and offer you peace for your heart and mind. Although you have no heir to carry on, Uther will have."

The Merlin gazed at the crown and a hint of a smile tugged at the corners of his mouth. "Uther's son will be a great

king, and this country shall know peace for the first time."
He gazed back into Ambrosius' eyes. "What you do now
Ambrosius has value, and will be remembered."

Outside the tent, Uther approached with Gorlois, Duke
of Cornwall. As they reached the tent, Uther laid his hand
on the flap to enter, his gold armlet reflecting a nearby
torchlight. He paused, then turned with a look of controlled
anger on his face. "You rode in with so few men. Where is
the rest of your army?"

Ignoring Uther's disposition, Gorlois replied flippantly,
"They will get here when they get here."

He brushed past Uther and proceeded into the tent, letting
the flap fall closed behind him, directly into Uther's' face.

Gorlois was a large, burly man with hawk-like features,
gray hair and a full beard covering his face. He entered with
a flair, wearing a deep green cloak with gold border. A large,
gaudy ring was apparent on his right index finger.

Uther entered behind him, his face filled with contempt
as he watched Gorlois approach Ambrosius with a great show
of arrogance.

Ambrosius rose from his chair and took a few steps
toward Gorlois. The two men clasped forearms in greeting
as Ambrosius said, "It is good to see you Gorlois. The
strength of your army is greatly appreciated."

The Merlin also rose, and bowed slightly in Gorlois'
direction.

Gorlois' demeanor suddenly exhibited discomfort, and
he cleared his throat in an attempt to clear away his
nervousness. He glanced at Uther before saying to
Ambrosius, "I am loyal to my King, but in all honesty, I left
half my army in Cornwall."

Uther glared at Gorlois, his distrust of this man instinctive.
Gorlois felt Uther's unrelenting stare and quickly said to
Ambrosius, "No disrespect meant to you, or your... prophet."

He glanced at the Merlin, then tense, he looked back at Ambrosius saying, "But I am not convinced that the Saxons will attack here. I had to have peace of mind knowing my own lands are protected."

Uther was barely able to contain himself. He groaned and turned away, attempting to calm his emotions.

Ambrosius closed his eyes and sighed heavily. Then he looked at Gorlois, and though the look was disapproving, he nodded saying, "I understand your hesitancy to believe."

Ambrosius turned, intending to return to his seat at the table, but hesitated. Turning back to Gorlois, the look in his eyes became extremely intense, and he said, "I assure you, as I have assured my brother, that you shall see for yourself the truth shortly, for it is forthcoming."

Ambrosius then took his seat and pointed to the other chairs at the table. "Please sit. Let us decide together our defense... lest the Merlin be correct."

The corners of the Merlin's mouth twitched as he secretly enjoyed Ambrosius' comment.

The Merlin casually took his seat while Gorlois moved to the chair opposite Ambrosius and sat down heavily. Uther, several paces behind the Merlin, remained standing.

"Sit brother," Ambrosius urged. "It will be a long night."

"If the Merlin cares to move, I will sit. He occupies the position to your right, where I rightfully belong," Uther stated flatly, staring intently at the back of the Merlin's head.

Gorlois cleared his throat, obviously becoming uncomfortable at the prospect of a confrontation between Uther and the Merlin.

Ambrosius started to rise, but the Merlin held up his hands as if to surrender. He rose instead and turned to face Uther, bowing graciously. He said, with a tone of distaste, "Please, we have much more to discuss besides who sits in which chair."

He then turned to Ambrosius, placed his hand on his chest and bowed slightly saying, "I most humbly accept the chair to the King's left."

Again returning his attention to Uther, the Merlin remarked, "I am concerned about the strategies of war, not the geography of this table."

Ambrosius covered his mouth to cover a faint smile, realizing that Uther was somehow threatened by the Merlin's presence. He had never before known Uther to be threatened by anything... or anyone.

"May we all take our 'proper' places now?" Ambrosius asked, slight amusement in his voice.

The Merlin gracefully moved to his seat, as Uther, visibly embarrassed by the confrontation he had caused, thought to himself, "Why do I allow him to annoy me?"

Then he shrugged off his feelings, and without a word, he strolled over to take his place at the table thinking, "Ah well, it will all take care of itself when the Saxons invade from the south, and not as the Merlin has prophesied."

Gorlois, with a smug look on his face, had thoroughly been enjoying Uther's discomfort.

Ambrosius let out a sigh, then directed his attention to the Merlin. "Merlin, when do you anticipate the Saxon landing?"

"On the morrow, shortly after nightfall," the Merlin replied. "They will attack in the dead of night to try to catch you off guard."

Gorlois offered his opinion. "If this is true, then we should be waiting on the shore for the barbarians and drive them back into the sea before they have a chance to attack."

"They will only come again," Uther interjected, his warrior instinct taking hold. "No, we will wait for them here." He glanced at the Merlin. "If... they come, we will be ready for them." After a brief pause, his gaze was redirected to Ambrosius as he continued, "Gorlois' men could wait amongst the trees, attacking from the rear. We will meet them head-on and catch them in the middle. That way they cannot turn tail and run. There will be no place to run to."

Ambrosius nodded in agreement, then asked, "What of Lot and Leodogranz? Do we still lack their support? And what of Uriens of Devon?"

Uther leaned back in his chair and snorted in disgust. "Lot, the mighty Scottish Lord hides in Scotland behind the skirts of his new wife Morgause. Their marriage was to bring about an alliance, but Lot's only concern was for the Duke's holdings in Guent. Since the Duke's death two moons past, Lot has taken over the lands there where he allows his cousin, Leodogranz to reside. For this, Leodogranz would kiss his feet in public. He revels in his new surroundings, for he likes the feel of British soil under his boots. But neither of them could care less for the future of Britain. They had better wake up from their dream world, for 'if' the Saxons were to attack and defeat us here..." He again glanced at the Merlin. "...which they will not, Guent would be sacked, should they decide to move north."

Ambrosius leaned forward with his elbows on the table and began to rub his temples.

Uther took a long, deep breath, then said, "As for Uriens, I have heard nothing. We have always had his support in the past."

"I rode through Devon on the way here," Gorlois stated, pleased with himself for having the needed information. "Uriens fears that he is in a vulnerable position no matter what direction the Saxons attack from. He stays to protect his own."

Ambrosius stood up, fuming, his face turning red with anger. "Protect his own!" He shouted, slamming his fist down on the table, jarring everything on it.

Gorlois and Uther both jerked and sat up attentively.

Ambrosius leaned on his fists as he continued, "Everyone is so damned worried about protecting their own that they do not see that their self-centeredness not only hurts us, but themselves as well. Divided we are weak. Only together will be defeat Hengist's bloodthirsty appetite. We fight to protect all of Britain, not just bits and pieces!"

He took a long, deep breath, calming himself, and eased himself back into his chair. He looked to the Merlin for reassurance. "Merlin, what do you make of all of this?"

The Merlin replied confidently, "Uriens is loyal. He may surprise you and aid you when you least expect it. Leodogranz' strength of character, and his destiny will eventually bring about his loyalty." The tone is his voice changed to one of extreme intensity. "As for Lot, his wife is power hungry." He turned to look at Uther. "Because of her, he will be your Judas, and betray you."

Gorlois raised his brows, his dislike for Uther unveiled as the self-satisfied look on his face covered him like a blanket.

"Betray me?" Uther questioned, taken aback and totally dismayed.

"Yes Uther," the Merlin replied while nodding his head. Then he gazed into Uther's eyes, and with a somewhat softened tone in his voice, he said, "I know that you do not respect my ways Uther, but a time will come when you will ask for my favour, and I shall grant my favour for the good of all Britain. Know now, that in this lifetime you and I will not walk side by side, but we will learn to respect each other."

Uther held the Merlin's gaze and opened his mouth to question him further. Then suddenly, he decided to remain silent for he felt something unknown and inexplicable stirring within him. He quickly brushed away the sensation and excused it as anticipation of the potential battle ahead.

Ambrosius rose from his chair, stretching to try to relieve the stress in his aching muscles. He was content as he said, "I believe we have come to an agreement then. We will wait for them here. Gorlois will station his men inside the tree line, and wait for my signal to attack. On the morrow we will defeat the Saxon barbarians. Tonight, we rest."

Uther stood up, and his voice held a fierceness as he said, "I want it understood that Hengist, the great Saxon leader, is mine. I want his golden braid as a souvenir."

Gorlois chuckled. "He is all yours Uther. But if you need any assistance holding him down while you cut that braid off his head, let me know. I would be happy to oblige."

Uther's eyes grew dark, changing from blue to gray, his jaw clenching. "I will not only have his hair. I will have his head."

৯৯•৯৫

The next evening as the moon was rising, a lone rider, sweat pouring from both himself and his horse, rode into camp. "The Saxons have landed!" He shouted several times.

He reined in at the King's tent and Ambrosius immediately appeared from within. He grabbed the reins to steady the horse as the rider slid from the saddle. "How many?" Ambrosius inquired eagerly.

Several soldiers began to gather around as the rider shook his head in disbelief and replied, "A thousand. Mayhaps more."

"By Christ! Find Uther!" Ambrosius bellowed.

Uther emerged from within his tent half dressed and hurried toward Ambrosius, dragging his shirt and attempting to put on his boot. A woman's face peered out from the tent, pouting as she cried out, "Uther, what about me?"

Uther yelled over his shoulder, "Get the hell out of here

now!"

The rider shook his head in disapproval, and Ambrosius gave him a look of total disbelief.

"Good God Uther!" Ambrosius growled. "Only you would find a wench and bring her to the middle of a battlefield!"

He grabbed the rider by the arm and shoved him toward Uther's tent. "Get her out of here!"

The rider ran to do Ambrosius' bidding.

Then to Uther, Ambrosius said with intensity, "Hengist has landed. He brings a thousand barbarian pigs with him."

Uther raised a brow, which was a distinct mannerism of his, and rubbed his chin thoughtfully as he said, "I'll be damned. Your prophet was right."

"We will all be damned if you do not organize the troops at once!" Ambrosius roared. Then he shouted, "Gorlois!"

ৡৡ●ৡৡ

Meanwhile at the sanctuary, Ygraine and Morella were at evening prayer with the sisters. This had become a nightly ritual, as Mother Marta had been encouraging both of them to take their vows and join the sisterhood.

Morella, with eyes closed and head bent reverently, was in silent prayer, her wispy, shoulder-length red hair falling toward her face.

Ygraine's mind was whirling with her fire visions. Her cheek rested on her clasped hands as she stared absently into space. She unconsciously let out a sigh, drawing a sidelong glance from Morella. She gazed momentarily at Ygraine's face, strands of stray auburn curls sprinkled with golden highlights framing her flawless skin, a tiny beauty mark on her right cheek. Ygraine's lips were slightly parted, her lower lip a bit fuller than the upper. A person could get lost in her eyes, and suddenly Morella found herself doing so. She shook her head while elbowing Ygraine to shake her from her reverie.

Ygraine's head jerked up, and Morella's large blue eyes twinkled as she whispered, "Thinking about him again?"

Ygraine brushed her long braided hair over her shoulder as she whispered back, "Oh... I cannot stop. He is in my mind night and day."

Morella leaned closer, still whispering, a grave look in her eyes. "Well, he'd better be coming soon. You're seventeen. You're getting old."

Ygraine's eyes widened. "I am getting old? What does that make you, a crone?" She leaned into Morella, giving her a playful nudge.

They both covered their mouths to suppress the laughter that threatened to bubble forth.

Then Morella drew her brows together in a frown as she said seriously, "All I know is there's got to be more than this. We've been here far too long. I feel like a caged animal. I'm not spending the rest a my life praying."

Ygraine nodded in affirmation. "Nor I."

ৡৡ●ঔৡ

The moon was high and almost full, spilling bright light onto the battlefield.

Gorlois' men were in place, and Ambrosius' were ten deep, stretched across the outside of the stronghold. There were archers lining the fortress wall.

Ambrosius, Uther, and Gorlois were on horseback, the animals stamping their feet impatiently, sensing the anticipation of their riders.

Gorlois drew his mount near Ambrosius and said, "I should have listened to your prophet and brought my entire army. I will never doubt him again."

Ambrosius replied, "It is not the number of men that concerns me. In that respect, we are evenly matched. It is the difference in the way we fight that troubles me. We are disciplined warriors. They are hackers."

"Hackers or not," Uther said, his eyes sparkling. "We will shock the hell out of them."

Uther was feeling excitement running through him, and it was evident in his voice as he said, "I want to see the look in Hengist's eyes when he sees us waiting for him." Then he scanned the area quickly and asked, "Where is the prophet?"

Ambrosius pointed to the crest of a hill, high above the rear of the fortress. "There."

Though there was quite a distance between them, Uther and the Merlin made eye contact. Uther raised his sword in acknowledgment. The Merlin nodded once.

There was a low thunderous noise, and the ground began to rumble. The echoing of the Saxon's savage screams could be heard as they neared the stronghold.

Ambrosius shouted, "Gorlois, ready your men!" Then he laid his hand on Gorlois' shoulder and said, "Good luck my friend."

Gorlois nodded, suddenly feeling a sense of pride, and turned his mount, quickly closing the distance between himself and his men.

The Saxons were all on foot, except for Hengist who straddled a magnificent, muscular, flaxen war-horse. They flooded onto the clearing.

"Do not give the signal to charge until they are halfway between us and Gorlois," Ambrosius instructed Uther.

Uther did not reply. His gaze was on Hengist, a giant of a man unclothed from his waist up. He was extraordinarily tall, his lithe, muscular body bronzed from the sun. His golden hair was braided and hung from the top of his head to the middle of his back.

Uther's mount began stomping anxiously, and scraping at the ground with his hooves.

As the Saxons reached the center of the clearing, Hengist's horse reared, ready for battle.

Uther's eyes lit up, and he said, "I still want his braid, but now I want his horse too!" He flashed Ambrosius a brilliant smile as he raised the banner of the Red Dragon, which he claimed as his own, and yelled, "Charge!"

As Uther raised his banner, the moonlight reflected off of the gold band on his wrist causing a flash of shimmering light.

Simultaneously, Ambrosius raised his banner of the Lion as the signal for Gorlois to attack.

There seemed to be no element of surprise, but when Gorlois' men charged in from the rear, Hengist, who was headed determinedly toward Uther, suddenly turned his mount in Gorlois' direction. Gorlois met him halfway.

Hengist let out a primal scream, and with no effort at all, drove his spear through Gorlois' left side, just under his rib. He fell from his mount and lay writhing in pain on the ground.

Hengist let out another, triumphant scream then turned and made his way into the thick of the battle, hacking away at everything in his path.

Uther, witnessing the attack on Gorlois, filled with rage, and he rode purposefully after Hengist. Reining in suddenly, Uther remained at a standstill for a moment. Then, in a split second's timing, he made a choice that would change the course of destiny. The warrior in him should have chosen to pursue Hengist with a vengeance, but the heart in him chose to go to the aid of his ally instead.

One of Gorlois' men was attempting to drag him through the maze of bodies when Uther reached them. He was off his horse and had Gorlois, who was now unconscious, up and over his saddle in one swift movement.

Uther shouted to Gorlois' soldier, "There is a sanctuary in Avebury. Take him there. If he makes it that far, possibly they can help him."

Instantly, Uther began to experience an unsettling feeling in the pit of his stomach. He released a deep breath, and shook it off, then asked, "What is your name?"

"Callum sir," the soldier replied as he swung himself up onto Uther's horse behind Gorlois' limp body.

Uther gave the horse a firm slap on its flank shouting, "Godspeed Callum!"

As the horse galloped away, Uther turned in the direction of the Merlin. From the prophet's own mouth emanated the most blood-curdling cry Uther had ever heard. His skin began to crawl, and he shivered as the echoing scream, "No!!!!......" ran through his blood like cold steel.

෬ *Five* ෨

Before dawn Callum arrived at the sanctuary with Gorlois draped lifelessly across Uther's saddle. He slid from the horse's back and began pounding on the door of the front gate. Several minutes passed before the window box slid open.

"Who dares to intrude here at this hour?" Mother Marta questioned sternly.

Callum nodded respectfully, then replied, "I apologize for the intrusion, but the Duke of Cornwall has been wounded, and I have been instructed by the High King's own brother to bring him here."

Mother Marta gazed past Callum, and seeing the form of Gorlois hanging across the saddle, she asked, "How do I know that man is the Duke?"

Callum immediately turned and pulled Gorlois' ring from his finger. He handed it to Mother Marta saying, "Here is the Duke's ring. It has his crest engraved on it. That should be proof enough."

She inspected the ring carefully and said, "Wait here. I will get someone to assist you in carrying him inside."

As an afterthought she said, "I will hold on to the ring for now."

She closed the window box and quickly made her way to the cottage. She rapped on the door, which drew an immediate response from Rodric.

"I am sorry to wake you at this hour, but I need your assistance," Mother Marta said, offering him an apologetic look.

Corelia peeked past Rodric, her concern evident. "What is it Mother Marta?"

"The Duke of Cornwall has been wounded," Mother Marta replied. "The High King's brother sent him here to be tended to. The Duke is unconscious. His man will need assistance carrying him inside."

"Rodric, go," Corelia urged, pushing him out the door. "I'll get my herbs and salves. I may be able to help. Where will you take him?"

"I will have a bed brought to the receiving room. That will have to do," Mother Marta replied.

Rodric went with Mother Marta, and Corelia quietly began to gather up her healing herbs, a small bowl, and pestle.

Ygraine, having partially overheard the conversation, quietly slid from bed, not wishing to disturb Morella. "What has happened?" She whispered.

"Go back to bed child. It's nothing for you to be concerned with," Corelia whispered back.

"But I want to know," Ygraine pleaded.

"You heard me Ygraine. Go back to bed," Corelia scolded her firmly.

Ygraine stood and watched silently as Corelia finished gathering her things and left the cottage.

Morella sat up, rubbing her eyes to clear away the drowsiness. "What's all the commotion?" She asked.

Ygraine replied, with a tone of deep concern in her voice,

"I overheard Mother Marta. It seems the Duke of Cornwall has been wounded. Everyone's gone to help."

Ygraine began to pace back and forth, wringing her hands together. She stopped suddenly in front of Morella, who was now sitting on the edge of the bed, and held her hands out for her to witness as she said intently, "Morella, my hands are on fire."

Morella got up from the bed and took Ygraine's hands in her own. She looked at Ygraine in disbelief and said in bewilderment, "Your hands are burning!"

Ygraine pulled her hands away and retrieved her robe from the foot of the bed. As she was putting it on, she said with determination, "I am going to help this Duke. Come with me Morella. I fear I shall need all the support I can get."

Morella snatched up her own robe, struggling to put it on as she ran after Ygraine, who was wasting no time.

Once at the receiving room, they stood outside the door with their ears pressed to the wood, listening.

Inside, Mother Marta, Rodric, and Callum watched as Corelia washed the Duke's wound. "He's bleeding bad." Corelia stated, shaking her head. "The wound goes straight through."

The Duke began to stir, and he moaned as the pain awakened his senses. Becoming fully conscious, he focused on Corelia and grabbed her wrist fiercely. "Where am I?" He forced the question through clenched teeth.

Corelia drew in her breath sharply, and winced in pain. Rodric immediately reacted, and moved to her side, but Corelia looked up at him and shook her head. Rodric stepped back, and Corelia proceeded to pry Gorlois' fingers from around her wrist as she said with assurance, "You're safe. You're in a house of God. Now lie still, or you're sure to bleed to death."

The blood began to ooze out of the wound. Gorlois looked down at the gaping hole in his side and went completely pale. Instantly filled with fear, he became light-headed. He looked up at Corelia, his eyes pleading. "Can you do something for me woman?" He asked breathlessly.

Corelia looked into his eyes, and even though she saw the look of death in them, she reassured him with a slight smile and said, "I'll do everything I can. Just lie still while I finish cleaning the wound."

When she was confident that the bleeding had slowed, she moved a short distance away to a small table and began to grind some of the herbs together with the pestle to make a salve.

Gorlois' breathing was ragged as he fought to stay conscious.

Mother Marta went to his side. She picked up a cloth and began to gently dab his forehead while praying quietly.

"He's bleeding bad again!" Callum's panic-stricken voice interrupted.

As Corelia turned around to look, the door creaked open, revealing Ygraine with Morella cowering behind her.

Rodric spun around. "Good God, what are you doing here?"

All eyes settled on Ygraine, except the Duke's, who was losing his inner battle for control. He began to cry out, as a mixture of pain and fear overtook him.

Everyone's attention reverted back to him, and Ygraine took this opportunity to rush to his side. Morella stood in the doorway, afraid to move.

All were frozen in their place, watching intently as Ygraine sat next to the Duke and took his face gently in her hands. She leaned close to him, looked into his eyes and said, "You must trust me, for I shall take away your pain."

Their eyes locked briefly, and in his weakened state,

Gorlois nodded, as he became mesmerized. Breathing heavily, he stared, realizing that he had never seen more beautiful green eyes than hers.

Rodric and Corelia exchanged a look of confusion as the others looked on.

Ygraine closed her eyes and placed her hands directly onto the bleeding wound. Perspiration began beading up on her face, and within seconds, the bleeding ceased. No one moved or made a sound as the Duke's breathing calmed.

Ygraine removed her hands, and once again leaned close to his face. "Is there still pain?" She asked softly.

Gorlois smiled as a peacefulness washed over him. His voice revealed his relief as he replied, "You must be an angel, for my pain is gone, and yours is the face of heaven."

He looked around the room, and his senses became clearer. Then he took Ygraine's hands in his and raised them so that he could look upon them. He said, with a sense of awe, "My blood is on your hands. They drip red with my life force that you have saved. I do not know who you are, but I do know that if it were not for these hands, I would be a dead man."

As he held her hands and gazed at her face his heart began to feel something unfamiliar. His whole body began to tremble as a tingling sensation ran through him.

Uncontrollably, he blurted out, "I love you, and I will have you for my bride. On my own blood I swear to worship you the rest of my days."

Corelia gave Rodric a worried glance and moved to Ygraine's side. She placed her hands on her shoulders, and gently lifted her from the bed, whispering next to her ear, "He's delirious. He doesn't know what he's saying."

Gorlois and Ygraine's eyes were still locked as she slowly backed away, Corelia guiding her. Looking over her shoulder, Corelia motioned for Morella to come near. As she reached them, Corelia released her hold on Ygraine and reached for her hands. Gazing upon them, she whispered, "You're a healer child."

Ygraine did not respond, but continued to stare at Gorlois.

"Take her back to the cottage," Corelia instructed Morella. "I'll be along as soon as I bandage him up."

Ygraine was silent as she continued to back out of the room, still staring. Once outside, Morella questioned her with wide-eyed hopefulness. "Is he the one?"

Ygraine's mind whirled. She put the back of her hand to her forehead as she cried, "I am so confused!" She turned and ran back to the cottage.

❧❀•❀❧

It was a long night for both Ygraine and Gorlois. Though his pain was gone, Gorlois was restless, and sleep would not come to him. What did come, over and over, was the face of an angel. It haunted him and had his senses reeling. "I must have her," he thought to himself. "Whatever it takes, I must have her."

Ygraine had gone directly to bed after quickly washing the blood from her hands, and she pretended to be in a state of deep slumber. She was not prepared to answer any questions, and she was certain everyone had plenty of them.

Morella decided to hold her questioning until morning, even though she knew that Ygraine was not truly asleep. She crawled into bed next to her, and quickly fell asleep herself.

Ygraine's head pounded. Visions of the beloved face she had seen in the fire for so long were now mingled with the face of Gorlois. From the first time she saw her King in the fire, she knew she loved him. Now she found herself wondering if he existed at all, or if it were all her imagination.

She felt something for this Duke that she had touched, but the feelings were different than those she felt for her King.

"What if he never comes for me," she thought. "What if he lives only in the fire... only in my mind? I cannot wait forever. Morella was right. I am getting old. I desire to share myself with a man and have a child. What if this Duke was not delirious at all, and asks for my hand in marriage? What will I do?"

Corelia and Rodric interrupted her thoughts as they entered the cottage. Seeing that Ygraine and Morella were already asleep, they decided to retire and wait to speak of this night's events on the morrow.

Ygraine waited until the sound of their breathing became deep, and she was certain they were asleep before quietly slipping out of bed. She settled herself in front of the fire, hoping to find answers within the flames.

"Sweet King, come to me," she whispered, gazing into the fire.

Nothing appeared, and Ygraine felt consumed with panic. Her heart skipped a beat, and she placed her hands over her chest. "I cannot lose you! I have waited too long!"

Suddenly, a face she had not seen since her fifth birthday arose in the flames. It startled her, and her body jerked. Upon recognition, she leaned forward and peered deeper into the fire. "Merlin?" She asked softly.

"Yes Ygraine, it is I, Merlin," he replied.

"I have not seen you in quite some time. You have changed," she said, noticing his black hair, now was slightly streaked with silver.

"Much has changed," he stated firmly. He paused, then said, "You have not needed me Ygraine. But know that I will always come to you in your time of need."

"Why?" She asked, his comment confusing her. "Who are you that you should be concerned for my well being?"

"For now, just know that I am watching over you," he replied.

A moment passed, and he said, "I am part of a great, divine plan to bring peace to Britain, as are you Ygraine. It is our destiny to do so."

"Destiny?" She asked, her voice strained. "I thought my destiny was to be a queen, and be with my King, who I have seen and held in my heart all these years."

"It is your destiny to be a queen, Ygraine," he assured her. "But you will not be the wife of a petty king. You will be wed to the High King of all Britain, and you shall give birth to a boy child who will be the greatest king these lands have ever known. However, events have taken place that may alter the process slightly. But the outcome will be the same. I will make certain of that. The choices you make now will determine what road fate takes."

Ygraine shook her head. "Your words confuse me. Petty kings, high kings. I am confused! Confused and tired. Tired of being behind walls, not knowing what exists outside of them. I desire more, and I cannot wait any longer for destiny to come knocking at my door." She raised her chin high and said, "I shall create my own destiny."

"Your stubbornness and impatience may cause you pain in the end Ygraine," he warned. "But as I have said, the choice is yours."

The Merlin's face faded slowly away.

Ygraine rose to her feet, feelings of desperation suddenly taking over, clouding her judgment. She quietly, but very quickly left the cottage and ran in her bare feet and sleeping gown to the receiving room where Gorlois lie awake.

She eased the door open, only to find him staring right through her as she entered. They stared at each other in silence for what seemed like an eternity. Then suddenly, Ygraine rushed forward and stopped just short of his bedside.

"Did you mean what you said to me?" She asked, breaking the silence, her eyes pleading. "You are looking at me now the way you looked at me before... with eyes of love. Do your eyes speak the truth, or does your pain confuse you."

"You and I both know that I have no pain," Gorlois replied, still staring at her. "If my eyes reveal what my heart is feeling, then they speak the truth."

Ygraine knelt down beside him, placing her hands over his heart. She whispered, "Does this heart beat for me?"

Gorlois' heart began pounding. "For you, and no other."

A single tear slipped down her cheek, and Ygraine laid her head on his bare chest and began to weep. "Take me with you. Please take me with you."

"I had not planned on leaving without you," he said softly. He reached out to stroke her hair, but hesitated, feeling a sudden twinge of discomfort at the intimacy. He overcame the feeling, and began to run his fingers through her hair.

She breathed in the scent of him as she drifted into a calm place, his fingers relaxing her as he continued to run them through her hair. Sleep came quickly to claim them both.

๛๛●๛๛

The sound of the chapel bell ringing woke Corelia up with a start. Rodric stirred and sat up slowly, rubbing his eyes. "God I'm tired," he mumbled.

Corelia sat up and rubbed the back of her neck, yawning. "What a night. I wonder how the Duke is faring." She let out a sigh, then said, "I suppose I'd better have a look."

Getting out of bed, Corelia noticed that the place next to Morella was empty, and she bolted to her feet. "Where's Ygraine!" She screeched.

Rodric was immediately out of bed. "Morella, where's Ygraine!"

Morella sat upright, and her head began to spin from being startled out of a sound sleep. She opened her mouth to speak, but no words came forth.

"The Duke!" Corelia exclaimed, rushing toward the door. "She's gone to him. I can feel it."

Rodric was at her heels, followed by Morella, who was now wide awake.

The door to the receiving room was ajar, and when the three reached it, Corelia pushed it wide and found a very shocked Mother Marta standing just inside the doorway.

The three stepped inside and found Ygraine and Gorlois sound asleep. Ygraine was still kneeling next to him with her head on his chest. Gorlois' hands were lost in her unbound hair.

Mother Marta gave them a worried look, then gazed back over at Ygraine with Gorlois, and found that she could no longer hold her tongue. "What is the meaning of this?" She demanded loudly.

Ygraine's eyes flew open. She was momentarily unclear of where she was. She realized all too quickly her surroundings, and who was watching, and jumped to her feet.

"Mother... father... I... I...," she stammered.

"God in heaven, what's going on here?" Corelia questioned, her puzzled look mirroring everyone in the room.

Ygraine began to breathe heavily, feeling like a hunted animal backed into a corner with no place to run.

Gorlois reached for her hand and gave it a gentle squeeze. He looked up at her, smiled, and said, "This is as good a time as any."

She nodded slowly. For the first time in her life, she was speechless.

"Time for what?" Rodric demanded.

"Time to ask for your daughter's hand," Gorlois replied. Then more firmly, he said, "But know this. She comes with me, with or without your favour."

Morella let out a squeal and ran to Ygraine. She threw her arms around her, and began jumping up and down, dragging Ygraine with her. "It's him, isn't it? It's him!"

Ygraine's heart thudded, and her lower lip began to quiver as she replied, "Yes, it is he."

Corelia rushed to Ygraine's rescue. "Stop bouncing her around. Can't you see she's over-excited?" She put her arm around Ygraine and began to soothe her. "It's all right sweet child. Let's go back to the cottage and talk about this."

Ygraine allowed herself to be led toward the door, the others silently preceding them out of the room. As Corelia and Ygraine were about to depart, the Duke's voice halted them. "Wait!" He shouted.

Ygraine and Corelia turned around. Gorlois smiled and said "I have just realized that I do not even know my bride's name."

"Her name's Ygraine, and I'll decide whether or not she's to be your bride," Corelia informed him sternly before turning on her heel and ushering Ygraine from the room.

Mother Marta decided to go into prayer, as she was worrying how the Merlin was going to react to all of this. Corelia and Rodric had the same concern.

Ygraine soon put their minds at ease. She decided to take full charge of the situation, and upon entering the cottage, she made her plans very clear.

Before any questions could be asked, she held up her hands and said, "I have decided to marry the Duke."

A look of surprise crossed everyone's face.

"I did not come upon this decision without giving it great thought," she continued.

"I also spoke with my guardian, Merlin, who said it was

my choice to do whatever pleases me."

"Your guardian?" Corelia asked, dismayed.

"Yes," Ygraine replied. "He is the one who came to me in the fire when I was five, and he will come again should I need him."

Rodric and Corelia were both still troubled by all of this, and Corelia questioned her further. "You say he spoke to you?" When Ygraine?"

"Last night. When everyone was asleep. He came to me as he did before. He told me the choice was mine to make, and I have made my choice. I shall marry the Duke."

"What about us?" Morella asked excitedly. "Can we go too?"

Ignoring Morella, Ygraine took Corelia and Rodric by the hand. "Do you not want to leave this place? Father, you have been caretaker here all my life. And you," she said looking at Corelia. "You have done nothing but take care of us all. Do you not want more?"

Corelia and Rodric both shrugged their shoulders, not knowing what to do or say. Ygraine released their hands and turned to Morella. "I know you want more."

Morella knelt before Ygraine, taking both her hands and laying her cheek against them. "Please don't go without me. I'll die here if you do."

Corelia's heart wrenched at the sight of Morella pleading with Ygraine.

To Morella, Ygraine said, "Raise from your knees. You are like a sister to me. Therefore, you will never again kneel to me." She cupped Morella's chin in her hand and whispered, "You are far too pretty to be left here to suffer a life of prayer."

Ygraine smiled, and Morella rose and responded with an encompassing embrace.

Then Ygraine turned to face Corelia and Rodric, determined to make them understand. "I was born here, but

I do not want to die here. This chance may not come again, and I do not want to be sitting here years from now wishing I had taken it."

She gazed into the depths of Corelia's eyes, attempting to reach her heart. "I want to have a child. So badly, that the desire for it burns inside of me. I cannot wait any longer to live my life. I have passion within my soul that is seeking to vent itself. There is a hunger within me that needs to be shared, and I wish to share it with the Duke."

Corelia did not respond, and Ygraine's expression became intense as she said, "I love you both, but we are at a crossroads. I am leaving this place, and with all my heart I hope that you will choose to come with me."

Corelia let out a deep, quivering sigh and threw her arms around Ygraine. "Wherever you go, I go with you. We are family, and we are bound together."

Rodric joined them, stretching his arms to encompass them both. Teary-eyed, he said, "Yes, we go where you go."

Morella put her hands together in prayer and raised her eyes heavenward as she whispered, "Thank you."

৩০৯০●৩০৯৩

Gorlois had sent Callum back to Avon for news of the outcome of the battle, and to deliver a message to Ambrosius that he was alive and well.

That evening, Ygraine was sitting at his bedside applying clean dressings to Gorlois' wound when Callum returned.

He was anxious for the news and pulled himself upright when Callum appeared in the open doorway.

Gorlois said to Ygraine, "My strength is already regained. In two more days I will be able to ride, and we will be on our way home... to Tintagel."

"Home." Ygraine repeated the word as if it were foreign.

Then she thought, "I should be happy to be going to this new home, but a sadness lingers in me." Visions of the face she deeply loved swam before her. "Will I ever release you from my heart?"

Callum cleared his throat, and Ygraine rose and stood beside Gorlois, continuing to tend to his wound.

"Come closer," Gorlois said as he motioned for Callum to enter. "What news do you bring?"

Callum, smiling, moved halfway across the room. He was obviously pleased with the information he had. "Good news my Lord. We've defeated the Saxons. Drove them back into the sea, what was left of them. Uriens came to Ambrosius' aid with five hundred men!"

"I'll be damned!" Gorlois exclaimed. "That prophet of Ambrosius is priceless!"

That remark drew Ygraine's attention fully, and she looked up from her ministering. "Who do you speak of, if I may ask?"

Gorlois saw no harm in her question and responded, "The High King holds counsel with a prophet. They call him the Merlin."

Ygraine's face lost all color, and her mouth dropped open. While attempting to regain her composure, she asked, "What does this King look like?" She was certain that Gorlois would describe 'her King'.

"What does he look like?" He was surprised at her question, but answered her in spite of his puzzlement. "He looks like a king. He looks... kingly."

Gorlois began to chuckle, as he realized he had never been asked to describe another man before, and he was having difficulty doing so.

"Let me see," he said, stroking his beard, attempting to find the right words to appease Ygraine. "He is a large man... with Roman features, I suppose you would say. Deep, reddish brown hair." Then proudly, he stated, "He has a scar on his face that would honour any man."

Ygraine's heart sank, and now more than ever, she felt that 'her King' was no more than a mere dream. She lowered her head to hide her disappointment and said, "Oh, I see." She held back her tears as she quickly finished her task then said, "I will leave you now so that you may speak more privately."

She hurried from the room, and Gorlois shrugged his shoulders, excusing her behavior as not desiring to hear war talk.

Then he motioned for Callum to come even closer. "What news do you bring of Hengist?" He questioned, half hoping to hear that the barbarian was dead. The other half was hoping to meet him again in battle to seek revenge.

"He fled," Callum replied. "They say he will gather more men and come back to hack us to pieces!" His voice grew louder. "The next time I want a chance at him myself!"

Gorlois let out a sigh and placed his hand on Callum's arm. "You are loyal. You could have left me to die and gone after the barbarian quenching your own thirst for Saxon blood."

Callum lowered his head, secretly wishing that he could take full credit for saving the Duke. "Truth is my Lord, I tried to drag you to safety. If it weren't for the High King's brother, you'd never have been brought here at all."

"Uther?" Gorlois asked, shocked.

"Yes, Lord Uther," Callum replied. "He grabbed you up like a grain sack and threw you on his horse and told me to bring you here."

In deep thought, Gorlois stroked his beard. "I did not believe that Uther had a heart. I owe as much to him for saving my life as I do to Ygraine."

Gorlois involuntarily shuddered at the thought of being

indebted to the Pendragon. Somehow that thought did not sit well with him at all. He had always viewed Uther as an arrogant war-dog, and hoped that the day would never come when he would succeed Ambrosius.

"Hmmm," Gorlois said aloud, speaking more to himself than to Callum. "Life takes odd twists and turns. You think it is all planned out, then just like that...," he snapped his fingers, "...everything changes."

Suddenly thinking of Ygraine, Gorlois raised his eyebrows and said, "I can hardly wait to see what is next!"

ଓଃ *Six* ଽ

Gorlois decided that he could not wait to have Ygraine in his bed, and informed her upon leaving the sanctuary that there would be a simple ceremony the day after their arrival at Tintagel, her new home.

The journey to Cornwall was on horseback, and to both Ygraine and Morella, very fascinating. Corelia and Rodric thoroughly enjoyed witnessing their reactions, for every sight and sound was new and exciting. It was as if all was seen and heard through the eyes and ears of children.

Gorlois was mesmerized by the innocence, and could not take his eyes from Ygraine as he watched her eyes light up over and over.

However, Ygraine grew apprehensive as they drew nearer to Tintagel. The castle was built on a headland, and was reachable from the mainland by a road crossing a narrow neck of rock. She slowed her horses pace, as she was unaccustomed to riding, and the crossing seemed quite precarious. Gorlois was unaffected by the apparent dangerous conditions, and rode on a few lengths ahead.

The smell of the sea, and the sound of the booming surf

echoing amongst the surrounding cliffs, began to stir some deep emotion within Ygraine. The sun was setting, and at first sight of Tintagel castle, silhouetted against a darkening sky painted with shades of red from the suns last rays, she felt her heart stop momentarily. She had seen this castle before in her fire visions. She suddenly felt torn between feelings of joy and more confusion. As she gazed upon, and felt its familiar presence, she knew somewhere deep within her that this was 'home'.

"If this is my destiny," she thought. "Then why does this man that I am about to wed appear so differently?"

Morella had a hard time containing the pleasure she was feeling. She drew her mount close to Ygraine's and whispered excitedly, "You were right Ygraine. I may not be a queen, but I am happy nonetheless to make that my home." She pointed to the castle, then a thought crossed her mind, and she said quietly, "I heard the sisters talking once about how the High King, Ambrosius has no heir. I'll bet the Duke is going to be High King someday, so you'll be a queen just like you said. After all, the Duke was wounded in battle defending the High King. I'll bet they're close, you know, allies."

Ygraine mulled over Morella's words, then whispered, "I suppose you could be right."

For now, this thought appeased Ygraine. Somehow she had to forget 'her King' as she had envisioned him and enter into her new life with Gorlois contented. She had made her choice. Now she had to accept it.

$$\wp\, \widetilde{\wp}\, \bullet\, \widetilde{\wp}\, \wp$$

The receiving room at the sanctuary had been returned to normal. All remnants of the passed few days had been cleared away, except one.

A hooded, cloaked figure entered the room. Mother Marta was waiting with her back to the door. Sensing the Merlin's presence, she turned around slowly. No words were exchanged. He extended his hand, into which she placed an object. He nodded, his eyes thanking her. Then he turned and left.

Gorlois' ring would prove to have great value in the future.

ふ々●ぐ々

The following day was filled with anticipation for Ygraine. The ceremony was to take place after sunset. Therefore, she had all of one day to prepare for the event she had dreamed of her entire life.

"I need more time!" Ygraine whined. "This is not at all the way I thought this day would unfold. I do not even have a proper gown to present myself in."

She leaned against the casement of the window facing the sea and breathed in the salt air, attempting to calm herself.

Morella had been given this room, next to the Duke's chamber above stairs, where Ygraine had spent the night with Morella. Hereafter, Ygraine would be sharing the Duke's chamber.

Ygraine had requested this room for Morella, as she was not accustomed to being away from her and felt the need to have her nearby. She had reasoned with Gorlois that it was the sensible thing to do, as Morella would be Ygraine's attendant, and therefore, should be close at hand.

Corelia and Rodric were housed on the ground floor near the kitchen, as Gorlois had taken a liking to Corelia's spirit, and had decided to give her full charge of the servants and household.

Rodric was content to be back in the stables, working amidst the scent of horses that he so loved and missed. He was up at the crack of dawn, and was already spending time with the stable-master acquainting himself with his new duties.

Corelia was in the kitchen giving orders for preparation of the wedding feast, which would take place after the ceremony.

The Duke had left the castle early and was not expected back until that evening.

Morella was attempting to comfort Ygraine. As she walked toward her, she said in a soothing tone, "Calm down. There's plenty of time to get yourself ready. We have all day."

Ygraine let out a sigh, turning away from the window. She confided in Morella, "It is not the 'day' I am concerned with." Then she gave Morella a fearful look.

"Oh, get that pitiful look off your face," Morella chided, putting her arm around Ygraine's shoulders and steering her toward the bed. "I wish I was in your shoes."

She sat on the bed and pulled Ygraine down next to her. "What is it you're afraid of?"

Ygraine laid her head against Morella's arm. "I am afraid that I may not satisfy him. I have no knowledge of how to please a man." Raising her head, and gazing into Morella's eyes, she continued, "I know that I have passion within me, and sometimes it frightens me to think of what might happen, should it ever be unleashed. But I have nothing to compare this night to, except my dreams." She lowered her eyes and pouted. "I am quite sure that he has had plenty of experience."

Morella thought to pacify her and said, "All I know is that I know you, and I've seen the look in your eyes when you've thought about him all these years. You'll know what to do."

That reminder of the beloved face she fought so desperately to forget brought tears to Ygraine's eyes. Morella mistook them as tears of anticipation of the night to come. If she only knew the truth of what Ygraine was really feeling. She was actually grieving on this day of her new life with Gorlois.

A rapping on the door snapped Ygraine from her misery temporarily. Morella went to the door, and upon opening it, Corelia rushed in carrying a beautiful white gown over her arm.

"This was just delivered!" Her voice was filled with excitement. "The Duke had it sent for you."

Ygraine gently touched the fine lace with trembling fingers.

Corelia was immediately worried. "You're shaking child."

Noticing Ygraine's tear-streaked face, she hurriedly put the gown across the bed and took Ygraine in her arms. "What's this all about now?"

Ygraine fell into Corelia's embrace and began to cry uncontrollably.

Corelia looked at Morella and questioned her with her eyes. Morella shrugged and said, "If you ask me, she's all upset over nothing. She's worried about pleasing the Duke."

"Oh!" Corelia exclaimed, her eyes wide, realizing the reason for Ygraine's behavior. "Well of course she's worried." She patted Ygraine on the back gently. "I was worried too, the first time."

She took Ygraine's face in her hands and said, "Stop your crying and listen to me."

Ygraine took a deep breath, regaining control of herself, and Corelia continued. "You're a beautiful woman, and the Duke loves you. I can see it in his eyes when he looks at you. You'll see that nature has a way of taking care of these things. When two people love each other, things just happen naturally. You don't have to know anything. Just feel.

Tonight is going to be a night you'll never forget."

Corelia took Ygraine's hand and placed a gentle kiss upon it. "I wish I was your age again and it was my first night."

Ygraine smiled, letting her mother's words soothe her for now.

"I know what'll make you feel better!" Corelia said joyously. "A nice warm bath in rose petals."

"Oh, you always know what to do to make me feel better," Ygraine said, hugging Corelia. "What would I do without you?"

"Well, that's one thing we'll never have to find out," Corelia stated firmly. "Now, lets get you prepared for your wedding."

ೲ☙●❧ೲ

The ceremony was held in the small chapel on the castle grounds.

Gorlois waited impatiently for Ygraine's arrival. He was anxious to be done with both the ceremony and the feasting, for he could feel an almost animalistic hunger growing inside of him as he thought of his virgin bride. By the time Ygraine entered the chapel, his thoughts were causing a swelling in his loins, and when he laid his eyes upon her, he thought he would explode. He had never seen anything so beautiful in his life.

The chapel was aglow with candlelight, making Ygraine's gown appear golden in colour. The satin material clung to her upper body snugly. The sleeves were long, coming to a point over the top of her hands. The waist was cut in a low V-shape to her hipline. The rest of the gown flowed full to the floor. The bodice was low, revealing the full swell of her breasts above the scalloped lace trim. Gorlois' attention was immediately drawn there, as Ygraine's chest rose and fell with each breath she took. Her hair was pulled away from her face and twisted in a knot. A single long, thin braid hung seductively over her breast. Her veil covered her face and was as long as her gown in back.

Although several of the town folk had been invited for the feasting, the ceremony was private with Rodric, Corelia, and Morella the only ones in attendance.

Rodric slowly walked Ygraine to the altar, and with tear-filled eyes, offered her hand to Gorlois. Gorlois covered her right hand with his, but his gaze was still upon her decolletage.

Gorlois forced himself to draw his eyes away as the priest draped a white linen cloth embossed with a shimmering gold cross over their wrists. He anointed the cloth with holy water, and began what turned out to be a mockery of a marriage ceremony.

Gorlois continually interrupted the priest, prodding him to hurry along. By the time their vows were exchanged, and he had placed the gold wedding band on Ygraine's finger, he was perspiring profusely. He lifted her veil and kissed her hungrily, devouring her lips.

Until that moment, Ygraine had felt that she was somewhere else entirely. That same feeling continued throughout the feasting, which was as short as the ceremony.

The massive hall was filled with guests enjoying the wide array of fine foods, wine, and ale while listening to the melodic harp being played in a far corner of the room.

Ygraine, seated at the feasting table, had barely touched her food when Gorlois, who was seated next to her, announced, with a pompous attitude, that is was time for the bride to be prepared for bed.

Ygraine's empty stomach gnawed as she looked up from her plate. Beads of perspiration appeared above her upper lip as fear consumed her.

The guests turned their attention to Gorlois, raising their glasses in a toasting manner.

Corelia, who was seated on the other side of Ygraine, noticed her distress. She immediately stood up and assisted Ygraine to her feet. Unsteady, Ygraine grabbed on to Corelia's arm for support. Corelia wrapped her arms around her saying, "It's going to be all right child. It's going to be all right."

Rodric filled with a mixture of emotions, and he rose from the feasting table and gazed across the room as Corelia guided Ygraine out of the hall.

Gorlois took a swig of his ale, wiping his mouth with the back of his hand as he watched them depart.

Morella was unaware of the tension her family was experiencing. She was caught up in her own flirtations with Gorlois' handsome Captain-at-arms, who had come to offer his congratulations.

In the Duke's chamber, Corelia helped Ygraine out of her gown and into her sleeping attire.

The room was sizeable and royally decorated. The furnishings were all made of wood, hand-carved and painted gold. A cedar chest was against the far wall near a door that led out to a parapet. Two large windows were on either side of it, facing the sea. The waves could be heard crashing on the rocks below.

Many furs and deerskins adorned the bed, which was quite large, the headboard intricately carved. Two high-backed chairs covered in rich red satin brocade, faced the fireplace, opposite the bed where a roaring fire blazed. Despite the warmth emanating from it, Ygraine's body trembled.

Corelia could not help but notice. However, she thought it best not to comment on it, as she did not want Ygraine to become upset, and she knew that the slightest little thing could send her into tears again. She pulled the fur blankets back on the bed, and helped Ygraine to settle in. Both remained silent as Corelia removed the pins from Ygraine's hair, then retrieved the comb that Rodric had given Ygraine years before from the bedside table. She began combing her hair, hoping it would relax her. All the while Ygraine stared blankly into the fire, a knot forming in the pit of her stomach.

After several moments, Corelia placed the comb back on the table and kissed Ygraine softly on the forehead, then left without a backward glance. It was the hardest thing Corelia had ever done. She wanted to hold Ygraine in her arms and soothe her worries, but Ygraine was not a little girl anymore. She was grown, and after this night she would be a woman.

Ygraine continued to tremble. Her trembling increased as she heard Gorlois' heavy footsteps in the corridor. He knocked once, then entered before she could reply.

He stared at her from across the room, and the look in his eyes sent chills through Ygraine's body. She leaned back against the pillows and pulled the blankets up tightly about her chin.

Gorlois began to remove his clothing, and Ygraine closed her eyes tight, unable to look at him.

"What is wrong with me?" She thought frantically. "I am a woman, and I shall look forward to being with my husband," she reprimanded herself silently.

Opening her eyes, she found Gorlois fully undressed and standing at the bedside. He startled her as he threw the blankets away from her.

"Husband! I fear that you have consumed far too much ale!" She exclaimed, once again noticing a look in his eyes that she had never seen in anyone's.

He was immediately on top of her, tearing away at her gown. She struggled beneath him, but soon lost the battle.

She opened her mouth to protest, but he covered it with his own, forcing his tongue inside as he roughly grabbed at her breasts.

Ygraine reached out for the comb and attempted to use it as a weapon as she hit him with it several times, but he soon forced her legs apart with his knee and penetrated her, ripping her soft flesh. She cried out in pain as he quickly planted his seed within her. He grunted loudly, lost in his own pleasure, before collapsing on top of her. He lay there, breathing heavily for several moments before rolling away from her. He was asleep before Ygraine fully realized what had happened.

She stared upward, tears of disappointment running from her eyes as her hand opened and the comb fell to the floor. The inside of her thighs throbbed, and her stomach churned. She got out of bed, and barely made it to the chamber pot before vomiting.

❧ *Seven* ☙

The following nine months dragged by as the child Ygraine carried grew in her womb.

Gorlois never came again to her bed after that first night. It was whispered throughout the castle that he had taken up with one of the serving wenches and spent his nights with her when he was home.

To Ygraine's delight, he was gone much of the time, as the Saxon's continued to invade. Ambrosius would drive them back, only to have them lick their wounds and come back for more.

Her only joy came from envisioning that the child she carried would be all that the Merlin had prophesied.

She spent more and more time alone. Morella tended to her needs, but would be off fulfilling her own desires as soon as she was done. She was often seen flirting with several of Gorlois' men, and she seemed to always be smiling. Ygraine was glad to see that Morella had found something in the way of passion that she had not.

Morella had also taken up the duty of midwife for the servants, and found great reward in bringing in new life.

Rodric was rarely seen, as there was much work to do in the stables. Gorlois' men came and went regularly and were in constant need of fresh horses.

Corelia busied herself with household duties, creating quite a different atmosphere than when they had first arrived. The castle was always alive with fresh or dried flowers and candlelight.

Ygraine was so grateful that those she loved were at peace here in this place. She never shared her first night experience, knowing full well it would have caused discord between her loved ones and Gorlois. She carried the pain of that night secretly within herself.

She spent long hours in front of the fire, but little came to her. Once, she thought she caught a glimpse of 'her King' mixed with a vision of a red dragon, but it quickly faded.

She began to accept this life she had chosen, although depression came to her often. She anxiously awaited the child's birth, hoping it would fill the void she felt in her heart. Little did she know, it would also be a disappointment.

The child was born early. Gorlois was away battling at Ambrosius' side. Ygraine had gone into labour several hours after sunset, and the child was born just before dawn.

It was planned that Corelia would midwife the child, but Morella pleaded for the honour. Ygraine agreed, but Corelia never left her side.

Ygraine was glad that Gorlois was away. She wanted to share this 'first' experience with loved ones.

Rodric paced outside the chamber door, just as he had done so many years before when Ygraine was born. As he was recalling that night to his memory, a cry echoed from within that was somehow very reminiscent of the Merlin's cry on that night of Ygraine's birth.

Ygraine's scream sent shivers through Rodric's body. He flung the door open, afraid of what he might see.

Ygraine, covered in perspiration, had a look of terror on her face as she stared wide-eyed at the child Morella held. The babe had been wrapped in blankets, and Morella was attempting to hand it to its mother. Corelia was on the bed, her arms around Ygraine, trying to calm her.

"It cannot be, it cannot be," Ygraine was mumbling, shaking her head violently, as if becoming hysterical.

Then suddenly, she shouted, "Get it away from me!"

The sound of Ygraine's shrill voice made the babe jerk, and it began to scream.

"Take her," Morella pleaded. "She needs to feel her mother."

Ygraine looked up at Corelia, her eyes full of fear, and cried, "That is not my child. Tell her that is not my child. Merlin said it would be a boy child. That is not mine. Oh God, what have I done?"

The babe continued to scream as Corelia held Ygraine tightly in her arms, patting her back gently and stroking her hair. In desperation, Corelia asked Morella, "Didn't one of the kitchen maids give birth recently?"

"Yes," Morella replied, confused.

"Take the babe to her to suckle for now," Corelia instructed, tears filling her eyes. "I don't know what's wrong. I fear she's lost her mind."

Rodric was still standing in the open doorway, staring at the scene in front of him with a pained expression on his face. As Morella hurried past him and down the corridor, she heard Ygraine screaming, "Merlin!... Merlin!"

The babe calmed down immediately upon feeling the maid's breast against her cheek. She nuzzled against it and began sucking as soon as the nipple found her tiny mouth. Morella stayed in the maid's chamber, almost afraid to return to Ygraine's.

Corelia gave Ygraine a calming potion and stayed with

her, stroking her hair until she fell asleep. Even in slumber, she continued to murmur the Merlin's name over and over.

Corelia left her to rest and went about her morning duties, leaving Rodric seated outside the door, should Ygraine wake before she returned.

She did wake, after sleeping only a few hours. Her mind and vision were foggy from the potion, but she remembered all too well the events of the morning. She lay in bed for several moments, gazing across the room at the fire, her eyes revealing the coldness she was feeling in her heart. Then, she eased herself out of bed and cautiously made her way to kneel on the hearth, staring intently into the flames.

"Merlin!" She called out angrily. "You said you would come to me in my time of need. Where are you?"

His shadowy form appeared, and his voice was an echo. "I am with you Ygraine."

Suddenly overwhelmed with her emotions, tears welled up in her eyes. Light-headed, and her vision still a bit blurred, she lowered herself to sit on the hearth, and she began to tremble.

"I know you are unclear, but I do not understand you," the Merlin said, his voice penetrating. "How can you turn a child away simply because it is not as you had expected? I question your faith Ygraine."

"Faith... destiny," she said, her voice strained. "You speak these words so easily. I am barely eighteen, and I feel like an old woman. All I had to look forward to was the boy child. She paused, and her voice quivered as she asked, "Why has that been taken from me?"

"Nothing has been taken from you Ygraine," he stated. "You made a choice that has altered the course of destiny. Find your faith Ygraine. When you do, you will find peace within."

The Merlin's form faded away, and Ygraine sat for several

moments contemplating his words. Suddenly realizing the wisdom within them, she rose to her feet, and though she was still weak, she rushed to the door. She found Rodric sitting just outside dozing, and eased past him. As she ran down the corridor, he jolted upright at the sound of her footsteps. He jumped up and ran after her.

She rapidly descended the main stairway to the lower level and quickly passed the kitchen. Corelia caught sight of her there and rushed out after her, just in time to meet up with Rodric. They both followed and stopped in the open doorway that Ygraine had entered.

Ygraine's babe lay sleeping in a cradle in the far corner of the room. The maid was sitting in a chair rocking her own curly, golden haired babe. Morella was asleep on the maid's bed, but woke when Ygraine entered.

Ygraine slowly walked toward the cradle. Inside, lay the tiniest little angel. She had a full head of black hair, and wee features like an elf child except for her eyes. Even in slumber, Ygraine could tell that they were quite large.

Ygraine touched one of her little fingers and felt her heart explode with love. She picked the babe up, and as she woke, Ygraine put her to her breast. The babe began sucking, and Ygraine could not contain her tears of regret at how she had treated this, her own blood.

Morella put her face in her hands and began to weep as well. Corelia could not hold back her tears either, and Rodric felt as if the floodgates had been opened up, as he also gave in to his feelings.

When the babe had finished nursing, Ygraine turned around, holding her babe close to her. "I am so sorry," she said, looking at the drawn faces of the three people she loved most in the world. "Please forgive me. I have been self-centered and unfeeling. I have been living in a dream world, but no more. I shall learn to live in the moment." She gazed down adoringly at the babe in her arms. "This child is now my world, and I will love her forever."

Ygraine closed her eyes and thought again of the Merlin's words, and vowed to have faith in her life as she now knew it to exist. After all, how would she ever conceive another child with a husband who shared another woman's bed? No... She would have to be content with this precious girl child.

She looked down at the babe sleeping soundly in her arms and smiled. She kissed the babe's cheek and said lovingly, "I know that there is much to gain from all of this. Therefore, I give you the name Morgaine."

ᏽ᠍᠍᠍ᢌ ● ᠍ᢌᏽ

Ygraine spent the next two years doing little else but loving her daughter. They were inseparable. Ygraine was even more grateful that Gorlois stayed away, as she preferred to share her bedchamber with her little girl.

After Morgaine's birth, Gorlois came once to see the child. Ygraine was lying on the bed resting one evening when he entered the room, without knocking. She was immediately on her feet, as he went straight to the cradle next to Ygraine's bed, and picked up the babe.

Morgaine awoke and let out a whimper, drawing up her legs and chewing on her fist. Gorlois held her out at arms' length, scrutinizing her, then made a face revealing his distaste. "This child does not resemble my bloodline, nor yours, from what I can tell. She looks more like the King's prophet than she does you or I. They say he is the spawn of the devil. Mayhaps she is also."

Morgaine began to cry, and Gorlois immediately handed her over to Ygraine. She ignored his comment, overwrought with discomfort at his mere presence. She calmed the babe and laid her back down in the cradle.

As Ygraine turned to face Gorlois, she noticed a familiar look in his eyes that made her even more uneasy. He took a couple of steps toward her, and Ygraine immediately backed away, right up against the bed. Gorlois stopped, letting out a loud sigh. He turned away from her and walked toward the fireplace, sitting down heavily in one of the chairs in front of it.

"You do not have to fear me Ygraine," he said sorrowfully. He lowered his head into his hands, rubbing his forehead. "I know that I have hurt you, and in a way, deceived you." He lifted his head, gazing across the room at her. "I was taken in by your beauty and your power. I was overwhelmed by the situation I found myself in. At that time, I thought a wife and family would bring me contentment. In fact, it was not until the morning after our wedding night that I realized those things are not for me."

He shook his head saying, "I am ashamed of the way I treated you, but it is my way. The only way I know. I would ask your forgiveness, but in truth, I have not yet forgiven myself. In staying away from you, I serve my penance."

He paused, staring at her, the fear still quite evident in her eyes, then said, "Many a night I wanted to come to you, but I cannot stand the look of fear in your eyes when you look upon me."

He lowered his eyes dejectedly, and Ygraine realized that he had been carrying the pain of that first night with him as well. She took a deep breath and went to kneel near his chair. She laid her hand gently on his arm and said softly, "I wanted so much for it to be different between us. But as you have said, it is not in your nature to be any other way. I have felt sorry for myself, for I have missed the tenderness I so longed for. But as I look at you now, the sorrow I feel for you is deeper. You wallow in misery because you refuse to see beyond the patterns of your life."

She stood up, and with great intensity said, "You may live your penance the rest of your days, but until you find it within yourself to change, you will never know forgiveness. You must learn from the error of your ways, not excuse them."

Gorlois looked up at her, and his voice was strained, as if he were holding back his emotions. "You are wise beyond your years Ygraine, and I will take what you have said to heart. I make no promises to myself, but I did make a promise to you once to worship you forever, and I have broken it. I make you another promise now, and I hope you believe me when I say, that I will never hurt you again. I see that you are content being separate from me, and so I shall honour your feelings and keep my distance.

He rose from the chair and walked toward the door. He turned to look at her before leaving and said, "I hope that some day you will look upon me with different eyes."

They saw very little of each other after that night. Gorlois purposely avoided her at all costs, and oddly enough, she did not converse with him again for nearly two years. Not until after the death of Ambrosius.

ଔ *Eight* ଶ

As the High King lay dying, the Saxons were gathering strength. Hengist's son Herne, who was reputed to be as barbaric as his father, was expected to join him.

Ambrosius had always foreseen for himself an honourable death on the battlefield, which years ago he would have chosen. However, this King who held a passion for his country, decided to simply lie down and die. He was tired of warring, and he saw no light at the end of the dark tunnel he was living in.

He had left the stronghold at Avon and gone home to Viroconium. He had been bed-ridden for a fortnight. There were no physical signs of illness, but day-by-day, the life force drained from him.

He had sent for Uther, and on this night of the fourteenth day, Ambrosius was to name his brother heir to the throne.

In the High King's chamber, Ambrosius lay in his bed.

The entire room was bathed in a rich golden colour as the glow from the fire mingled with the soft hue of the many candles burning. Heavy, gold velvet curtains covered the windows, and soft, light coloured furs covered the bed and floor. Ambrosius' crown was on the bedside table.

Uther paced back and forth at the foot of the bed, his emotions raw. He was filled with frustration and fear, and he could not stand to see Ambrosius in his weakened state.

"My fire has gone out," Ambrosius whispered, his voice very weak and shallow.

Uther stopped pacing, and his voice shook as he said, "Then re-ignite it!"

Ambrosius slowly shook his head. "I choose not to." Then he smiled warmly at Uther, his eyes tear-filled as he said, "If I had been more like you brother, I would have more to live for."

Uther moved to Ambrosius' side and knelt down, his eyes burning with the love he felt for him. "If I had been more like you brother, I would not be so terrified of taking your place." He glanced at the crown, and let out a stressful sigh. "I am a strong follower, but you are a great leader."

Ambrosius returned Uther's gaze, his face radiating with warmth. "Some day you will have an heir Uther, and he will be a mixture of us both." A deep sense of pride filled Ambrosius as he continued to gaze into his brother's eyes. "I should have liked to witness his reign of power."

Uther raised an inquisitive brow and opened his mouth to question Ambrosius, but the King's attention had been suddenly drawn to the foot of the bed. Uther followed Ambrosius' gaze, but saw nothing. He touched his arm and asked gently, "What is it brother?"

Ambrosius continued to stare, and he smiled as if what he saw pleased him greatly. "I thought that I would fear this dark hour, but in truth, I welcome it." He paused, and his eyes began to lose their focus as he surrendered to this moment of bliss. "A dear friend has come to guide me through the door to the other side."

Uther looked again. This time he could have sworn that

he saw a faint apparition resembling the Merlin, but it disappeared as quickly as it had come. When he looked back at Ambrosius, his eyes were in a cold stare.

Uther held his breath, waiting for Ambrosius to blink. He did not. Uther thought his heart would explode, and his throat constricted with a pain he had never felt before. He reached over and gently closed Ambrosius' eyes. Then he raised his hand, and held it close to his face saying, "I will meet you on the other side, dear brother. But first I will finish what you have begun."

He kissed Ambrosius' hand, and fought back the tears that threatened to escape his eyes as he lowered his head for a moment of silent prayer. Then he rose to his feet and gazed down at Ambrosius lovingly.

With reluctance, he picked up the crown. He stared at it while taking in a deep breath, exhaling loudly, his anxiety apparent. Then he shook his head, and he set the crown upon Ambrosius' chest. He took in another deep breath. Exhaling fully, he could feel the fear slowly draining from his body. "I accept the throne," Uther stated with assurance. "But I shall not wear the crown." He paused, then said, "There is no man alive that deserves it more than you. You will always be my king."

He smiled affectionately, then turned away and left the chamber.

Once outside, Uther stood looking up at the banner of the Lion blowing in the wind on its staff. He slowly lowered it, and held it tightly in his hands before replacing it with his own, the Red Dragon.

A roll of thunder was heard, followed by a shooting star, its fiery trail blazing across the sky.

Uther dropped to one knee, and he swallowed hard, his gaze fixed on the heavens as he said, with great passion, "I hear the roar of the Lion as he crosses over, leaving in his stead the Red Dragon. Have faith, that I shall fulfill my destiny and bring peace to Britain."

As he filled with courage, a gust of wind blew over him, and his gaze moved to his banner snapping in the wind. As he took in a deep breath, he heard the sound of horse's hooves approaching. He rose to his feet and turned to see Gorlois riding up.

Uther frowned slightly and moved to mount his own horse that was tethered to a nearby post. He was settling himself on his saddle and tucking Ambrosius' banner safely away inside his cloak as Gorlois reigned in at his side.

Gorlois' voice revealed his concern as he said, "I received word of the High King's illness. May I pay him a visit? I bring news of Hengist."

Uther closed his eyes briefly, willing himself to keep both his sadness and his dislike for Gorlois under control. As he opened them, his sorrow was evident as he said, "You may pay your respects. Ambrosius has passed."

Gorlois was shocked, and he shook his head in disbelief. "I had no idea his illness was fatal." Then he laid his hand on Uther's arm compassionately and said, "I am sorry. I know you shared a strong bond."

Another gust of wind caused the banner to blow hard, whipping and snapping. It drew Gorlois' attention, and as he looked up and saw the Red Dragon, he made a face of disappointment.

Uther looked down at Gorlois' hand, stunned at his show of sympathy, and noticed that his ring was missing. "It seems that you have lost something." He remarked.

Gorlois pulled his hand away, grunted, and said heatedly, "One of the Saxon thieves must have taken it when I was wounded by Hengist." He paused, then said, "That was some time ago."

"Yes, I remember it well," Uther said, raising a brow in

acknowledgment. Then, a bit of arrogance seeped into his voice as he remarked, "I hear a woman saved your life."

Gorlois smiled wryly. "That is partially true." Then leaning closer to Uther, his mood turned more serious. "I know what you did for me that day. I could never find it within myself to give thanks to you before. But now that you are about to be crowned High King, I suppose I had better express my gratitude to you now."

He extended his hand to Uther. Uther hesitated, then, as he slowly reached out to clasp it, Gorlois said smugly, "The woman who shares the honour of saving my life is now my wife."

Uther pulled his hand back and snickered. "I heard you had taken a wife. They say she is so beautiful, you keep her hidden. Afraid of losing her?" He taunted.

"Enough talk of women!" Gorlois growled, as he pulled his mount away from Uther's.

"Ah, you are right," Uther agreed. Then turning somber, he asked, "What news do you bring of Hengist?"

Again, Gorlois moved closer to Uther, and he lowered his voice as he replied, "He is holed up in a church west of Barry, off the coast of Glamorgan. My man tells me that he is with a wench, getting his fill before his son joins him. Herne is not expected to land for at least ten days. I would like to organize an ambush."

"No!" Uther shouted, losing control. "He is mine!"

He grabbed Gorlois' cloak at his throat, and pulled his face so close to his that they almost touched. "Tell no one of this, do you hear me?" Uther forced the words through clenched teeth. He released his hold on Gorlois, and his eyes were cold as ice as he said, "I know you seek revenge for yourself, but I seek it for Ambrosius."

Gorlois' face was beet-red, revealing his shock at Uther's outburst. He cleared his throat and nodded in agreement.

As he regained his composure, he squinted his eyes and warned Uther saying, "I will keep silent, but this is your test Uther. Get Hengist, and we will follow you. Fail, and you may end up with a skeleton army."

Uther smiled, more to himself than to Gorlois, and said with conviction, "Do not worry. I will get him."

Uther started to ride off, but reigned in suddenly, turning his mount to face Gorlois. "One more thing," he said, his impetuous nature revealing itself. "Bring your wife to my coronation. I would like to inspect her beauty myself."

Before Gorlois could reply, Uther rode away. Gorlois glared after him, his lip curled in contempt.

ᔕᕉ●ᕉᔕ

It was early morning, and Morgaine was asleep in Ygraine's bed. She began to stir, as Ygraine and Gorlois argued, their voices raised.

"I will not go!" Ygraine said, pacing back and forth in front of the fire.

Gorlois was seated near the fire. "You have to go. You have no choice," Gorlois said flatly. "The King himself requested your presence. That arrogant..." His voice trailed off.

Ygraine stopped pacing and glared at Gorlois. "No choice?" She asked, an incredulous look on her face. "There is always choice! Who is this King that makes demands of such insignificant meaning?"

"Ambrosius' brother, and new High King, Uther the Pendragon," Gorlois replied sourly.

Ygraine took a step back, and she suddenly felt as though the breath had been knocked out of her. She took in a long, deep breath and a chill went through her. She turned to face the fire for a moment while regulating her breathing. "Well,

Uther the Pendragon," she repeated the name with disdain as she shivered. "I will not meet your demands."

"There is penalty to pay, should you refuse the High King's request Ygraine," Gorlois warned.

Ygraine turned back to face him, and with chin held high stated, "Then I shall pay the penalty."

Gorlois rose from his chair, his voice slightly raised as he said emphatically, "You are being ridiculous woman!"

Morgaine whimpered, rolled over, and began to suck her thumb.

Gorlois was becoming uncomfortable, and he tried desperately to reason with her. "I do not like this any more than you do, but we must be rational. Besides, the other nobles will be accompanied by their Ladies. It would be questioned, should I be present without you."

He walked toward the door as Morgaine awoke and sat up. She began to rub the sleep from her eyes, then looked at Gorlois and became frightened. She immediately crawled from the bed and ran to Ygraine.

Ygraine took her in her arms and held her close while patting her on the back to comfort her. She gave Gorlois a look of repugnance and said, "It is a shame our daughter cowers from her own father. She does not even know who you are."

Gorlois did not respond to her remarks, but said, "You will be ready to leave in the morning."

He left the chamber, and Ygraine began to feel panic rising within her. She paced in front of the fire, gently rocking Morgaine in her arms, overcome with anxiety. Then she sat in a chair facing the fire with Morgaine on her lap. She tried desperately to calm herself, but all she could think of was that she would be away from her daughter for the first time, and the thought sickened her.

Morgaine's voice penetrated Ygraine's thoughts. "Look,"

she said, pointing her little finger toward the fire.

Ygraine's heart leapt, suddenly realizing that Morgaine also had the sight. "What do you see?" She questioned her gently, leaning forward, but not seeing anything herself.

Morgaine replied excitedly, "A dragon... a red one." She turned to look up at Ygraine with wide eyes. "He is coming for you."

ᔕᔕ ● ᔕᔕ

The coronation was held in the cathedral at Londinium as the season was changing from summer to autumn. The cathedral was full, and all its occupants were becoming impatient. Britain's new High King was over and hour late for his own coronation, and whispered predictions of his tardiness were spreading through the crowd.

Gorlois and Ygraine were seated three rows back from the front facing the altar. Ygraine had a clear view of the Archbishop who was seated next to the altar, and she noticed that he was visibly perspiring.

She tried desperately to close out the gossiping voices, but could not help over-hearing. From somewhere behind her she heard a man say, "He has a temperament more like a dog in heat, rather than a king." Another man said, "He cares more for his women than his country."

Ygraine felt herself blushing, then shook her head in disgust as she smoothed the folds of her plain black gown. She was completely noticeable in this crowd of Ladies who were immaculately coifed and dressed in all their finery. Also, Ygraine had deliberately worn her hair loose as an open act of disrespect, her long auburn waves cascading down her back. She did not care for anyone telling her what to do, but moreover, she was still upset at being away from Morgaine.

She smiled to herself as she recalled the events of the morning and prior evening, and thought of just how irritated she was indeed feeling.

She and Gorlois had been given lodging in the town near the Cathedral, and unfortunately, had to share a room so as not to cause suspicion of their marital bliss. Gorlois did, however, sleep on the floor, somewhat against his wishes. He was secretly hoping that being away together might put Ygraine in a different frame of mind. He was mistaken. She was so disgruntled that she had gone directly to bed after their arrival the night before, and had pulled the covers up over her head to shut him out.

Today, she had the audacity to present herself in a black gown. Gorlois was appalled. "You cannot wear black to a coronation! It is unheard of! You are not attending a funeral Ygraine!"

She raised her nose in the air and simply said, "It reflects my mood." She whisked passed him, and he began to dread the day ahead.

Thinking now of her actions, she wanted to laugh aloud, and she covered her mouth to suppress the temptation.

The voices of those around her were again seeping into her consciousness, and she found herself longing desperately for this coronation to speedily reach its end so that she could go home.

A sudden commotion outside the Cathedral drew everyone's attention to the entrance.

Ygraine's entire body began to tremble uncontrollably as Uther entered straddling a splendid steed. Almost in a state of panic, she quickly glanced at Gorlois, then immediately back to Uther, placing her hand over her heart.

Heading toward the altar bareback, Uther proudly held his banner of the Red Dragon in his left hand, while clutching a long, blonde braid in his right. He held the braid above his head, and the sunlight filtering in through the high, stained glass windows, caught the gold band on his wrist, causing a flash of light.

Ygraine could not take her eyes from him, and she felt as though her heart was visible to all as it beat wildly in her chest.

With only the strength of his legs, Uther halted the horse halfway to the altar as Uriens, awestricken, rose from his seat in the front row and stepped forward. "Is that the Saxon's braid?"

Uther flashed him a broad smile and said proudly, "Yes, and this was his horse. It is mine now, and so is this." He held the braid high for all to witness and shouted, "For my brother!" He gazed down into Uriens' large brown eyes, and finished softly with, "And my country."

In that moment there was a kind of soul recognition between them, and an instant bond was formed.

Murmurs rose as the doubtful crowd began to speak amongst themselves.

Uriens immediately dropped to one knee next to the horse and bowed his head saying, "I swear loyalty to you, my King." Then looking up into Uther's eyes, he concluded, with integrity, "I followed your brother. Now I will follow you, with honour."

Silence now filled the room, and the Scottish Lord, Lot rose from a position near the rear of the Cathedral and shouted, "How are we to know from where that braid came? It could be from Hengist, or it could be from one of your whores Uther, for all we know."

An obscure woman standing behind Lot rested her hand on his shoulder possessively.

Uriens quickly rose to his feet and spun around as Uther turned his mount in Lot's direction.

"Well, well... Lot." Uther spoke the words with distaste.

His disfavor of this man was unmasked as he spat out, "It belonged to the Saxon. I assumed there would be those of you who would require proof. Look outside. Hengist's head rests in a basket for you to witness." Then in a softer tone, "I thought it would be improper to bring it in, as there are Ladies present."

The horse, sensing its rider's surge of energy, suddenly reared, revealing its magnificent muscular strength. Uther grabbed onto the horse's mane with the same hand holding the braid, and masterfully controlled the animal beneath him. He then proceeded slowly toward the altar.

Murmurs again filled the Cathedral, and several men rushed outside. Their voices could be heard clearly as they confirmed Uther's words. "It is Hengist! The barbarian pig has been slaughtered!"

A cheer arose within, and again Uther raised both his banner, and the braid as he continued on.

He stopped just short of the altar, as his attention had suddenly been drawn to something a few rows back. A woman was staring at him, and he was instantly mesmerized by her.

His heart leapt in his chest and his body began to quiver. Then all at once, his heart was on fire, and he suddenly found it hard to breathe. Feeling light-headed, he closed his eyes for a moment. He took in a very long, deep breath, and when he opened his eyes, all else was invisible, but her. He stared openly at her, as a tear dropped from her eye. Sound and time stopped, and all matter took the form of slow motion as Uther dropped his banner and drew his sword from its sheathe. He pierced the braid with the end of the sword and held it out to Ygraine.

She reached for it, her fingers trembling. She took the braid, raised it to her lips, and kissed it. All the while, her eyes spoke words of love to him that she had felt for an eternity. Uther's gaze returned her every sentiment.

The sound of Gorlois' booming voice shook them from the euphoria of their silent world. "How dare you disgrace me like this in public Uther!" Then, thoroughly enraged, he shouted, "I will make you pay for this! I would prefer to do it now, but this is a house of God, and out of respect, I will wait for a more appropriate time!"

Uriens watched intently, prepared to defend his King.

Uther was undaunted by Gorlois' outburst. "Will you swear loyalty to me as High King?" Uther questioned, at that moment not caring what answer he received.

"Nay," Gorlois growled.

Uther shrugged. "Then save your strength, for I shall come to you."

His gaze left Gorlois and was immediately drawn back to Ygraine, who had not, for one moment, taken her eyes from him. Uther, deeply admiring her, took on the look of a starry-eyed boy.

Gorlois rose and roughly grabbed Ygraine by the arm, lifting her to her feet. Whispers filled the Cathedral, and all eyes watched as Gorlois hurriedly ushered Ygraine toward the entrance.

Uriens stepped back, and took his seat as they passed him.

Ygraine stared over her shoulder at Uther as they exited, while clasping the braid to her heart.

‹ॐ *Nine* ॐ›

It was evening when the Merlin entered the small candlelit chapel where mortal men were forbidden.

Angels carved into the stone walls seemed to serve as sentinels in this hallowed place, where worshippers of the Goddess gathered. A peaceful place, the only sound that could be heard was that of water trickling in a nearby stream.

Viviane, high priestess of this Isle of Avalon, was waiting for him. She stood behind the high, candlelit, stone altar, a sheer vision of beauty and grace. She was tall and slim, her long, wavy, black hair blending with the simple, black woolen dress she wore. A large Celtic cross hung from a chain around her neck, and rested over her solar plexus.

She met him halfway between the altar and the entrance, and welcomed him with outstretched arms. He took both her hands in his and brought them to his lips. He had a pained expression on his face as he stared into her familiar brown eyes.

Noticing his appearance, Viviane said with compassion, "You still grieve for her, do you not?"

The Merlin took a step back, still holding her hands, and

gazed upon her fully before replying, "The pain is deeper when I look at you. The resemblance is so strong."

Viviane spoke softly, giving him a look of sympathy. "Yes, I know, and I share your grief. Even after twenty years, I find myself missing my other half. It is said that when you lose a twin, you lose a part of yourself. Sometimes I feel that is so."

The Merlin's deeply embedded misery was unhidden in his eyes as he said, "I lost part of myself also. I fear I shall never be whole again." He closed his eyes, and a tremor ran through him as he whispered to himself, "Oh, Evanona."

Viviane gave him his time of silence, closing her eyes to join him for a moment's meditation. Then she opened her eyes, gently squeezed his hands, and said reassuringly, "She waits for you on the other side."

He took in a deep, quivering breath, exhaling fully, and opened his eyes. He forced back the emotions that threatened to erupt within him and said "She was not destined to die in childbirth."

She squeezed his hands again and said, "She could not bear life without you, and so, out of free will she made another choice."

All of this the Merlin already knew, and as a result thereof, he had allowed a seed of torment to be planted inside of him all those years ago, and it was rooted deeply within.

The numbness returning, he nodded, his eyes appearing hollow as he released her hands.

Nonetheless, a warm smile illuminated Viviane's lovely face and she said, "Come, I will show you what you have journeyed for."

She turned and walked gracefully toward the altar. The Merlin followed her silently.

Behind the altar, she lowered herself to her knees and began to lift a piece of the stone floor beneath it. The Merlin dropped to his knees and helped her to push the stone away, revealing an earthen space the length of the altar.

He reached inside and pulled out a long, heavy object that was wrapped in white cloth. He rose and lifted it, laying it upon the altar. As he unwrapped it, he drew in his breath sharply and said, "It is magnificent."

"Yes, it is magnificent," Viviane agreed, smiling as she gazed down admiringly at the sword. "I am glad you are pleased. It has been awaiting its time to be wielded."

Warmth filled her being as she pulled her gaze away and looked at the Merlin, whose eyes were fixed upon the sword. She said, "I shall never forget the night it appeared, all those years ago when Ygraine was born. I knew in my soul that my dear sister had passed, and I came here to bless her union with the Goddess."

The Merlin shifted his eyes from the sword to her face. A radiant light glowed from within her eyes as she continued, saying, "As I entered, there it was, lying upon the altar. I put it to rest in the arms of Mother Earth, knowing that one day you would come to retrieve it."

The Merlin nodded appreciatively, and again his eyes became riveted on the sword as he said, "It was a gift from Archangel Michael, patron of the soldiers." Slight amusement was revealed in his eyes as he stated, "It is ironic, for as Michael has been denoted for slaying a dragon, this sword shall be wielded by the Dragon."

The sword was massive, the blade of unyielding metal, razor sharp. The cross-guard and hilt were finely sculptured, a rare black diamond encrusted in the center. A dragon's head was intricately carved on the pommel. Two fiery red rubies rested in the eyes of the dragon.

There was an opening above the altar, revealing the moonlit sky. The Merlin grabbed the sword by the hilt and held it up, pointing it toward the heavens. His voice reverberated though the chapel as he shouted, "Caliburnus*, sword of Michael!"

A sudden gust of wind filtered down through the opening, causing the candles to flicker, and a distant roll of thunder was heard.

Viviane raised her arms upward, feeling the divine power of this moment pulsating through her body.

The Merlin laid the sword back on the altar, and slowly raised his hands and eyes to the sky above as another, much louder rumble of thunder was heard.

A moment passed, and Viviane watched in awe, as a piercing crack of thunder preceded a bolt of lightening that shot down through the opening into the sword. It seemed to come alive as the energy moved through it, the dragon's eyes gleaming.

Viviane closed her eyes, silently thanking the Universe for allowing her to witness such an event.

As she opened her eyes, the Merlin lifted the sword again, pointed it heavenward, and shouted, "Excalibur!"

*Caliburnus: Medieval Latin for Excalibur.

❧ *Ten* ☙

Gorlois and Ygraine squabbled the entire journey back to Cornwall, and their quarrelling continued after arriving back at Tintagel. Gorlois was furious, and could not understand Ygraine's resistance in giving up the Saxon braid that she now carried with her at all times.

Upon arrival, Ygraine went immediately to her chamber. Gorlois followed close behind.

Corelia had taken Morgaine to market, and although Ygraine was anxious to see them, she felt an increasing urgency to be alone. There had been no time to sort out what had happened, and she felt a desperate need to do so. All she knew was that 'her King' was real, and he loved her. Of that she was certain.

Gorlois continued to vent his anger as they entered the chamber. "I have been openly disgraced! Why can you not see my side of this? That... that... thing you carry so near you is a disgusting reminder of how I have been ridiculed!"

Ygraine headed toward a chair near the fire, and as she turned to sit, Gorlois lunged at her, attempting to take the braid from her. "Give it to me now Ygraine!" He demanded.

She pulled back, holding the braid tightly to her chest, and glared at him. "I will not!" She raised her head high in defiance and said, "It was a gift from the High King, and I shall keep it!"

Her head was spinning, and she collapsed into the chair, rubbing her temples. She looked up at Gorlois with pleading eyes and said, "Please leave me. I am weary and desire silence."

Enraged, he spun around on his heel and stomped from the room, mumbling obscenities under his breath, and slamming the door behind him.

As he was passing Morella's room, her door quickly opened. Morella grabbed him by the arm and pulled him inside.

"What has happened?" She asked, closing the door. "I didn't hear the words, but I couldn't help over-hearing the sound of your voice penetrating the walls."

Without thinking, Gorlois related all of the painful events to her. He paced the length of her room, speaking with his hands as well as with words. When he was finished venting his frustration, he sat down heavily at the foot of her bed, his head in his hands.

Morella sat beside him and attempted to comfort him by putting her arm around his shoulders sympathetically.

Her closeness was soothing to Gorlois, and he turned to face her, intending to thank her for her kindness. Instead, the intimacy that he was feeling consumed him. She was so close. Her scent penetrated his senses. He fought for control of his mind, but his emotions were stronger.

He kissed her once, then again, as she did not resist. All reason was lost as he took her face gently in his hands and tenderly kissed her eyelids, her nose, her cheek, then back to her mouth. He ran his fingers through her hair, feeling totally lost in her essence.

She was in her robe, and as he untied it, it fell open revealing her naked body underneath.

Morella was aflame under his touch as his hands roamed, stopping to caress her breasts. She leaned her head back, and he carefully laid her down.

He began to kiss her neck, and Morella sighed as waves of pleasure washed over her.

He took his time touching and tasting every part of her. He traced a line with his tongue between her breasts and down her stomach. He sucked on her navel, sending chills through her body. Then he moved his tongue lower, stopping between her thighs. She arched her back as her pleasure mounted. Her body moved rhythmically as his tongue created a fire within her, and she finally cried out in ecstasy as she reached her peak.

He raised to look at her, and the sweat on her body glistened. The sight of her was intoxicating, and he stared at her, in awe, as she lay breathing heavily with contentment.

Drawing his gaze away, he laid his head on her stomach, feeling her pulse beating rapidly beneath him. The sound was hypnotic, and Gorlois felt as though he was drifting far away. As her breathing slowed, he raised his head, shaking away the feeling, and stood up.

Morella, totally enthralled, sat up slowly and reached out for him. Gorlois backed away.

She furrowed her brows in confusion and said, "It is only right that I should please you in return."

Gorlois looked down at her and smiled warmly as he replied, "I have received more pleasure than I ever thought possible."

He turned and walked toward the door. As he reached it, he turned back to her and said, "Thank you."

Her voice quivered as she attempted to hold back her emotions. "I always wished I was in her shoes."

At the mention of Ygraine, Gorlois suddenly felt sad, and for the first time, he thought of how it could have been between them.

He left feeling at odds with himself as a mixture of contentment, and remorse surrounded him.

C3 *Eleven* 80

The Saxons had temporarily retreated after the death of Hengist. Herne would need time to reorganize before returning to avenge his father.

The Saxon's were the last thing on Uther's mind. He had returned to Viroconium after the coronation, and could think of nothing else, but Gorlois' wife.

After what had taken place in Londinium, this warlord was a changed man. He walked the halls of the keep, lonely for the first time in his life. How could he have ever lived without her? Her haunting face was embedded in his memory, and somehow he felt it was a very old memory. Deep inside, he knew this woman, even though he had never seen her before the coronation.

He could not stand being without her, and thought frantically of how he could steal her away from Gorlois without causing himself humiliation. He did, after all, need to be concerned with his reputation now that he was High King.

When he had reached his wits' end after days of seeking, and finding no answers within himself, he decided to send for the Merlin, who was reputed to reside in a cave north of Guent. For the first time, Uther felt the need for Ambrosius' prophet.

Uther had barely gotten the message off to summon him, when the Merlin arrived. Uther was in the great hall roaming aimlessly around the room with his hands clasped behind him. He was in deep thought, and was startled at the sound of the Merlin clearing his throat.

He turned to find the Merlin standing casually in the entranceway.

How on God's earth did you get here that quickly!" Uther questioned, visibly shocked.

The Merlin raised a brow. "You sent for me?"

"My messenger left here only a short time ago," Uther replied, scratching his head in confusion.

The Merlin moved forward toward Uther. "Obviously I did not receive the message, for it has not yet been delivered." Reaching him, he looked deeply into Uther's eyes and said, "But I heard your call."

Uther shook his head in bewilderment, then he grinned and said, "I will not pretend to understand you sir, but I am grateful for your appearance."

Uther waved his hand nonchalantly toward the fire as he moved in that direction, where a settee and large armchair faced each other. "Please... sit."

The Merlin moved toward the chair, but stopped just in front of it. He turned around and gave Uther a quizzical look and asked, "Are you sure this chair is facing the proper direction?"

"What!" Uther exclaimed, momentarily confused by the question. Then he recalled his and the Merlin's confrontation about 'table geography', and he burst into laughter. "Touché!" He remarked, raising a brow.

The Merlin repressed the smile that almost appeared, and

pleased with himself, he relaxed into the chair.

Uther poured two goblets of mead at a nearby table and handed one to the Merlin before sitting down on the settee. After taking a swallow, Uther began to explain. "The reason I have called you here..."

The Merlin held up his hand to halt his speech. "I know why you have summoned me. I knew that a day would come when you would ask for the aid of Ambrosius' prophet, and that day is here."

The Merlin raised a brow, then casually took a sip of his mead while Uther stared at him intently, impatiently waiting for him to continue.

The Merlin set his goblet aside on the table next to his chair and said, "I will offer you my aid for the welfare of Britain."

Uther leaned forward. "Are you aware of the happenings at the coronation?"

The Merlin replied, "What I am aware of is your desire for Ygraine, the Duchess of Cornwall."

Now Uther was completely engrossed in the Merlin's words, and he leaned even closer asking, "How do you know these things?"

"It matters not," the Merlin replied. "Now silence yourself and listen to me."

Uther leaned back, attempting to relax as the Merlin continued. "You are destined to be with Ygraine."

Uther bolted straight up and opened his mouth to speak, but the Merlin held up his hand to silence him. "Had you let destiny take its course, and allowed Gorlois to die on the battlefield, as was his destiny, we would not be in this awkward position now."

Uther's face lost all colour as he remembered the Merlin's scream that day on the battlefield when he had gone to Gorlois' aid.

The Merlin picked up his goblet and took another sip, then said, "Gorlois was taken to the sanctuary, as you instructed, and met his lovely bride there."

Uther leaned back and closed his eyes, silently cursing himself.

"Do not linger on the past," the Merlin said, waving his hand as if to send the thought away as he set his goblet back down. "We have the future to discuss."

Uther, downtrodden, opened his eyes and took a long swallow of his mead. The Merlin took pity on him, and decided to quickly put him out of his misery by saying, "I will help you attain your desire Uther..."

Uther's eyes lit up, and the Merlin finished his statement. "But in return you must grant me your favour."

Uther quickly rose to his feet and said ardently, "I would do anything, for she is the flame of my heart."

"I know that feeling well," the Merlin whispered. He paused for a moment, then shook his head to rid himself of the memories that threatened to enter his mind. Now agitated, he said, "Sit down Uther and listen to me!"

Uther sat, and the Merlin quickly calmed himself. After reaching for his goblet and taking another sip of mead, he said, "Ygraine will conceive a child who is destined for greatness. You will father that child."

Even though his heart was racing, Uther kept quiet and stared at the Merlin as he proceeded. "Because of the state of affairs to come, the child's parentage will be questioned. For that reason, and others, I must have your permission and your word that you will allow me to take the child at his birth."

Uther again stood up. He had a concerned look on his face as the Merlin gazed directly into his eyes and said, "I will make sure that he is protected and brought forth to claim the throne as your heir when the time is right." He paused, then asked, "Do you agree?"

Uther let out a deep sigh, then turned away and walked to the window, staring out. After a moment, he turned back around and replied, "As I said, I would do anything. But what of Ygraine's feelings? Will she agree to give up her child? And what of Gorlois?"

The Merlin rose from his chair, set the goblet on the table, and stated confidently, "Ygraine will agree. As for Gorlois, his destiny is about to catch up with him."

Uther and the Merlin stared at each other for several moments, then Uther turned back to the window and looked out. The Merlin took a few steps toward him and said, "Ygraine will be your queen Uther."

Uther continued to stare out the window for a few more moments, then turned back around again, a grin now spreading across his face. "Then it is done!"

The Merlin merely nodded.

Excitement was now running through Uther, and he questioned, "When will you make the arrangements?"

The Merlin revealed a slight smile and replied, "Meet me on the night of the sixth full moon from now at Tintagel. There is a cave at the foot of the cliff nearest the sea. A sharp crag juts out above it, covering its identity. You will find it. Your heart will lead you."

Uther's grin was replaced with a frown. "Can it not be sooner? Six moons is a long time to wait."

"We will not be making alterations this time," the Merlin responded flatly.

Uther understood his words perfectly and nodded in agreement. Then a puzzled look crossed his face as he walked back to where the Merlin was standing. Reaching him, he said, "The course of destiny has been altered, but you once said that I would request your favour. Was it in regards to this matter?"

The Merlin replied, "As I have said, you are destined to be with Ygraine. However, your meeting would have been under different circumstances."

Uther raised a brow. "What circumstances?"

The Merlin hesitated, then he decided to explain to Uther the pre-ordained course of destiny. "Had you followed your spiritual heart rather than your sentimental one, you would have pursued Hengist as you were destined to."

Uther listened intently, thoroughly drawn in by the Merlin's words. He continued, "You would have suffered a wounding by Hengist, but you would have also had the pleasure of receiving a healing by a fair maiden at the sanctuary."

He paused as Uther let out a deep groan, then said, "Gorlois would have died on the battlefield, and having left no heir, Tintagel would have become the property of the High King, which he would have gifted to his brother upon his betrothal to the lovely maiden."

Uther groaned louder, running his fingers through his hair as he shook his head. Then he gave the Merlin a questioning glance and asked, "Why would your favour have been required?"

The Merlin was silent for a moment before replying, "I am sorry Uther. Some things are better left unsaid."

Uther gazed intently at him, and the Merlin thought it best to quickly change the subject. He gestured toward the door with his hand and said, "I have something for you Uther. Please come outside."

Without hesitation, the Merlin strode from the room with Uther at his side.

Once outside, Uther stood and watched as the Merlin removed the sword that was strapped to his saddle. Unveiling it, he pulled the cloth away that was covering it and held it up. The sunlight reflected off of it, illuminating its brilliance.

The rubies looked like pools of blood as the eyes of the dragon gazed at Uther.

Uther's eyes bulged as the Merlin handed it to him saying proudly, "May I present... Excalibur."

Uther reached slowly for the sword, grabbing the hilt that fit his hand perfectly. The muscles in his arm protruded as he raised the heavy mass. The sun kissed the rubies in the sword, and the band at Uther's wrist, causing a simultaneous blazing flash of red and gold light. For an instant it appeared as though a flame had been kindled.

Uther lowered the sword and said, with genuine appreciation, "There are no words that I can find to express my gratitude." He was taken aback by the Merlin's gift, and asked, "Why have you given this to me?"

"It will belong to your son one day Uther," the Merlin replied. "It is very powerful, but it needs to have the Pendragon vibration in order to fulfill its destiny. Your touch will ignite it so that it may be passed down at the proper time."

Uther could not take his eyes from the sword. He felt as if it were an extension of himself, for its comfort within his grasp was superb. He began play-acting with it, wielding it as if he were defending himself in battle.

The Merlin swung himself onto his saddle. He leaned over and extended his hand to Uther and asked, in a very serious tone, "On your honour as both man and King, do I have your word concerning the child?"

Uther lowered the sword and stepped closer. He looked up, and the Merlin gazed deeply into his eyes, as if he were looking directly into his soul. Uther clasped his hand firmly, returning his gaze and replied, just as seriously, "You have my word."

❦ *Twelve* ❧

Gorlois was obsessed and had left Tintagel on a quest to gather forces against Uther.

Ygraine was also obsessed, once again, with 'her King', and now that she knew his identity it was harder than before to contain her longing.

She spent less time with Morgaine. In Ygraine's absence, the child had become quite fond of Corelia, and now spent much of her time enjoying being spoiled by her grandmother.

Corelia wanted all the details of the coronation, but Ygraine was not ready to share the experience. She put Corelia off, feigning exhaustion from the journey, and promised to tell her everything when she had completely regained her strength.

To Ygraine's surprise, Morella asked no questions at all. In fact, she made herself even more scarce than she had before. Ygraine tended to her own needs most of the time, and was actually grateful for the solitude.

"Will he come for me as Morgaine has seen?" Ygraine found herself questioning.

At times she even wished that Gorlois were dead so that

she would be free. Then she would pray for forgiveness for having such feelings.

After several days of being consumed with thoughts of Uther, not knowing how she could possibly live without him, but also feeling that she must, she decided to call upon the Merlin. She had not communicated with him in over two years, but she was confident that he would answer her plea.

She positioned herself in front of the fire in her chamber, forcing herself to relax. After taking several deep breaths, she leaned forward in her chair and searched the flames. She peered deep into them, softly speaking his name. "Merlin... Merlin, please come to me."

He immediately responded, "The present tone of your voice is far easier on my ears than the last time you summoned me."

His reply came not from the fire, and Ygraine jumped to her feet, spinning around to find him standing directly behind her. She drew her breath in sharply. His powerful presence shocked her, causing her to grab on to the chair to steady herself.

She quickly regained her composure and asked haughtily, "Do you not knock?"

He shrugged and replied, matter-of-factly, "It is a waste of time."

Ygraine stared at him in dismay. "Forgive my surprise, but I did not expect to have sight of you in such... solid form."

He laid his hand on the back of her chair, gesturing with his other hand for her to sit as he raised his eyebrows and asked, "Still relying on expectation Ygraine?"

She lowered her eyes shamefully and sat down. As he took the chair opposite her, she looked up and replied softly, "No, I do not... and I have accepted the choices I have made. Though I have not been overly content, I have learned to live in the moment. In that, I have found peace."

She paused, closing her eyes for a moment as feelings of frustration suddenly arose in her. Then she looked at him, the softness leaving her voice as she continued. "Until now. Now I find no peace."

She rose from her chair, feeling more frustration rising to the surface. Looking down at him, she questioned, "Was I being tested? Have I proven myself worthy enough to fulfill destiny, or is there more fire to pass through?"

He did not respond, and she turned away, gazing into the fire, her voice lowering to a whisper. "I have the sight, and sometimes it is a curse to me." Turning back to him, she asked, "How could I not have expectations, when I have the ability to see certain aspects of my life stretched out before me?"

He still did not respond, and Ygraine moved back to her chair and sat down, her emotions now under control. She tilted her head and looked deeply into his eyes. "You seem to take an odd interest in me." She paused, then inquired, "Should you not be counseling our new High King? After all, that was your position with Ambrosius, was it not?"

The Merlin rose from his chair, picked up the poker and began to casually stoke the fire. He steered clear of her foremost remark and replied, "As a matter of fact, I am here on behalf of our new High King."

Ygraine's eyes widened and her heart began to flutter. She swallowed hard and asked anxiously, "You have been with him?"

He glanced over his shoulder and replied, "Yes."

"He is a great warrior, is he not?" Ygraine questioned, her mind drifting, as she retrieved the braid from a velvet pouch that hung from her waist.

The Merlin put the poker down and turned to face her. "Not these days," he remarked.

Alarmed by his reply, she leaned forward with a worried

look on her face. "Is he not well?"

The Merlin let out a sigh. "He is... lovesick," he stated with a tone of disgust as he sat back down.

Ygraine felt as though she would swoon, and she leaned back into the chair, closing her eyes and holding the braid to her heart. "Oh, my heart beats for him," she said, with a look of agony on her face.

As he watched her, a slight smile lit his face. He was thoroughly enjoying her euphoria. Then when she opened her eyes and looked at him, he immediately replaced his smile with a look of sternness. He shook his head sympathetically and said, "I will be glad when destiny's course has been righted. It is such a drain on me to be dealing with such sensitivities."

He shifted his position in the chair, making himself more comfortable, and cleared his throat. With a serious tone, he said, "Listen to me Ygraine."

The quality of his voice made her sit erect, listening intently.

Then he explained. "Many years ago I had a vision. I saw peace in these lands brought about by a boy king who would rule in a way that no other has. This vision was given to me because our people are in great need, and I have the power to carry out this prophecy. As I once told you, you will give birth to that boy child... and Uther will father him."

Ygraine let out a long sigh, unable to contain her feelings of relief and delight.

"So you see Ygraine," the Merlin continued. "The choices you made did not change destiny, they simply shifted its course."

Tears of joy filled Ygraine's eyes, and she nodded, understanding his words.

He leaned forward slightly, his gaze intent upon her as he said, "Destiny unfolds easily to those who allow. In your attempt to control, you have suffered and created a chain of suffering."

He again rose to his feet, moving back to the fire. He gazed into the flames for several moments, preparing himself for her reaction, before turning around and saying, "Unfortunately, there are more prices to pay for choosing unwisely... and you and Uther will pay that penalty."

Ygraine wiped her tears away, and she suddenly felt the joy drain from her heart as she gazed at him, trepidation now filling her.

Without another moment's pause, he said, "You will make a sacrifice that will be hard for you, but you have also been blessed by giving birth to the girl child, who was to be yours and Uther's second child. She will soothe your loss."

Ygraine's brows creased with concern. "My loss? What must I forsake in order to be with my beloved?" She was eager to sacrifice anything to be with Uther, but she was suddenly fearful of his response.

"You must give up the child," he replied firmly.

Shocked, Ygraine's mouth dropped open. "Why must I give up the child?"

Her mind reverted back to the day she had refused Morgaine, and the thought of feeling that kind of separation again terrified her.

Her eyes revealed her turmoil, and the Merlin had an urge to comfort her.

However, he moved back to his chair and sat back down, in spite of his fleeting desire. Nonetheless, his voice did soften as he said, "Had events taken place as was envisioned, Gorlois would not have been a participant. Because of his involvement, there will be questions. For many reasons, the child will need to be protected."

Ygraine put her hand to her mouth as she attempted to suppress her tears. He endeavored to soothe her by saying,

"Do not hold yourself solely responsible for this Ygraine, for Uther was equally responsible for the shift as you."

"I would do anything to be with him... but to give up the child..." she said, her voice trailing off as she shook her head. "I do not believe I can do so."

The Merlin leaned forward, a grave look in his eyes. "Ygraine, his life will be in danger."

Her eyes widened in horror, and he stated, "Again, it narrows down to choices."

He stood up, and she had not realized until then, the full extent of the power that he exuded. He stared down at her intently and said, "I urge you to make the highest choice this time."

She stared back at him, and a tear dropped from her eye. "For the first time in my life, I feel I have no choice." She raised the braid and brushed it against her cheek. "I cannot allow harm to come to the child, and I see no life without the Pendragon. I will do as you ask."

He nodded and said, "I hope that you will not take offense Ygraine, but I must have your word."

Her eyes filled with fire and she rose from her chair, holding the braid out in front of him. Her fist shook as she said, "On this, my most cherished possession, I give you my solemn vow."

Their eyes locked for several moments. The sound of the door opening broke through the thickness in the air.

Morgaine stood inside the doorway, momentarily uncomfortable at seeing a stranger in the room with her mother. They turned and watched as Morgaine slowly moved forward, sizing up the Merlin as she did. She seemed mesmerized by his presence, and to Ygraine's surprise, not the least bit frightened. When she reached them, she stared up at the Merlin and said sweetly, "Hello grandfather."

He stared back at her, unable to remove his gaze, but did

not reply.

Ygraine immediately scooped Morgaine up and wrapped her arms around her protectively. With an apologetic look on her face, she said, "I fear she is confused." Then to Morgaine, as she laid her wrist against the child's forehead to check for fever, she said softly, "This is not your grandfather, my sweet."

The Merlin and Morgaine were still locked in each other's eyes. This was causing Ygraine discomfort, and her voice quivered as she asked, "Why do you look at her that way?"

"She has the sight," he replied, his eyes penetrating Morgaine's.

Ygraine took a few steps back, suddenly feeling very nervous. "She is not part of the bargain." Her words were very firm and clear.

Continuing to stare into the depths of Morgaine's soul, he stated, "Of course not." He paused, then said, "I see her destiny in her eyes." Finally breaking eye contact with Morgaine, he looked at Ygraine and said, "She has chosen quite a powerful one."

Before she could reply, he turned away and walked toward the door. Ygraine called out after him, "What is to happen now?"

He turned as he reached the door. "In six moons, Uther will come to you. In the meantime, continue to dream Ygraine. When the time is near, you will know it. You will see it in the flames."

He opened the door, then turned around again, as if he had forgotten something and said, "Someone close to you has deceived you. Your ability to forgive will be strongly tested."

"Who?" Ygraine asked, concern in her voice.

The sound of the door closing was his reply.

༅ *Thirteen* ༄

Gorlois made his way north to Scotland, riding like the wind over the moors, heading purposefully toward the home of Lot in Lothian.

Lot was the most likely candidate to align against Uther. Gorlois had heard rumors that Lot and his wife, Morgause had left the coronation shortly after he and Ygraine. Therefore, Lot had not sworn fealty to the new High King.

Lot graciously welcomed Gorlois into his home, but to Gorlois' astonishment, Morgause was permitted to be present during their meeting.

They met in the great hall, and Gorlois was grateful for the blazing fire to warm him. But there was a coldness in this place that was more than climatic. The low hanging clouds that could be seen through the windows blended with the grayness of the drab furnishings, adding to the iciness.

Morgause was waiting as he and Lot entered the room. She was standing on the hearth, but there was no warmth surrounding her. She appeared to Gorlois to be carved of stone, for her face was expressionless, and almost gray in pallor.

An involuntary shiver ran through him, and he suddenly felt the need for a strong mead to soothe him. It was not offered.

There were two chairs in front of the fire, and Morgause waved her hand as a directive for the two men to sit. She, however, remained standing.

Morgause stared at Gorlois for what seemed like an eternity. Her eyes were as expressionless as her face, and he found himself trying to figure out what colour they were, but was unclear. They seemed colourless, taking on the grayness of her complexion. Her reddish hair was pulled tight and bound at her neck. She had a matronly appearance, which contradicted her age. There was a familiar look to her mouth, but overall, he found nothing attractive about her. In fact, she bore quite a resemblance to her father, the Duke, who was not considered to have been overly attractive himself when he was alive.

Lot ran his fingers through his jet-black hair, and he began to play with his goatee, seemingly nervous.

The sound of Morgause's voice, which held a masculine tone, and was as cold as the look in her eyes, broke the silence. "Stop fidgeting," she demanded, her attention having shifted from Gorlois to Lot.

Lot cleared his throat and placed his hands on the arms of his chair, perfectly still.

Morgause, satisfied that she now had his full attention, shifted her focus back to Gorlois. "Your messenger arrived yesterday," she said, staring at him intently. "Am I to understand that you have come here seeking our allegiance?" Before Gorlois could reply, she immediately continued, "Why should we align with you?"

Gorlois opened his mouth to speak, but Morgause persisted. "Do you seek the throne, or do you gather strength for personal reasons?"

Gorlois shifted his position in the chair and looked at Lot as he said, "You bore witness to my disgrace at the coronation."

Lot nodded, and nervously straightened the cuff of his sleeve. Gorlois, agitated with him, turned back to Morgause. "I seek revenge."

Morgause smiled, and Gorlois feared that her face would crack. "Ah," she whispered, tilting her head back slightly and stroking her throat. "Revenge has a sweet taste, does it not?"

Gorlois was beginning to think that she was totally mad, and silently berated himself for coming here.

Morgause glared down at him, taking on an air of arrogance as she said, "We do seek the throne, and when it is time, we will not require assistance from others. If it is revenge you seek, I suggest you find it on your own."

She brushed passed him, and again a shiver went through him. She stopped midway to the door, as an apparent pleasant thought crossed her mind. She turned, and there was a crazed look in her eyes as she said, "Mayhaps you should consider sneaking into his bedchamber and murdering him in his sleep."

Gorlois did not turn to acknowledge her, and as she exited, cackling, he jumped to his feet.

Lot, who had seemed to lose his tongue, was also on his feet instantly, escorting Gorlois out of the room saying, "I apologize, but as Morgause has said, this is your battle."

Gorlois had no reply.

Once outside, he swung himself onto his horse and galloped away, thinking to himself, "That is the closest thing to hell that I have ever seen, and she is surely a servant of the devil!"

❧ *Fourteen* ❧

Gorlois spent the next six months with his men in heavy training. He had decided to do as the she-devil had suggested and wage his own war against Uther. He was obsessed with the thought of revenge, and spent every waking hour on the training field preparing.

Ygraine spent every waking hour dreaming, as the Merlin had suggested. The winter had been long, but as the weather became calmer now with the approach of spring, she found contentment in being out of doors. She went for long walks, sometimes taking Morgaine with her.

Even now, the child shared Ygraine's bedchamber, and her bed, as they both still found great comfort in their closeness. However, Ygraine was feeling the necessity to change their sleeping arrangements. She was hoping to be sharing a bed soon with the Pendragon, and thought it best that Morgaine get used to sleeping alone.

As the sixth full moon approached, Ygraine decided to speak to Morella about offering her chamber to Morgaine. She wanted her daughter as close as possible, and since Morella spent most of her time elsewhere, it seemed the appropriate solution.

It was evening, and Ygraine had tucked Morgaine in for the night. She heard the door to Morella's room close, and quietly knocked on the adjoining door between their chambers.

There was no reply, and Ygraine knocked again, this time harder. The door opened slightly, and Morella peered out.

"Yes, what is it Ygraine?" Morella questioned softly, immediately lowering her eyes.

"May we speak?" Ygraine replied. "There is an imperative matter that I wish to discuss with you."

"What matter?" Morella asked, quickly raising her fear-filled eyes to meet Ygraine's.

Because of Morella's feelings of guilt concerning Gorlois, she immediately assumed that Ygraine was referring to the secret, intimate tryst between them. Knowing that Ygraine had the sight, she had feared that she would gain knowledge of the situation, and dreaded being confronted by her.

Morella opened the door slowly, allowing Ygraine to enter. She stepped into the room, wringing her hands together, a bit worried about broaching the subject. Moving past Morella, she walked to the center of the room, turned around and said, "I came to ask you to take another chamber."

"You want me to leave?" Morella asked, her eyes welling up with tears as she turned away from Ygraine.

Ygraine was confused by Morella's response, and opened her mouth to speak when Morella turned back around. "So, you know." Morella stated, then rushed on with her confession. "I meant no harm, I swear to you Ygraine. I only thought to comfort him. I knew you'd find out, but I assure you, it only happened once, and that was some time ago. I've stayed away from him since... and you. I couldn't face you." She looked at Ygraine with pleading eyes. "Please forgive me. I couldn't bear it if you didn't forgive me

Ygraine."

Ygraine stared at Morella silently for a moment in confusion, then said, "I know not what you speak of."

Then suddenly, the Merlin's words concerning deception hit her with a heavy blow. She shook her head as Morella's chattering began to make sense to her. She took a few steps toward Morella, looking at her with eyes of disbelief. "What are you saying to me?" Ygraine demanded.

Instantly, Morella realized that she had offered information that Ygraine knew nothing of. She covered her mouth with her hand, wishing desperately that she could retrieve her words. She stared wide-eyed at Ygraine, afraid to speak further.

"You have been with my husband Morella?" Ygraine asked, her voice quivering with anger. She moved even closer to Morella and asked, "How could you do so?"

As an act of self-defense, Morella raised her head high, closed the remainder of the distance between them and said, "How can you question my behavior concerning your husband when you love another?"

Ygraine narrowed her eyes and looked at her questioningly.

Morella continued, "I've seen you wandering the halls carrying the High King's gift pressed to your heart. Your husband was disgraced by him, and yet you remove yourself from his presence, and think instead of the one who has humiliated him. You waited your whole life for Gorlois. How could you turn him away now? You don't deserve him, and I assure you, you won't find another as passionate as he."

Morella paused and took a deep breath, feeling strength in her defense of Gorlois. Then she squinted her eyes and spat out, "You are selfish Ygraine!"

Ygraine automatically slapped her hard across the face,

stunning Morella, who immediately placed her hand on her stinging cheek.

"How dare you speak to me of selfishness?" Ygraine hissed, as she stepped back from Morella. "You think you are so knowledgeable, and yet you know so little. Did you know that your 'passionate' Lord brutally raped me on our wedding night, and we have not been together since?"

Morella's face went pale, and her mouth dropped open slightly.

"Did you know that he shares the bed of a serving wench instead of mine?" Ygraine asked with contempt.

Morella turned away and slowly walked across the room, sitting down on the edge of her bed. She placed her hand over her stomach as it began to churn.

Ygraine followed after her, her eyes burning with unshed tears as she said, "I did not wait my whole life for Gorlois. I chose to be with him, not only for myself, but for us all. I thought the man I had waited for my whole life, did not really exist. I have since found out that he does exist, and yes I love him. I have always loved him."

Ygraine's heart was pounding hard, and she could not recall ever feeling so filled with rage. She stepped back, and her voice was strained as she said, "The Pendragon will come for me. Until then, I want you out of this room! After I am gone, you may share my chamber with your Lord, for all I care."

Morella rose from the bed, her knees shaking, and her eyes filled with tears. She tried to steady herself, but could not. She lowered herself to kneel in front of Ygraine, then bent and kissed her bare feet. Looking up at Ygraine, she then began to cry and said, "I didn't know. Please don't turn me away."

Ygraine was still seething. She stepped back from her and said coldly, "I told you once never to kneel to me again."

Morella looked up at her, feeling hopeful. "Yes, we are sisters."

"We are not sisters!" Ygraine shouted. "You have deceived me." She shook her head pitifully. "I cannot forgive you."

Ygraine turned away and went back into her own chamber. She could hear Morella's sobs as she closed the door behind her.

Morella immediately moved to the main level of the castle near Rodric and Corelia's quarters. She was so upset, that she confided all of the events to Corelia, but thought it best not to involve Rodric.

Corelia soothed Morella and assured her that in time Ygraine would feel differently.

Corelia allowed a few days to pass, then went to see Ygraine.

They sat in front of the fire speaking quietly so as not to wake Morgaine, who had fallen asleep in Ygraine's bed.

Corelia's face was drawn and her eyes were filled with sadness as she said, "You've kept to yourself so much. I should have known something was wrong. And when you didn't tell me about the coronation, I thought it was because it was a boring affair."

Ygraine raised her eyebrows. "Oh, I assure you it was far from boring."

Corelia reached over and took Ygraine's hand, squeezing it. Her voice quivered and she fought back her tears as she said, "I wish you had told me about your first night."

Ygraine let out a low chuckle. "I fear it would have been Gorlois' last night."

Corelia also chuckled as she again squeezed Ygraine's hand. "You've got that right!"

Releasing Ygraine's hand, and leaning back in her chair, Corelia again turned serious and asked, "What's going to happen now child?"

Ygraine replied, "The Pendragon is coming for me, and he is coming soon. That is all I can tell you now, for that is all I know. When the time grows nearer, I shall know more."

Corelia nodded, then with a sympathetic tone in her voice, she asked, "Can you not find it within your heart to forgive Morella? She loves you Ygraine."

Ygraine's face hardened, and she abruptly looked away. "I cannot... not now."

Corelia's disappointment was evident, but she held her tongue. She stood, and as Ygraine turned her head back, Corelia kissed her on the cheek and said, "Why don't you let me take Morgaine to her new room. You need some time alone."

Ygraine smiled and gazed over at Morgaine. "As you can see, she prefers my bed, but she will soon get used to her own."

Corelia walked over to the bed and scooped the child up into her arms, then headed toward the adjoining door. Upon reaching it, she turned back to Ygraine and said, "Search deep inside yourself Ygraine before you decide not to forgive Morella. Think about what your intentions are. I'm not excusing his behavior, but no matter what's happened between you and Gorlois, he's still your husband, and you think to let another take you from him. Does that make you any different than Morella?" She paused, and said, "I think not. You've made choices for passions' sake, and you'll continue to. Don't condemn Morella for doing the same."

Corelia held her gaze on Ygraine for a moment, then smiled and said, "Goodnight my sweet."

Ygraine returned her smile, and Corelia entered Morgaine's chamber, closing the door behind her.

Ygraine felt torn. She was still angry, but she was also confused. She looked into the fire and said, "I am certain of one thing. I love you Pendragon."

As she spoke the words, Uther's face appeared in the flames. Her heart soared at the sight of him, and she felt his presence was very near. She became excited, for she knew in that moment that on the morrow the full moon would bring them together.

She reached toward the fire, wanting so badly to touch his face, when suddenly it changed to the face of Gorlois. She pulled her hand back quickly and stared intently at the picture being painted in front of her.

Gorlois was astride his horse on a bridge, and there were several of his men scattered amongst the trees behind him.

As the vision faded, she heard Gorlois' voice. "The war is between us Uther, not our men. Meet me on the night of the full moon at Slaughter Bridge. Come alone, when the moon is at its highest. If you cross over, Cornwall is yours, and all that goes with it."

Ygraine rose from her chair and yelled into the fire, as if he could hear her. "Deceiver! You shall take your dishonour to your grave!"

She knew instinctively that Uther had accepted the challenge and would be en route.

She immediately scrolled out a message of warning for Uther. Then hurrying to the door and opening it, she found one of the servants in the corridor and instructed her to find Rodric and send him to her.

When Rodric arrived, Ygraine was bent over a table affixing a seal to the rolled up parchment in front of her.

Rodric walked over to her, and she blew on the wax before holding the message out to him. With a sense of urgency in her voice, she said, "I can trust no one else. Please take this to the High King. He will be riding toward Cornwall alone."

Rodric just stared at her, obviously confused by her request. Ygraine let out a sigh of desperation and laid her hand on his forearm saying, "Please father... you must leave now and head him off."

Rodric took the parchment from her, but he was still confused as Ygraine said, "He will be riding a giant of horse the colour of corn-silk." She paused, drawing a mental picture of Uther, then said, "You will know it is the King by his eyes."

Rodric looked down at the parchment in his hand, a blank expression on his face. "I don't understand Ygraine."

She grabbed his shoulders, giving him an intense look in an effort to make him realize the importance of his task. "An ambush awaits him."

Rodric's eyes widened, and he took a step back. He was appalled at the indication, but knew that Ygraine would not speak an untruth. "An ambush against the High King?"

Ygraine nodded. "Yes. You must go straight away and speak to no one. Do you understand?"

He nodded his head, as he filled with a sense of gallantry. "Don't worry Ygraine. I'll get it to him"

He turned to leave, and Ygraine exclaimed, "Wait!" Her inner voice spoke, and she hurried to the cedar chest against the wall. She opened it and retrieved one of Gorlois' cloaks and took it to Rodric. Handing it to him, she said, "Take this with you and give it to our King. My guidance tells me that he shall need it."

As Rodric left, Ygraine turned back to the fire and said, "God help you Gorlois, for I shall kill you, should you harm one hair on the Pendragon's beautiful head!"

ᗧᗣ●ᗣᗢ

Rodric rode through the night reaching North Devon at dawn.

Riding hard, he made his way down the narrow Roman

road, the horse's hooves pounding against the dirt. The morning mist rose from the surrounding foliage, drops of dew settling on the heavy overgrowth.

A figure on horseback appeared in the distance, and as Rodric neared him, he felt certain that it was the High King. Rodric slowed his horses pace, as did the approaching rider.

Rodric's horse was dripping wet and breathing heavily as he reigned in near Uther's mount.

Uther remarked, "Good God man! Do you wish to kill the beast beneath you?"

It was definitely the High King, for as Ygraine had said, there was no mistaking his horse, or the eyes of the Pendragon.

Rodric was panting, sweating as profusely as his horse. He leaned forward, gazing into Uther's eyes. "Sire?"

Uther hesitated a moment, then nodded.

Rodric bowed his head respectfully, then immediately withdrew the message from inside his coat and said, "I bring news from my Lady Ygraine, sire."

Uther, startled, grabbed the message from Rodric. As he unrolled the parchment and read it, his jaw tightened, his ire clearly distinguishable. Then lowering it, he reached out and laid his hand on Rodric's shoulder. His gratitude was apparent as he said, "I give you thanks for your haste." He backed his mount a few paces away from Rodric's saying, "Tell the Lady Ygraine that I shall thank her personally."

Rodric nodded, feeling a deep sense of pride for accomplishing his mission. Then he retrieved the cloak from inside his saddlebag and handed it out to Uther. "Sire, Ygraine said you'd be needing this."

Uther urged his mount forward, took the cloak from Rodric, and wrapped it around himself and his own cloak. Then he spurred his mount and was out of sight before Rodric had time to catch his breath.

ౡ౾●ఌ౾

Uther rode directly to the home of Uriens. It was early morning when he arrived. The guards immediately opened the gate, and Uther made his way to the outer bailey.

Uriens was on the training field. Many of his men were gathered around watching intently as he and one of his men engaged in swordplay.

As Uther approached, Uriens powerfully knocked his opponent to the ground. His men began to laugh and cheer.

The sound of Uther's horse approaching caused them all to turn around. Reigning in, Uther began to clap his hands, grinning broadly.

Realizing it was the High King, the men immediately bowed respectfully.

Seeing Uther riding alone concerned Uriens. He instructed his men to continue, then went to greet him straight away.

Uther did not dismount, and Uriens grabbed the reins to steady his horse. Beads of perspiration dripped from Uriens' brown curls as they clung to the nape of his neck. He was ruggedly handsome with features that were finely chiseled, his body solid and muscular.

His concern obvious, Uriens said, "Pardon me sire, but are you mad riding out alone? The High King should never be without protection!"

Uther, still grinning, pretended to be offended as he replied, "Have you not heard? I am fearless."

"You are arrogant," Uriens remarked lightheartedly.

Uther chuckled, nodding his head. "That too."

Uther's mood then turned solemn, and he handed the message to Uriens. While reading it, Uriens' face turned red with anger. He looked up at Uther, and said between clenched teeth, "I will defend you."

Uther nodded appreciatively. "I knew that I could count on your loyalty. I would have defended myself man to man, but I do not have the time to engage in a full-fledged battle. I have other important... personal matters to attend to at Tintagel castle."

Uriens raised a brow and gave Uther a questioning look. Then suddenly, he recalled the events at the coronation, and deep inside he knew what Uther's intentions were. How could anyone forget his open display of desire for the Lady Ygraine? "Oh, I see!" Uriens exclaimed. "Well, I shall make sure the King is not interrupted."

Uther again nodded gratefully.

The sound of swords clanging as the men continued their practice drew his attention, and both he and Uriens watched for several moments. Then, Uther raised a brow, and it was evident that a brilliant thought had entered his mind. He gazed back at Uriens, and a warm smile spread across his face. He retrieved his own sword from its sheath on the horse's side just as Uriens turned back to him.

Uriens' eyes lit up at the mere sight of Excalibur.

Uther raised the sword with both hands above Uriens' head, and his voice resonated as he said, "I call upon God as my witness."

Uriens' mouth dropped open, and he stared at Uther in astonishment, overwhelmed with the realization of what was taking place. He quickly pulled himself together, and knelt on the ground, bowing his head.

Uther touched the tip of Excalibur to Uriens' right shoulder saying, "As reward for loyalty and chivalrous duty to both crown and country, I deem thee the High King's champion in war."

Uriens' men noticed what was occurring. Filled with awe, they turned their attention to their liege Lord and the High King.

Uther then touched the sword to Uriens' left shoulder and said, "As High King and protector of all Britain, I knight thee, Sir Uriens."

Uriens' men dropped to one knee, bowing their heads reverently.

Uriens took the tip of the sword lovingly in his palm and kissed it. Then looking up into Uther's eyes, there was a silent exchange of deep respect.

As Uther slid Excalibur back into its sheath, Uriens rose to his feet. With his head held high, he said, "I will meet the Duke on Slaughter Bridge... and slaughter him." He spun around and began barking orders at his men.

ℰℰ • ℰℰ

After the knighting, Uther rode to Tintagel, letting his heart lead him to the cave where the Merlin awaited his arrival.

The path to it was narrow and treacherous. The sea pounded on the rocks below, and Uther had to lead his horse rather than ride him. The sun was setting, and the weather had taken a sudden turn. A freezing rain pelted against him, and he drew the cloak tighter about him for protection as the wind battered his body.

Entering the cave, Uther guided his horse, to which he had given the name Andromeda, next to the Merlin's, just inside the entrance for shelter. He was soaked, and he shivered as the wind howled outside. He was grateful for the fire that blazed, spreading its warmth throughout the cave.

The Merlin sat on the cave floor, peering into the fire in front of him. Uther squatted down near the fire across from him, warming his chilled bones.

"You shake like a fawn taking its first steps," the Merlin remarked.

"I quiver with anticipation," Uther shot back at him.

"I see," the Merlin responded, half-smiling as he continued to stare into the fire.

"Gorlois plans an ambush," Uther informed him, briskly rubbing his hands together over the flames.

"I know," the Merlin replied.

"Ygraine sent word to warn me," Uther continued.

"I know," the Merlin again replied.

"Uriens comes to defend me," Uther said proudly.

"I know," the Merlin stated firmly.

"You are beginning to grind on my nerves," Uther growled.

"I know," the Merlin said, looking up from the fire at Uther and raising his eyebrows comically.

Uther shook his head and laughed as he sat on the ground, stretching out his legs. "I think my brother kept company with you for entertainment's sake."

Taking offense, the Merlin's face grew stern, and he said firmly, "Ambrosius kept company with me for Britain's sake."

He glared at Uther, and Uther immediately offered him an apology. "I know my brother respected you, and even though I may not show it, I do as well."

The Merlin merely nodded, then said, "I see you wear the Duke's colours." He observed the deep green cloak with gold border while reaching into a pouch and retrieving Gorlois' ring.

"Yes," Uther replied, as he removed the sodden cloak and laid it out on the ground to dry. "Ygraine sent it with her warning. She said that I would need it, and I must say it provided me much protection. It shielded me from this damn freezing rain, and it kept my travel through Cornwall unhindered."

This time the Merlin did smile, but more to himself than

to Uther. "I am proud Ygraine," he whispered.

Uther gave him a quizzical look, and the Merlin immediately regained his serious demeanor. He handed the ring to Uther saying, "This was the Duke's. Put it on."

Uther stood and took the ring, inspecting it closely as he sat back down. He raised a brow, then grinned, thinking of how Gorlois had surmised that the ring had been stolen. "You are quite resourceful," he said while placing the ring on his own finger.

The Merlin bowed his head slightly, accepting the compliment, then said, "When night falls, and the Duke is gone, you will enter the castle above from the rear. There is a path that leads up. Take my horse. It will attract less attention than that beast, Andromeda."

Uther gawked at the Merlin in amazement, wondering how on God's earth he knew these things, for he had not revealed the horse's name to anyone.

As if reading his mind, the Merlin waved his hand nonchalantly, and continued on. "There is a postern gate with only one guard posted. The road to it is dark and unguarded. The entrance is used only by the Duke, and leads to the kitchen and servants quarters. Pull the cloak's hood closely about your face and make the ring visible. The guard will ask no questions. He will assume the Duke is having one of his many trysts with the maid he seeks fulfillment with. Once inside, let your instincts guide you to the main entrance. Ascend the stairway there. Ygraine's chamber is at the end of the corridor."

He paused, staring intently into Uther's eyes, then said, "She will be waiting for you."

Uther nodded, taking in a deep breath and releasing it loudly.

The Merlin leaned back against the wall of the cave, pulling his cloak tightly around him and closing his eyes.

He said casually, "Rest a while." Then he opened one eye to peek at Uther. "You will be up all night."

Uther again raised a brow, then laughed, but his heart began to beat wildly as he thought of being with Ygraine. He leaned back and closed his eyes, attempting to calm his nerves. "Soon," he thought to himself. "I will hold you in my arms and never let you go."

❦ *Fifteen* ❧

All in the castle slept as Uther, his heart pounding, ascended the main stairway, taking the steps two at a time. He pulled the cloak's hood back, wiping the rain from his face as he hurried down the corridor. Ygraine had the door open before he reached it.

"Come inside quickly," she whispered, then closed and barred the door behind him.

"How did you know..." He was unable to finish his question regarding the ambush, for Ygraine touched her fingertips to his lips to silence him.

He kissed them gently, then took the same hand and turned it over, placing a kiss on the inside of her wrist.

It was as if he had fused some sweet potion of passion directly into her veins. All at once, her body seemed to go limp. Weightlessly, she leaned against him, and sensing what she was experiencing, Uther pulled her to him in a crushing embrace.

His lips found hers, and she opened her mouth to receive the warmth of his tongue. He had waited so long to taste her sweetness, and now he could not get enough.

Pulling away slightly, he whispered against the corner of her mouth, "I love you Ygraine."

"And I you," she whispered back.

He tore the cloak from his back, and tossed it onto the floor. Scooping her up in his arms, he carried her effortlessly across the room and placed her upon the fur covers on the bed.

The only light came from the fire that blazed, filling the room with golden warmth.

Lost in the feeling, Ygraine closed her eyes and lay perfectly still, sensing his eyes tracing every part of her body through the sheer sleeping gown she wore. He scanned her features, and as she opened her eyes, he wondered to himself how such an innocent face could hold eyes so full of fire.

He knelt down next to the bed and took her hand in his. Holding it close to his face, he gazed lovingly into her eyes as he said, "Before I take thee Ygraine, on bended knee I make you a promise."

He paused, taking in a deep breath in an attempt to slow his racing heartbeat, then continued, "I should have liked for us to be wed first, but I cannot endure another day without knowing what it would be like to be one with you."

He brushed the back of his other hand against her cheek and his eyes reflected her smoldering ones as he said, "I pledge before God and all that I believe in, to love you always, and no less than I do at this very moment. I shall marry you on the morrow, even though Gorlois' body has not yet grown cold." He shook his head slowly. "I cannot live through another night without you beside me."

Ygraine sighed and whispered, "I love you more than life itself."

As she spoke the words, her minds' eye brought about a vision of Uther. He was laid out upon a raised stone slab, his body gray and cold.

Her heart leapt, and her throat constricted in pain. With sadness suddenly consuming her, she said, "A time will come when death shall part us, and I shall have no desire to live without thee. The breath you draw is the same breath I draw. My heart cannot beat if the blood does not flow through yours."

Uther kissed her hand gently, then said softly, "My sweet love, do not speak of death on this night when we shall attempt to create new life."

Uther tried to lighten the heavy look in her eyes by flashing her a boyish grin. "Tell me that you will be my queen, for I cannot wait another moment to feel your body near mine."

"I am your queen, Uther the Pendragon," she whispered.

A tender smile spread across his face, a sense of deep euphoria coming over him. He rose, removed Excalibur from the sheath at his side, and placed it at the foot of the bed.

Ygraine's attention was instantly drawn to the sword. She recognized it from her childhood fire vision, just as she had recognized this man, who was now sitting next to her running his fingers through her hair. Its fragrance engulfed him as he leaned over and buried his face into her soft curls. Her scent made his senses reel, and he drew away, shaking his head to ward off the dizziness that threatened to overtake him.

"What is it my love?" Ygraine questioned softly, while running her fingertips across his forehead.

He let out a low chuckle, and again shook his head, for he could not voice what his mind was thinking. Uther's reputation with women was well known, and he had never spent this much time 'talking' to any woman. By now, he would have already had his way, and would have been quenching his thirst with a goblet or two of ale.

"Nothing is wrong my sweet," he assured her. "But I

feel as though this were my first time bedding a woman."

Ygraine smiled wryly and said with candor, "As we both know, this is not your first time... but perhaps it is the first time you brought your heart with you as well as your loins?"

Uther momentarily blushed, for the first time in his life, at her stinging retort. He searched frantically in his mind for some kind of reply, but could find no words.

Ygraine, noticing the blank look on his face, began to giggle. "Is there something you thought to say, my Lord?" She taunted.

"You are not queen yet Ygraine. I may change my desire," he teased.

"I am all that you desire... and more," she replied, the lightness in the air making way for sudden intensity. Her eyes were ablaze with passion as she gazed into his. "Make me one with you, my precious King. Make me yours... now."

He rose and lifted her from the bed, along with one of the soft, deerskin covers. He carried her across the room and laid her down upon it in front of the vibrantly glowing fire. His eyes penetrated hers as he said, "I not only want to touch you Ygraine, I want to see your body beneath my touch."

As she returned his gaze, her desire for him began to radiate from the very core of her being, her passion turning to molten lava that erupted and began to flow throughout her entire body.

Uther could feel the heat emanating from her, and unable to wait another moment, he knelt beside her and untied the ribbon at her neck. He noticed the pulse in her throat quicken as her gown loosened and slipped down over her shoulders.

Ygraine sighed as he leaned over to kiss her left shoulder. His tongue was hot as he slid it along her collarbone and kissed her other shoulder. Her breath became ragged as he made his way to her ear, nibbling on it gently. Then he cupped her head in his hands and he kissed her deeply while covering her body with his.

She ran her fingers down his back, and her body began to move against his. He pulled away slightly, slowly running his tongue down her neck. He kissed her chest, stopping to rest his head against it, listening to her heart beat. It was pounding, as was his own.

Then he slowly pulled her gown lower, exposing her breasts. He brushed his lips against her nipple, capturing it and sucking gently.

She gasped and arched her back as waves of heat ran up and down her spine. She had never felt this kind of passion igniting within her.

Reaching down, he took hold of her gown, and slid it up her body. She raised her arms to allow him to remove it.

Then he stood, and from her feet, he gazed down up her naked form, fully knowing that he had never desired a woman more. The firelight danced in her hair, and her eyes beckoned him.

He slowly undressed himself, his eyes never leaving her. Then naked, he stood before her, and Ygraine thought her heart would burst at the beautiful sight of him.

"I can stand no more," she whispered, as he knelt at her feet.

She sat up, and with cat-like movement, crawled upon his lap, wrapping her arms and legs around his body like a cocoon. He pulled her closer into him, their bodies becoming one.

ᵍᵒ᷉ᵒ●᷉ᵒᵉ

On Slaughter Bridge, amidst the bodies of Cornwall's slain men, a cry emanated from their leader, as if with his dying breath he saw that which his eyes could not believe.

"Ygraine... no...!!!" His scream echoed in the freezing cold night as a single drop of blood ran from his mouth, and a tear froze halfway down his cheek.

ை‍‍‍‍‍‍‍‍‍‍‍‍‍‍‍‍‍‍‍‍‍‍‍

On a hilltop overlooking the bridge, the Merlin stood, still as a statue.

Hearing the death cry, he turned toward the North Star as it suddenly appeared through the cloud-covered sky. Its silver radiance twinkled brightly, a faint golden halo encircling it.

He looked down at the pentacle he held in his hand, then lowered himself to one knee, bowing his head reverently, acknowledging that Britain's saviour had been conceived.

ɔ೩ Sixteen ೱು

U ther and Ygraine made love into the wee hours of
the morning. Their hunger for each other seemed insatiable.
That hunger would burn inside of them for the rest of their
days.

Outside, the clouds hung low as the night's storm left its
shadow. The skies remained gloomy, showing no evidence
of the approaching dawn.

Inside, the fire crackled, mingling its warmth with that
of Uther and Ygraine's. She was curled up on his lap in a
chair near the hearth, a fur coverlet wrapped around them
both. Her head rested on his chest, and she wished that time
would stop. She felt that morning would bring disruption,
and she dreaded it.

As she stared into the flames, she whispered, "Gorlois is
dead, is he not?"

"Yes, I feel that is so," Uther replied while tenderly
stroking her hair. "Does that displease you?"

"It does not," she responded with certainty, raising her
head to look into his eyes. "I know that he was husband to
me, but I feel no remorse. Is that wrong?"

His eyes roamed over her face and he shook his head slowly. "He was not for you my love," he said warmly, gently brushing the back of his hand over her cheek. "Things have been righted, and Gorlois has given in to destiny's grasp. He was fortunate to borrow extra time in this world, enabling him to gaze upon this enchanting face."

Ygraine tilted her head back and closed her eyes, allowing herself to enjoy the sensations his fingers were causing her as he continued to lightly stroke her face.

"When my end has come, I will seek to borrow time also," Uther said softly.

He took her face in his hands, and as she opened her eyes, he gazed deeply into them saying, "May we live a long life together Ygraine, for I shall never tire of spending precious moments with you."

He brushed his lips over hers, then laid his cheek against her cheek. His breath was warm as he whispered next to her ear, "Even death could not part us. We are part of each other. Always have been, and always will be."

A quiet rapping on the chamber door stirred them from their rapture.

Ygraine's brow creased with concern, wondering who would disturb her at this early hour. "Yes?" She called out.

Rodric's voice held a formidable tone as he replied, "I think you'd better come downstairs."

Ygraine sighed heavily, her bliss suddenly replaced with anxiety. She slowly crawled from the haven of Uther's lap and went to retrieve her robe, which was at the foot of her bed. Excalibur was also there, where Uther had placed it. As she donned her robe, she stared into the depths of the dragon's eyes that seemed to be looking right at her. As she turned away, tying the sash at her waist, Uther was heading for the door, completely dressed.

Rodric had a more than startled look on his face as Uther

opened the door, but showed his respect nonetheless. Bowing his head, he said, "Pardon the interruption sire, but I think the Lady Ygraine should come below."

Ygraine, now at Uther's side asked, "What is it father?" However, deep inside of her, she already knew what his reply would be.

Rodric raised his head to look at her. "It's Gorlois. His men have brought him home." He began fidgeting nervously, and cleared his throat. "He's... ugh... well, he's gone Ygraine."

Ygraine took in a long, deep breath and slowly moved past Rodric, Uther a step behind her. Rodric lowered his eyes and waited a few moments before trailing a short distance behind them.

As they neared the main stairway, Ygraine began to tremble as the sound of troubled voices reached her ears. She felt unsteady, and reached out to lay a hand against the stone wall for support.

Uther, noticing her distress, pulled her to him and wrapped his arms tightly around her. She shook uncontrollably, her teeth beginning to chatter.

His desire to protect her was overwhelming, and he whispered, "You do not have to do this my love. You may not wish to witness what awaits below."

His voice was calming to her, and she began to relax in his arms. She looked up at him and smiled, even though her lips quivered. She said softly, "From this day forward, all that we do, we do together."

Uther returned her smile and nodded in affirmation of her words. Then he took her hands and brought them to his lips. He kissed them tenderly and said with reassurance, "I am by your side... always."

She held onto his arm as they descended the stairs, should her legs become weak.

Several of Gorlois' men, Corelia, and Morella were gathered at the main entrance. The servants and more of Gorlois' men were crowding in, and the voices were growing louder.

As Uther and Ygraine approached, all eyes reverted to them. Various looks of shock, anger, and disgust covered their faces.

Ygraine, pale and filled with apprehension, looked up at Uther. He gave her a reassuring glance and put his arm about her waist to support her quaking body.

Morella, who was staring down at something on the floor inside the entranceway, turned her attention to Ygraine and Uther. She began to cry, and ran past them, down the corridor to her chamber. Everyone else slowly backed away from the point of Morella's interest, revealing Gorlois' body.

The servants gasped and began speaking loudly amongst themselves.

The sight of Gorlois' blood-soaked form made Ygraine's stomach lurch. The room around her suddenly became foggy, and the voices began to sound more like a dull chanting. The blood drained from her head, and Uther caught her, as she swayed and fainted.

Uther held Ygraine in his arms, and although he began to feel discomfort as everyone stared at him awaiting some explanation, he held his head high.

Corelia, not at all surprised, immediately rushed to Ygraine, taking her hand and patting it gently.

Rodric came into view from behind Uther and moved to Corelia's side, putting his arm about her shoulders.

One of Gorlois' men stepped forward and spoke with a demanding fierceness as he questioned, "What manner of deception is this?"

Uther, defensive, opened his mouth to speak, but was interrupted by the voice of the Merlin, who now stood in the open doorway. "The only deception here is on the part of one who obviously cannot defend himself against these accusations."

There was silence as the Merlin gracefully moved to stand over Gorlois' body. He looked down at him, and when he raised his eyes back to the crowd, he was void of emotion. He waved his hand over Gorlois in reference and said, "He has received justice."

Gorlois' man spoke again, angry and challenging, while pointing at Uther, who still held Ygraine in his arms. "It appears the King has taken another man's holdings. How do you explain that!"

The Merlin replied calmly, "Simply put, the Duke waged a battle and has lost." Then he addressed the entire crowd, the tone of his voice changing as he said firmly, "What once belonged to him, now belongs to the King."

"I think the King has killed the Duke to satisfy his needs!" Another man shouted.

Uther's jaw tightened and twitched, offended by the accusation, and he again attempted to speak, but was interrupted, this time by Uriens.

"The King has killed no one." Uriens spoke with conviction as he entered and made his way purposefully toward Gorlois' body. He stared down at him coldly, then looked directly at the accusing man and stated, "I killed the Duke... and you witnessed it."

He paused, waiting for the mumbling of the crowd to cease. Then pointing at Gorlois' man, he said, "As you are well aware, an ambush awaited our King, organized by him." Uriens nodded his head toward Gorlois' body.

The man lowered his head, and the rest of Gorlois' men became uneasy, knowing that Uriens spoke the truth.

Uriens scanned the crowd, his eyes intense. His gaze fell upon Uther, holding Ygraine in his arms, and his mouth dropped open slightly. He raised a brow and said, "Sire?"

They looked into each other's eyes momentarily, then both men exchanged a nod of understanding.

Finally receiving his opportunity to speak, Uther turned his attention to Gorlois' men and said with extreme intensity, "You should all hang for this."

He paused, as their eyes filled with trepidation, their tension apparent as they waited for the King to continue.

Uther let out a sigh and said, "But I have decided to spare you."

As relief washed over their faces, Uther continued, "What you did, you did out of loyalty to your leader. I respect that, but I cannot have those who have sought to betray me in my service. You now belong to no man's army. You will leave here now, and God help you, should I ever lay eyes on any of you again."

Gorlois' men all lowered their eyes and filed out of the room. The servants disbursed and hurriedly went about their business. Uriens nodded to Uther and went outside. He could be heard giving orders to his men to set up camp.

The Merlin moved toward Uther, and upon reaching him, glanced down at Ygraine. There was a stray curl hanging across her eye, and he gently brushed it away with the tip of his thumb.

Uther noticed a kind of warmth in the Merlin's eyes that he had never witnessed before.

The Merlin pulled his gaze from Ygraine, looked at Uther and said sternly, "I will see you both on Christ Mass Eve."

Corelia and Rodric exchanged a glance of puzzlement as a slight frown came to Uther's face. The Merlin turned to depart.

Stopping suddenly, he turned back around and looked at Rodric and Corelia while saying, "I believe you had better send for the priest. You have a funeral to attend to." Then he directed his attention back to Uther and said, "And a wedding."

Subsequently, he retrieved a black, velvet box from inside his cloak and placed it in Uther's hand. "Your gift for the bride. It will have greater meaning than the customary ring."

Uther tilted his head, questioning.

The Merlin responded, "It is a symbol of hope."

After one last glance at Ygraine, he turned and departed.

ᔑᔐ●ᔐᔑ

When Ygraine awoke in her chamber, Corelia was dabbing her forehead with a cool, damp cloth.

As she opened her eyes, Corelia's face was a blur. As her senses returned, she heard Uther's panicked voice. "Are you certain she will be all right?"

"Stop your pacing. Your wearing a hole in the floor," Corelia scolded him.

Corelia's voice then softened as she said, "She's just fine. She's coming to, aren't you my sweet Ygraine?"

Uther was immediately kneeling at Ygraine's side. He lifted her hand and kissed it. "You have been gone a while," he whispered. "I was beginning to worry."

Ygraine looked up at him, and her heart swelled with joy. Corelia was standing behind him, smiling down at her. Ygraine was feeling so loved that she had temporarily forgotten the events that had put her in the state she was in, but the memory came rushing back.

"Oh, what have I done?" Ygraine moaned. "I cannot believe that I swooned! I am so ashamed."

"Now, now," Corelia soothed. "You've got nothing to be ashamed of. Besides, it was for the best you weren't there."

Uther leaned closer and flashed Ygraine a grin, then

asked, "Was that your idea of togetherness?"

Ygraine let out a sigh of distress, and Corelia said sternly, "Don't be teasing her. She feels bad enough already."

Uther took Ygraine's face tenderly in his hands and kissed her deeply. Drawing away, he whispered, "Does that make you feel any better?"

Ygraine nodded her head slowly, feeling lost in the affection of her beloved.

Corelia stepped back and pretended not to be watching, but she was drawn in by the tenderness and intimacy. She had never seen Ygraine look so peaceful and content. Her husband lay cold downstairs, and another man had obviously shared her bed. In someone else's eyes, it might look sinful, but to Corelia it was a blessing. She had never seen the look of love so intense in anyone's eyes as she did in these two.

She permitted them their moment of bliss, then said firmly, "I hate to spoil your mood, but we've things to attend to."

Uther leaned over and whispered in Ygraine's ear, "Your mother speaks to me like a child, not a king. She has courage. I think I shall knight her."

Ygraine giggled, and Uther laughed aloud.

Corelia made a face, knowing that she was the subject of their laughter. She raised her nose and walked to the adjoining door. Turning, her voice was serious as she said, "Your father's gone for the priest. Should I dress your daughter for her father's funeral, or her mother's wedding?"

Uther stood up, and there was a look of surprise on his face as he said to Ygraine, "I did not know you had a child."

Ygraine replied to Corelia, "Dress her for a celebration." Then she gazed up at Uther saying, "For that is what this day shall bring."

Corelia nodded and entered Morgaine's room, closing the door behind her.

Ygraine sat upright and reached for Uther's hand. He took her hand in his own, and sat down on the bed next to her. She closed her eyes and took a deep breath. Opening her eyes, she said, "The night of our wedding, I conceived the Duke's child. But I want you to know that she was not conceived out of love. He brutally forced himself upon me, and we were never together again." She lowered her head and whispered, "My daughter did not know her father."

Uther took Ygraine's chin and gently lifted it. Her eyes were tear-glazed as she looked at him. "She shall know me," he said with assurance.

He put his arms around her and held her face close to his chest. She did not see the look of rage come over Uther's face as he envisioned the Duke, and thought to himself, "I should have killed you with my bare hands."

❧ *Seventeen* ❧

The chapel was aglow with candlelight. The night had brought the wind with it, and it whistled in through the cracks in the windows. The draught caused the candle flames to dance, casting eerie shadows against the walls.

By the time Ygraine entered with Rodric at her side, all that had come to pay their respects to the Duke had done so, and were gone. She stopped just inside, taking in the sight of what lay before her.

Gorlois' body had been washed clean, and he was covered to his neck with a fur blanket. He had been placed upon the altar, and the priest was sitting in a chair at his feet in silent prayer.

Morella was seated in the back of the chapel, dressed in mourning attire, her head bent.

Uther was not yet present, and as Ygraine approached the altar with Rodric, she found herself wishing desperately that he were.

Corelia and Morgaine sat in front, facing the altar, and she glanced at them as she passed by. To Ygraine's surprise, the child did not seem the least bit distressed. In fact, she was staring at Gorlois with a coldness in her eyes that Ygraine had never seen.

Corelia gave Ygraine a loving smile as they proceeded toward the altar, but Ygraine could not seem to settle her nerves. She clung to Rodric's arm, and he reached for her hand, squeezing it gently as he assisted her up the step to the platform of the altar.

Rodric had not spoken a word. He had remained silent from the time he had come for Ygraine in her chamber until now.

There was great sentiment in his voice as he gazed at Ygraine with sympathetic eyes and whispered, "Your mum told me everything."

He paused for some time, attempting to calm his breathing and restrain his erupting anger. He looked at Gorlois, and his voice became hoarse as he fought to keep his speech to a whisper. "If you weren't already dead Gorlois, you bastard, you'd be suffering at my hands."

He squeezed Ygraine's hand, a might too hard, and she winced in pain, pulling it from him. He quickly looked at her, realizing that he had hurt her, and his eyes became watery as he said, "I'm sorry. I got a bit carried away." A tear welled up and dropped from his eye, and he swallowed hard. "It's just that I love you so much."

He reached for her hand and kissed it gently, then took his seat next to Corelia, which left Ygraine standing alone.

Nervously, she reached into the velvet pouch hanging at her waist and retrieved the braid, needing the security that it seemed to offer her. She turned and fixed her eyes upon the door, waiting for Uther to enter. As she held her gaze there, something caught her eye in the back of the chapel on the opposite side of where Morella sat.

There was movement, ever so slight, but she was sure someone was there. She squinted, willing her eyes to adjust to the faintness of light. As they did, she recognized the maid that had taken Morgaine to her breast after her birth. Even in the dimness, Ygraine could make out the curly, golden hair of the child with her. She thought it strange that they should linger after the rest of the servants had gone.

The sound of the door opening drew her attention away, and she was elated at the sight of Uther standing in the doorway.

Uriens was with him, and as they stepped forward, Uther stopped in mid-stride, staring at Ygraine. By the look on his face, he was obviously pleased.

She was dressed simply in a light gray, woolen tunic with a bright red surcoat to honour the Red Dragon. Her hair was loose, ornamented with a dried ring of flowers that hung low on her forehead. What he noticed, and which pleased him most, was the braid she held tightly in her hand.

Uriens observed Uther's adoring gaze and whispered, "She is beautiful, my Lord."

Uther nodded, and stood admiring Ygraine for a few moments longer. Then he turned to look at Uriens, whose full attention had been drawn to Morella. He laid his hand on Uriens arm, who reluctantly pulled his gaze from her.

Uther smiled warmly and said, "I must thank you once again for your loyalty, and yet again for what you are about to do."

Uriens shrugged his shoulders and replied, "It appears somewhat awkward, but you are the King, and what the King does is correct." He smiled genuinely at Uther and said, "I am honoured to stand by you in witness of your marriage."

Uther returned his smile, and strode forward. Uriens remained where he stood, awaiting the proper time, when he would then come forth and stand at Uther's side. He glanced back at Morella, who was now staring at him. She immediately turned and lowered her head.

As Uther approached Ygraine, Morgaine turned to look at him. As he passed by, her face revealed an immediate affinity for him.

Uther reached for Ygraine's hand. Hers was trembling, and he took it in his own and held it tight.

"Have you paid your last respects?" Uther questioned softly.

"I have not," she whispered. "For I am in dire need of your support."

Uther nodded, smiling warmly.

Now feeling a sense of security with him at her side, Ygraine tucked the braid back into her pouch.

Turning toward the altar, Uther led her a few steps forward, close to Gorlois' body. He looked at the priest, who was no longer in prayer, and said rigidly, "We desire privacy."

The priest immediately stood and moved to the far end of the dais.

Uther leaned over to discretely speak his last words. "I have but one thing to say," he whispered coldly, pulling Gorlois' ring from his own finger. "Had it not been for this, it would not have been so easy gaining entry to your bedchamber."

He reached under the fur cover, retrieving Gorlois' cold hand. He forced the ring on his finger and glared down at him."

Ygraine removed her gold wedding band and placed it in Gorlois' palm, squeezing the already stiffened fingers shut. She whispered, "You and I came together for all the wrong reasons." She shook her head sorrowfully, then pulled the cover back over his hand.

Uther nodded toward the priest, who then rushed to stand in front of Gorlois.

Uther and Ygraine stepped back and descended the step,

giving the priest ample room to offer his last blessing.

To Ygraine, everything had suddenly gone into slow motion. To her, the priest's voice was muffled as he prayed aloud, walking slowly around Gorlois' body swinging a thurible filled with burning thyme leaves. The smoke lay heavy, and the smell permeated the air.

He then picked up a receptacle filled with holy water from a small table next to the altar and began sprinkling it over the body. The water looked like tiny diamonds as it cascaded outward. Afterward, he moved to the center of the altar, and again faced Gorlois.

To Ygraine, his voice was still a hum, the Latin he was speaking sounding totally inaudible.

Completing his benediction, he slowly drew a cross in the air with a fluid movement of his fingers. Then turning to face Uther and Ygraine, he traced the same cross in the air in front of them.

Uriens quickly strode forward, taking his place beside Uther, as Corelia rose and moved to stand by Ygraine.

The holy water was now being directed toward them, the tiny droplets reaching out.

It was as if there was no differentiation between the two ceremonies. One flowed directly into the other.

Ygraine stared at Gorlois, as the priest's voice droned on. She had lost all concept of time, and suddenly Uther was placing a chain around her neck. She looked down, and the gold band on Uther's wrist caught the candle's glow. To Ygraine, it looked like liquid fire. Then she looked at the pentacle resting against her heart, and she took it in her hand, holding it firmly within her grasp. As she looked back up, Uther's mouth formed the words "I do".

Ygraine replied in kind when it was her turn to do so, but she was unaware of her own voice as she spoke the words. It sounded completely foreign... a low, guttural monotone.

Uther took her in his arms and kissed her long and deep. Only then did she wake from her altered state.

She wrapped her arms about his shoulders, leaning into him. When he withdrew from the kiss, she laid her cheek next to his. Looking at Gorlois' face, she whispered to Uther, "I love you... forever."

☙ *Eighteen* ❧

The month that followed was blissful for Ygraine. Uther remained at Tintagel, awaiting the transfer of his troops from Viroconium. Therefore, he was able to spend much of his time with her.

During that time, Uther had done exactly as he had promised in regards to Morgaine. She took to Uther easily, and he greatly enjoyed his new daughter. He had even gone so far as to surprise her with a puppy. She was elated, and as Uther handed the chubby, whimpering pup over to her, she wrapped her arms about it, hugging it to her. However, a few moments later, she said, "Arianrod wants you."

Uther and Ygraine were completely shocked, but Morgaine was right. As soon as she put the puppy down, he immediately ran back to Uther, and from that day on, Arianrod followed Uther everywhere he could. Even so, Morgaine was not the least bit discontent. She basked in Uther's adoration. So much so, that it was as if he were her seed father instead of Gorlois.

Tintagel was now filled with an abundance of joy. Everyone seemed content except for Morella, whom Ygraine had seen very little of since the ceremony. Corelia had voiced her concern several times to Ygraine that Morella appeared to be suffering from depression.

"She will be all right," Ygraine had assured her. "She grieves for Gorlois. She will soon recover from her grief."

"It's not the loss of Gorlois that grieves her," Corelia had replied. "It's the loss of you that she suffers from. Have you not yet found it in your heart to forgive her? Gorlois is gone, and you've found happiness. Can you not make peace with her?"

But despite Corelia's rationalizations, Ygraine was still unable to forgive.

The full moon passed, and Ygraine was a fortnight late in receiving her flux. She knew in her heart that she was with child, but she wanted to be certain before telling Uther. She decided to wait, and as the second, then third full moon passed, she was sure of it.

She saw less of Uther now, as he was on the training field daily. Word had come that Herne would be invading soon, and Uther's army would be prepared.

Uther had been training late one evening, and Ygraine had decided to warm herself in a hot bath near the fire.

She had snuffed the candles and was enjoying the glow of the firelight. The flames reflected off of the water, making her body look radiant, the pentacle shimmering against her bare skin.

Upon entering their chamber, Arianrod following him, Uther was mesmerized by the sight. He stood staring at her, and when she looked upon him, she was also entranced. Even caked with mud, and his hair dripping with sweat, she thought him the most desirable thing in the world.

Arianrod went to lie in front of the fire as Uther moved to hang Excalibur in its place on the wall next to the bed. Then he stripped himself of the heavy chain mail that he wore.

Naked, he went to Ygraine and knelt down on the floor behind her. Her hair was piled on top of her head, and he removed the pin that held it there. He ran his fingers through it as it fell into the water.

Then climbing into the tub, he gently lifted her and slid his body under hers. He wrapped his arms around her and began to kiss the back of her neck. She sighed, feeling engulfed in his love for her.

He kissed her shoulder and slowly ran his hands over her breasts. Moving his hands further down her body, he stopped to caress her stomach. As he did so, he noticed her once flat belly now was slightly rounded.

He thought to tease her as he gently massaged her stomach and said, "Hmmm... I must be lacking in my duties as husband, or you would not be gaining this."

Ygraine smiled. "On the contrary, it is because of your husbandly duties that I have this," she said, placing her hand on top of his.

He drew his breath in sharply, and he held it momentarily before asking, "Are you with child?"

"I am," she replied, glowing as brightly as the burning embers in the fire.

He turned his hand over and entwined his fingers in with hers. He raised her hand to his lips and kissed it, but remained silent. After a few moments, he began to caress her stomach again, but still no words were spoken.

Ygraine leaned her head back against his chest, waiting for him to say something... anything.

Finally he broke the stillness, his voice revealing his inner turmoil. "This should be the happiest time of my life, but I know not how to feel. How can I open my heart to this, when it is but a temporary fulfillment?" He continued to stroke her stomach saying, "My son grows in you, and all I have to look forward to is losing him."

Ygraine had never heard such torment in his voice, and her heart ached because of it. She could not hold back her tears, and she let them flow as she shared in his pain.

She turned over in the water to face him, and the look in his eyes cut through her very being.

She rested her cheek upon his chest, and suddenly found herself grasping for some kind of hope. She looked up at him and said, "Mayhaps he will not take our child after all. Gorlois is gone, and things have been righted. What harm could come to him now? Besides, what better place for him to receive protection than in the High King's household? There is no reason we cannot raise him ourselves." She paused, and said, "We cannot give up hope."

Uther gazed into her eyes, wanting so badly to believe in her words. He took the pentacle in his hand that was resting between their bodies. He lifted it so that he could gaze upon it and said, "The Merlin said that this was a symbol of hope."

Ygraine tilted her head, her eyes questioning. "Merlin?"

"Yes," Uther relied. "He said that it held great meaning, and requested that I give it to you in place of a ring."

Ygraine smiled and reached up to caress his worried brow. "Merlin will change his mind. You will see... he will change his mind."

As the heaviness drained away, he gazed into her assuring eyes. He let the pentacle fall, and took her face in his hands. "You may be right. I cannot break my word to him, but if I have to, I shall beg him to leave the child. He would not say no to that."

He smiled at her, feeling confident now, and said, "We shall raise our son to be the great king the Merlin has prophesied. It is only right."

Ygraine returned his smile, gazing into his eyes. Then she laid her cheek back on Uther's chest. She took the pentacle in her hand, and holding it tight, she closed her eyes contentedly.

ら゜ずん●んごっ

The news of Ygraine's pregnancy had spread quickly throughout the castle. Corelia was ecstatic and spared no time sharing the information.

Ygraine felt that she should tell Morgaine herself, and did so one afternoon while they were alone.

She took Morgaine, who was now three, for a walk through the gardens. It was a beautiful day, and the flowers were in bloom. The air was full of their sweet scent and the birds were singing a wondrous tune.

They stopped to sit on a bench, and Ygraine pulled her daughter onto her lap, facing her, and kissed the top of her head. "You are so beautiful," she said, stroking the child's long black hair.

Morgaine still had the look of an elf child. Her features were so small, except for her eyes, which were deep blue, but sometimes looked as black as her hair.

Ygraine lifted her chin to gain her full attention and asked, "You love the Pendragon, do you not?"

Morgaine nodded enthusiastically. "I do," she replied sweetly. "I will love his son too." She smiled the smile of a child, but her eyes held the look of a woman. She pressed her little hand to Ygraine's belly and said, "This one."

Ygraine was taken off guard. She knew the child had the sight, but since her foretelling of the coming of the Red Dragon, she had witnessed no other incidents. Now Ygraine felt that the child's gift was far greater than her own, and she wondered from whom this gift of theirs was inherited. She had always believed that such gifts were ancestral, but she knew of no other relatives aside from Corelia and Rodric. She began to wonder why they had never spoken of any.

Morella's voice brought her back from her thoughts. "I heard the news Ygraine," she said, approaching the bench. There was a bounce in her step and a look of joy on her face. She stopped to pick one of the flowers before reaching them, then asked, "May I sit?"

"You may," Ygraine responded flatly. Then her tone changed as she said to Morgaine lovingly, "Run off and play now."

Morgaine hopped off of Ygraine's lap and took the flower that Morella now offered her, before running after a beautiful butterfly.

Morella sat down, wringing her hands together, and her voice revealed her nervousness as she said, "I know we've grown apart Ygraine. Much has happened, but can we not put the past in the past?"

Morella smiled at Ygraine, but her tension was still very present. "I'm happy for you, and no matter what you think of me, I love you still. I miss you Ygraine."

"Why have you come to me Morella?" Ygraine asked, her voice cold. "Why can you not leave things as they are? I do not feel the same towards you as I once did. I know that I am no Saint, but for some reason, I cannot bear your presence near me."

She saw the tears welling up in Morella's eyes, and her voice softened somewhat, for she truly had no desire to hurt her. "I bear you no ill will Morella, but what you did, sisters do not do... and we were like sisters. No matter the circumstances, it was wrong."

"I know how you feel towards me Ygraine," Morella said, her voice strained with emotion. "But, I've come to ask for your favour."

Ygraine tilted her head, questioning.

Morella slid a little closer to her on the bench, and looked at her with pleading eyes. "I've come to ask for your permission, and the honour of midwifing your child. I was there for you when Morgaine was born."

Ygraine's eyes widened at the request, disbelieving what was being asked of her. She furrowed her brows and said, "Things are different now than when Morgaine was born." She stood up and said sharply, "You know full well I will not allow it!"

She turned away and called out for Morgaine, leaving Morella sitting on the bench weeping, her face in her hands.

Later that evening, Uther and Ygraine were sharing their supper together in their chamber when Rodric pounded on the door.

Arianrod was asleep at Uther's feet, and he sat up sleepily as Uther called out, "Enter!"

The worried look on Rodric's face when the door opened made them both raise to their feet.

"What is it?" Ygraine asked, rushing to him.

"It's Morella," he replied, his voice shaky. "I fear something terrible is wrong. Your mum went to call her to supper, and her door's latched. There's no sound from within her room. Your mum feels something awful has happened, seeing as Morella was all upset today. She's still banging on her door."

Uther instructed Rodric to fetch an axe, and all of them rushed from the room, Arianrod trailing behind.

Ygraine's heart was pounding heavily as she followed after Uther, suddenly feeling horrible for the way she had treated Morella earlier.

When they reached Morella's room, Corelia was pounding on the door with her fist.

Uther gently guided her out of the way and started

pounding himself. "Morella, open the door!" He called out loudly.

There was no reply.

Arianrod began scratching at the door and whimpering as Rodric came running down the corridor with an axe in hand. He handed it to Uther, and with Ygraine and Corelia, he stood back to allow Uther plenty of room. After only two powerful swings, Uther broke the latch off the door, and it swung open.

"Oh God," Uther groaned, seeing Morella lying on her bed unconscious, blood dripping from her wrists, soaking the covers.

He rushed forward, and immediately began to rip pieces of cloth from Morella's skirt, as Arianrod laid near him on the floor, still whimpering.

Ygraine followed after, panic rising within her. Corelia and Rodric stood in the doorway, and Corelia put her hand over her mouth as she began to weep. Rodric put his arm around her comfortingly as his own eyes filled with tears.

Uther was frantically attempting to wrap Morella's wrists to stop the bleeding when Ygraine cried out, "No!"

She pushed him out of the way and tore the cloth away from Morella. She grabbed onto her wrists, one in each hand, a palm over each wound.

Corelia stopped crying and hurried to Uther's side. She saw the look of confusion on his face and said, "She knows what she's doing." She placed her hand reassuringly on his arm. "If anyone can save her, she can. She saved the Duke's life."

Uther ran his shaking fingers through his hair and said, "I had forgotten."

Arianrod stopped whimpering, rolled onto his side, and began to doze.

Ygraine was trembling from head to toe, and she was visibly perspiring, but Morella had stopped bleeding.

Ygraine looked up at Corelia and asked softly, "Would you please get some clean linen to wrap her wounds with?"

Corelia nodded and left to do what was requested of her with Rodric following close behind.

Uther just stood there, staring at Ygraine in disbelief. He was in awe of what he had just witnessed, and it was still evident on his face. He sat down on the bed next to Morella, across from Ygraine, and reached out to take Ygraine's bloody hands in his. He stared at them as he said, "You have a gift like none I have ever seen." Then his gaze moved from her hands to her eyes and he whispered, "Mayhaps, some day these hands will save me."

Corelia returned with the linens and brought them to the bedside where Uther sat.

He let go of Ygraine's hands and stood up. "Can I be of assistance?" He questioned absently as he stared at the blood on his own hands.

"I can manage," Corelia replied confidently as she began to bandage Morella's wrists.

She noticed that Ygraine had not stopped trembling and said to Uther, "Get yourselves cleaned up, then take Ygraine and go. Morella will be fine."

Uther immediately moved to the other side of the bed, and attempted to help Ygraine to her feet. She pulled away from him and leaned over Morella, cradling her head in her arms. Tears streamed down Ygraine's face as she held her. "I am so sorry," she sobbed. "God forgive me. Please, forgive me."

ೲೋ•ೋೲ

Ygraine was silent as Uther helped her up the stairway and to their chamber. She was still trembling, unable to calm herself.

Uther led her to a chair near the hearth, and she rested

her head back against the soft, fur coverlet that was draped over the back it. Then he stoked the fire, its warmth spreading through the room. Arianrod curled up in front of it, quickly falling asleep.

After adding a few more logs, Uther turned his full attention to Ygraine. He took the coverlet from the chair and wrapped it around her. He poured her a goblet of wine from a flask on the mantel, and her fingers shook as she took the goblet and slowly brought it to her lips. She closed her eyes, surrendering to the effect of the warm liquid as its essence began to relax her.

Uther squatted down beside her as she opened her eyes, and she knew by the look of him, that he was confused. He said softly, "I feel compelled to ask many questions, but I leave it up to you to tell me what you will."

"Oh," Ygraine whispered, reaching out to gently stroke his forehead, running her fingers down the side of his face. "I would hold nothing from you in secrecy... ever."

She paused, and set the goblet aside. Taking his hands in hers, she said sorrowfully, "If the truth be known, I am afraid that you will think me cold and cruel, for I have sat in judgment, and it was not my place to do so."

She closed her eyes and shook her head regretfully. "I thought that mine was the hand of God as I dealt out punishment to one who did not deserve it."

Opening her eyes, she gazed into Uther's as she said, "I should have loved her, no matter the circumstances. Love is forgiving and unconditional, is it not?"

"Yes it is," he replied assuredly. "And as a matter of record, I do not believe that God punishes."

Then before she could respond, he asked, "What did Morella do to provoke such judgment from you?"

Ygraine rose to her feet and replied, "In my eyes, she betrayed me. She took my husband into her bed... willingly.

But it should have mattered not, for he did not share mine. I should not have cared whose bed he crawled into."

"Was Morella aware of your lack of intimacy with Gorlois?" Uther questioned, raising to his feet.

"Not until recently," she replied.

"Then you were betrayed," he said firmly. "In her eyes there was no distance between you and Gorlois. From what I understand, you and she were as close as sisters... raised together. She had no right to do what she did. I have also heard that she makes no secret of her passionate nature, and has taken many men to her bed."

He turned away momentarily, rubbing his chin in thought. As he turned back, he had a quizzical look on his face. "Why has she never wed?"

Ygraine shrugged. "It seems silly, but the subject was never broached. She has seemed content with her life the way it is."

"Sometimes appearances are misleading," Uther stated, again rubbing his chin as he began to pace. Suddenly, a grin lit up his face, and he stopped and turned to face Ygraine. "I think she needs taming, and I think I know just the man to do it!"

Ygraine could feel Uther's exuberance. "Who?" She asked.

"Uriens," Uther replied confidently.

Ygraine titled her head, and Uther responded to her unspoken question. "The night of our wedding I caught him gazing at her with adoration. He desires her. I can tell."

"But will he accept her?" Ygraine questioned. "She has no rank."

Uther raised a brow, then shot her a mocking grin and said, "Neither did you!"

Ygraine smiled broadly and stepped close to him, putting her arms about his neck. Her face was very close to his as she said confidently, "You are right my Lord. But royal blood or no, I am Queen."

"My Queen," Uther growled, and scooped her up in his arms.

As he carried her toward the bed, Ygraine asked, "Are you certain of Uriens?"

"Positive," he replied, laying her down on the bed. "Now, enough talk of them," he said in a commanding voice.

He covered her body with his, and his voice softened to a whisper as he said, "I request the use of your gift. You see, I have this swelling that is in dire need of a healing."

Ygraine started to giggle, but he cut it off as his mouth covered hers.

A Merlin hawk landed on the window casement, and its shrill cry rang out before again taking flight.

Ygraine heard the cry, and the flutter of wings and thought, "Yes Merlin, it seems that I have many lessons to learn."

ço~ço~●~ço~ço

Morella spent the entire week in bed regaining her strength. Ygraine watched over her, but not to Morella's knowledge. Ygraine was feeling such remorse, that she could not bring herself to face her yet. She crept in to check on her while she was napping, which Morella did often.

Corelia had informed Morella of how Ygraine had stopped her bleeding, but Morella remained depressed. To her knowledge, Ygraine had not been to see her. Therefore, she felt that Ygraine had healed her out of responsibility, and nothing more.

Uther was right about Uriens. He was obsessed with Morella, a fact that Uther discovered upon visiting him at the week's end.

Uriens received Uther in the great hall, which surprised him. He had expected Uriens to be on the training field.

Instead, he was pacing the length of the room and he looked like he had not slept in days.

"Are you ill man?" Uther questioned, concern in his voice as he entered the hall.

Uriens did not reply, but shook his head as he ran his fingers through his hair. He continued to pace, kicking at the rushes on the floor.

Uther stood with his arms crossed, watching him for several moments. Uriens was heedless of the King's presence, lost in his own torment. When Uther could stand no more, he said in a commanding voice, "Stop... now, and tell me what ails you!"

Uriens spun around and responded with apparent frustration, "What 'ails' me sire? Morella!"

"Ah, ha!" Uther shouted jubilantly, walking over and slapping Uriens on the back. "I knew it!"

Uriens was completely taken aback by Uther's response, and he stood gaping at him, dumbfounded.

"Do not look so shocked," Uther said, grinning. "I could tell the way you looked at her, you wanted her."

Uriens suddenly looked quite ill. "Oh," he groaned. "This is far more than just wanting a woman."

Uther walked over to the fireplace and leaned back against the stone mantle with his arms crossed in front of him. His grin remained as he continued to watch Uriens.

"I cannot get her out of my head," Uriens whined, pulling at his hair dramatically. Totally demoralized, he lowered his head and slowly made his way to a chair near the fireplace. He sat down heavily and gazed up at Uther with a pitiful look on his face and said, "She plagues me night and day. At first, I merely thought about her occasionally. I was preoccupied with training my men. But of late, I can think of nothing else." He let out a deep sigh and asked fervently, "What am I to do?"

"Marry her," Uther replied, shrugging his shoulders as if it were a simple matter.

"Marry her?" Uriens questioned, his eyes wide. He looked at Uther as if he had gone mad.

Uther straightened, and walked passed Uriens. "You have my permission," Uther stated, striding toward the door.

Uriens quickly attempted to pull himself together. "But when?" He called out, standing and looking after Uther.

Uther turned. "Now is as good a time as any."

"Now?" Uriens asked, his voice quivering with excitement.

"Now," Uther stated with finality.

Uther strode from the room, and was mounting his horse when Uriens came rushing out of the house behind him. Uriens was on his horse, and off at a full gallop before Uther had settled himself on his saddle.

Uther shook his head and chuckled, speaking his thoughts aloud. "At least you do not have to wait six moons!"

ⸯⸯ●ⸯⸯ

When Uriens arrived at Tintagel, he wanted to burst through the gates.

Uther was a short distance behind him, and he saw Uriens dismount before his horse had come to a full halt. The animal was dripping wet, as was Uriens. He ran into the castle and emerged a short time later with Morella in his arms.

Corelia was running after him shouting, "Stop! Someone stop him!"

Uther quickly dismounted and rushed to Uriens' aid. He placed himself between Uriens and Corelia, holding up his hand to halt her. To Uriens, he grinned and said, "It looks as though it is the King's turn to defend his champion."

Uriens smiled and proceeded toward his horse with

Morella held tightly in his arms.

Then to Corelia, Uther said, "I have blessed their union. He loves her. It will be all right."

Corelia had a look of confusion on her face, but she nodded her head, for she noticed that Morella was not protesting. In fact, she looked quite happy in Uriens' arms.

As Uriens reached his horse, he looked down at Morella, who had not uttered a sound and said, "I love you, and I have received the High King's permission to have you as my bride." He gazed into her eyes and pleaded, "Can you learn to love me?"

"I already do," Morella replied, tears filling her eyes. "From the moment I saw you in the chapel, I loved you, but I never thought I was good enough for you."

Ygraine was on her way to check on Morella, and as she descended the stairway with Arianrod in her arms, she observed the wide-open door. Upon reaching it, she peered out just in time to see Uriens holding Morella in his arms, kissing her deeply.

Arianrod caught sight of Uther and began a desperate struggle to be released.

Ygraine put him down and he immediately ran toward Uther. She as well hurried to him, her shock apparent when she asked, "What is happening?"

"Uriens is taking his bride-to-be home," Uther responded arrogantly. He raised a brow and said, "I told you he would have her." Then he scooped Arianrod up into his arms, and he laughed heartily as the puppy covered his face with wet kisses.

Rodric led a fresh horse to Uriens, and he lifted Morella onto it. He nodded his thanks to Rodric, then pulled himself up behind Morella, straddling her.

"Wait!" Ygraine shouted in desperation.

Morella's apprehension was visible as Ygraine

approached.

Upon reaching them, Ygraine retrieved the braid from her velvet pouch. She took Morella's hand, placed the braid in it, and gently closed Morella's fingers around it. Then she kissed Morella's hand tenderly, and smiled up at her.

Tears ran from the eyes of both women, but no words were spoken. They each knew that they had been forgiven.

❦ *Nineteen* ❧

Morgause had spies constantly observing the comings and goings at Tintagel. She had developed quite a jealousy of Britain's new Queen, feeling that she, herself, belonged on the throne.

The messages that she received of the High King and Queen's bliss were nauseating to her. Also, she had been informed of the Queen's pregnancy, as Ygraine was now heavy with child, and Morgause's stomach churned at the possibility of Uther having an heir. However, there was much gossip of whose seed grew within the Queen. Because of the timing, it was uncertain whether the child she carried was of the King, or the Duke.

Morgause had only caught a glimpse of Ygraine at the coronation, and her curiosity at seeing for herself if the rumors of the Queen's beauty was true, overwhelmed her. As well, her desire to see the home of the High King was just as overpowering.

Unable to withstand her craving, she decided to pay a visit to Tintagel under the pretense of showing support to the throne.

She arrived with quite an entourage. However, Lot was not present. She had no patience for his sniveling at a time like this. Besides, she intended to make her visit short, even though the journey from Scotland was extremely long and tiresome. She did not think she could endure being in the Queen's presence for long without her envy consuming her, causing her to possibly become irrational.

She had sent word ahead of her arrival, and Ygraine was very apprehensive, having heard rumors of Lot's resistance in aligning with Uther.

Added to that, she had no desire for women's chatter at a time when she was consumed with worry for Uther. He had gone to his stronghold in Avon, as the Saxon ships were making their way up the coast, and Herne was expected to invade within the week.

Also, Christ Mass was fast approaching, and Ygraine knew that her child would be born then. In addition to worrying about Uther, she worried constantly about confronting the Merlin, should he present himself after the birthing.

The only good news that Ygraine had received was that Morella was with child. She had not seen her since her departure with Uriens, as he had married her immediately upon returning home. Therefore, there was no wedding to attend, and thus far, there had been no appropriate time afforded to visit. However, they stayed in contact through messenger, and the news was always pleasing, as Uriens and Morella were quite content.

Corelia was not aware that the guest about to be received was Morgause, the daughter of Evanona, and Ygraine's half-sister. Ygraine had simply informed her that the Lady of Lothian would be arriving.

Ygraine received Morgause personally, with Corelia and Morgaine. As she approached through the gate in her covered litter, they were waiting on the front steps. Morgause caught sight of them instantly, as she was spying out from behind the curtains at the magnificence of Tintagel castle.

The day was bitter cold, and Ygraine was wrapped in a heavy red cloak, the hood lined with rabbit fur. The white frame around her face gave her an angelic appearance, and Morgause cringed at the sight.

Corelia stood next to Ygraine, her arm wrapped possessively about her shoulders. Morgaine was huddled up against her mother, her cheek pressed to her swollen belly. Arianrod, now quite large, was sitting in front of them protectively.

Morgause took in the view and sneered, saying in a low, guttural voice, "One happy family. How touching."

As the litter halted and she was assisted from within, Morgause put on an air that was completely opposite of what she was feeling.

She went immediately to stand before Ygraine. In spite of Arianrod bearing his teeth as he began to growl, she bowed low, took Ygraine's hand, and placed a stiff-lipped kiss upon it. She slowly straightened and attempted to sound convincing as she said, "I know my husband does not align with our High King, but I, on the other-hand, most humbly serve."

Corelia instantly saw through her guise and made a face as if she had just smelled something extremely offensive.

With Arianrod still growling low, Morgaine peered up at Morgause, and frowning, drew nearer to Ygraine.

Morgause noticed the child's action, and her eyes betrayed her pleasant voice as she said, "Sweet child."

Corelia had seen enough. She abruptly took Morgaine by the hand and led her inside. Morgaine turned around as they were passing through the doorway and called Arianrod to come. Then she said to Ygraine, "Careful mama."

Ygraine was quite uncomfortable now, but she still felt the need to be gracious. After all, this woman was of noble blood.

"Please come inside," Ygraine offered as kindly as possible. "I am sure a mulled wine would be soothing after your long journey."

"I am grateful for your kindness my Queen," Morgause purred.

She followed Ygraine into the great hall where a welcoming fire blazed. Straight away, Morgause began to eye everything in the room.

A flagon of warm wine had been prepared, and was set on a table with two ornately carved goblets.

Ygraine removed her cloak, revealing a beautiful, emerald green gown underneath, and tossed it absently onto a chair. Even pregnant, she radiated both beauty, and royalty.

Morgause had to fight back her desire to claw at Ygraine with her fingernails, wiping that sweetness from her face.

She forced herself to smile as Ygraine said, "Please sit." She directed her to one of the chairs near the fire. "I will pour."

"I prefer to stand," Morgause replied. Then, "The Queen serving herself? I find that a bit odd. I would not think of being so... domestic."

Ygraine wanted desperately to sit, as her back was aching, but found herself desiring to be at the same level as this woman. If Morgause preferred to stand, then she would also.

Ygraine responded to her remark while she poured the wine. "I see no need to be served. It is no heavy task pouring wine."

Morgause shrugged and waved her hand as if to agree.

Ygraine handed her a goblet, then turned toward the fire, feeling the sudden need to warm her hands. As she did, the flames called to her. The vision came and went quickly, but the message was crystal clear. She saw Morgause pouring a black liquid from a small vial into a goblet. Ygraine spun around, and as she did, she caught Morgause attempting to do that which she had just seen in the flames.

Morgause had not expected her to turn around so quickly. Startled, she jerked, dropping the vial on the floor. She opened her mouth in an attempt to speak, but nothing came forth. She found herself speechless, and that annoyed her more than anything. She straightened, bracing herself for Ygraine's reaction.

"You have come here under false pretenses!" Ygraine shouted.

Morgause smiled shrewdly and replied, "I have come here to preview what shall be mine."

Ygraine took a step forward, her head held high. "You will leave my home now!"

Morgause turned to leave, but after taking only a few steps, she hesitated, as she had a second thought. She turned slowly around and walked purposefully toward Ygraine, stopping directly in front of her. She grabbed Ygraine's face and kissed her hard on the mouth, biting her lip.

Ygraine gasped, pulling away abruptly as Morgause stepped back. Ygraine's trembling fingers immediately went to touch her stinging lip, noticing the blood on her fingertips as she drew them away.

"You are mad," Ygraine hissed. "What is the meaning of this!"

Morgause tilted her head and replied matter-of-factly, "A simple rule of battle my love. One who draws first blood... wins."

She raised a brow, glaring at Ygraine, then turned and sauntered from the room. Ygraine stood staring after her, and when she heard the door slam, she fell heavily into a chair. Trembling, she closed her eyes and wept.

⌘ *Twenty* ∞

Uther sent messages twice weekly, and Ygraine always made the vassal wait so that she could send a message in return.

The Saxons had landed a week before Christ Mass, and Ygraine was worried that Uther would not be present at the birth of their son. She had informed him of her certainty that the child would be born on the eve of Christ Mass, and he had assured her that he would be there, no matter the circumstances.

The most recent message that she received appeased her somewhat, as it seemed that Uther's army had succeeded in driving the Saxons back. But from all accounts, when questioning the vassal further, it was a bloody battle and many men were lost.

It was but three days from Christ Mass when that last message came. Uther was intending to come home to Tintagel, but first he had preparations to make, should the Saxons attack again in his absence.

The morning of Christ Mass eve brought concern to Ygraine. She was sitting on her bed combing Morgaine's hair, but her mind was on the child in her womb.

Arianrod was asleep on the floor near the fire in front of Uther's favorite chair.

Ygraine waited with great anticipation for her labouring to begin. While praying silently to feel the first twinges of pain, Morgaine scooted away from her and climbed from the bed. She went directly to the window, as if something had suddenly drawn her attention there.

"What is it sweetness?" Ygraine asked lovingly.

Morgaine turned around, a look of awe on her face as she replied, "There was a bird and a dragonfly flying round and round each other."

Excitedly, she ran back and leaned on Ygraine's knees, propping herself on her elbows. Looking up at Ygraine innocently, she asked, "When is grandfather coming?"

Ygraine frowned, for Morgaine's questioned deeply distressed her. She stood up suddenly and a sharp pain radiated down her back. She grimaced and leaned forward as her hand went immediately to the point of discomfort. She let out a deep breath and straightened while rubbing her back with the palm of her hand, attempting to massage the pain away.

All at once, she felt a warmth between her thighs. She looked down to discover a puddle of water on the floor beneath her. She quickly nudged Morgaine toward the door and said, "Hurry, get your grandmother."

Morgaine scurried off to do her mother's bidding, and Ygraine slowly walked to the window and peered out. There was no bird, nor dragonfly.

She shuddered involuntarily and called out to the wind, "Pendragon, come to me. Please come to me."

Corelia, her eyes sparkling with joy, rushed into the room with a maid following. "What a wondrous time for the babe to come!" Her words bubbled out.

Ygraine turned around, her eyes pleading as she asked, "Has the Pendragon come?"

Arianrod's ears perked up, suddenly waking. He sat up and yawned, looking in Corelia's direction as if he were awaiting her reply as well as Ygraine.

Corelia gently led her from the window. "You'd be the first to know, I'm sure." Then patting Ygraine's hand, she said, "Don't you worry. My senses tell me he's coming."

The maid wiped the water up from the floor, then bowed before hurrying away to gather the necessary provisions for the birthing.

"I want to lie down," Ygraine said impulsively.

"You can't lie down," Corelia stated firmly. "You've lost your water. It's best we do a little gentle pacing to get things moving. This being your second child, he's liable to come quick. You don't want to slow things down by lying in bed."

Ygraine felt panic rising in her. "Yes I do," she said defiantly. "I will not have this child until I am ready, and I will not be ready until the Pendragon is here."

She pulled away from Corelia and crawled into bed. She winced as her first twinge of pain was felt.

Corelia stood with her hands on her hips staring at Ygraine for a moment. Then she pulled the covers up over her saying, "Have it your way. I know better than to argue with you. I just hope he comes soon."

Arianrod let out a slight groan, then lay back down and waited.

Ygraine laid in bed the entire day and well into the evening. She had eaten nothing since the night before, and she was beginning to weaken. Her pains were close together, and she willed her body to slow its process.

She was dripping wet, her breathing ragged as she desperately fought against nature. She trembled, and even though her shift was soaked, she felt chilled to the bone.

Corelia had put several logs on the fire to keep her warm, and she made every attempt to keep her comfortable, but her efforts were futile. As the night went on, Ygraine's conditioned worsened.

Corelia was distraught to the point of misery as she dabbed Ygraine's forehead with a damp cloth. As she wrung out the cloth in a basin near the bed and turned back to Ygraine, memories of Evanona came flooding back, filling her with more fear.

Arianrod suddenly got up and went to the door, scratching at it to get out. Corelia left Ygraine's side momentarily to open the door for him. He immediately ran down the corridor.

Rodric was pacing in the hall. He stopped and looked to Corelia, questioning with his eyes. She shook her head, tucking strands of hair back into the knot on top of her head, a look of disappointment on her face. The circumstances all too familiar, Rodric now filled with fear as well.

As she closed the door and turned back, she pleaded with Ygraine. "Please child, you've got to let go. Your husband is a warrior. There's no definite way of knowing if he'll be here. You're going to hurt yourself and the babe."

Suddenly Ygraine could stand the pain no longer. Her head tilted back, and she cried out in agony. As she did, the chamber door opened, and Uther rushed into the room.

Ygraine was so relieved to see him that she began to cry.

Rodric, filled with a sense of relief, took Arianrod, who was jumping up at Uther for attention, back out into the hall and closed the door.

Uther was in his chain mail and tabard. He had obviously been in it for some time, as the tabard was blood stained, and he was covered in grime. He smelled of battle and death, but Ygraine had never seen a sweeter sight in her entire life.

He laid Excalibur to rest against a nearby chair, the eyes

of the dragon lustrous, then went to her and knelt at her bedside.

"Do not weep my love," he soothed, gently brushing damp stands of hair from her face. "I am here."

Tears continued to flow from her eyes as Uther leaned over and placed a gentle kiss on her brow. As he withdrew, Ygraine cried out again, the pain becoming intolerable.

"It's about time," Corelia said to Uther reproachfully, pulling the covers from Ygraine and positioning her legs for the birthing. "She would have died with that child in her, had you not presented yourself."

Uther stared at her in terror, and noticing his fear, Corelia softened saying, "Make yourself useful. Get up behind her there, so she can lean against you."

Uther immediately helped Ygraine to sit up, and situated himself behind her, allowing her to rest against him. He wrapped his arms around her, and the metal was cold against her, but she was not about to complain.

"When your next pain comes, I want you to push hard, you hear me?" Corelia instructed.

Ygraine nodded, and Uther held her as her contraction came. Ygraine bore down and pushed with all her might. The child was more than ready, and with that first push, the babe's head crowned.

Ygraine, panting, laid her head back against Uther. The moonlight streamed in through the window, cascading across the bed. Ygraine's pentacle seemed to light up as it lay against her sodden shift, and it appeared as though it were a direct reflection of the radiant star that could now be seen through the window, a brilliant golden aura surrounding it.

"Again!" Corelia shouted, and with Ygraine's next push, the babe freed itself from its mother's womb.

Ygraine collapsed against Uther, and she began to weep again as she drank in the sight of her beautiful son. He was bathed in the light of the moon as Corelia held him up in her hands.

Uther's eyes were tear-glazed as Corelia cut the cord of life and rose to hand the still bloodied babe to its mother's reaching arms.

"Halt!" The Merlin's voice echoed through the chamber.

Ygraine sat straight up, and Uther jumped to his feet, both of them horrified as they stared at the Merlin standing just inside the closed door.

The Merlin's face was drawn as he quickly strode to stand before Corelia, who started shaking as she held the crying babe in her hands, not knowing what to do.

"Give me the child," the Merlin urged.

"No!" Ygraine screamed.

Uther's inner pain was unmasked as he looked down at Ygraine.

Then with pleading eyes fixed upon the Merlin, Ygraine cried out, "Please, I must hold him."

Uther gazed at his son, then closed his eyes, his heart wrenching.

The Merlin forced his own inner torment aside and, with a serious tone, replied, "It is better for the child to have no bonding with you Ygraine."

Then to Corelia he said, "This situation is as delicate as a piece of fine crystal. One wrong move and all will be shattered. Now give me the child."

Corelia looked at Ygraine, then at Uther, asking with her eyes for some direction.

Ygraine grabbed Uther's arm and cried out, "For God's sake Uther, do something!"

The emotion running through Uther was overwhelming. With a fierceness, he rushed forward, throwing himself at the Merlin's feet. He looked up at him with tear-filled eyes, and his voice was strained, revealing his obvious torture as he said, "I have never begged for anything in my life, but I will grovel at your feet if you will only leave the child."

The Merlin closed his eyes, drawing his brows together. The sight of Uther begging pained him greatly. After a moment, he opened his eyes and said in a commanding voice, "Rise Uther."

Uther slowly rose to his feet, and the Merlin attempted to explain as he gazed into Uther's eyes. "I do not take your child for any other reason than his own protection. There will be questions as to his validity as your heir."

Corelia took a blanket from atop the stack at the end of the bed and wrapped the crying babe in it, then held him to her bosom, rocking him gently.

Ygraine was beset with grief, and she began to sob. Uther went back to her side and sat next to her, pulling her into his arms.

The Merlin let out a deep sigh, and attempted to reason with them. "This child was conceived on the night of Gorlois' death. The intimacy shared between the High King and the Duchess of Cornwall was evident and witnessed by many the morning after. But can you convince all that this child is not the Duke's?"

Neither of them responded, and the Merlin shook his head. "I think not. But if you could, this child would then be decreed Uther's bastard. Which would you prefer?"

Ygraine let out a painful groan as she continued to weep in Uther's arms.

The Merlin continued, "Because of the way events have occurred, there will be questions, and this child will not be accepted. However, the time will come to pass when he will be. In the meantime, his protection is imperative."

Ygraine withdrew from Uther's embrace and her tears temporarily subsided as she looked at the Merlin. She knew that his words were true, but she still could not bear the thought of giving up her son. She buried her face into Uther's chest, and again began to sob.

Corelia held the whimpering babe close, still rocking him at the foot of the bed, attempting to quench his need for bonding. As the Merlin turned to face her, she looked back over at Uther and Ygraine, but she knew what had to be done. Her own tears poured from her eyes as she laid the babe, who again began to cry, at the foot of the bed and wrapped more blankets around him. She then retrieved Evanona's shawl from amidst the remainder of the blankets. She held it up to her cheek and closed her eyes momentarily before wrapping it around the babe. She lifted him and kissed his sweet face, then turned to hand him to the Merlin.

The babe instantly stopped crying, and great warmth spread over the Merlin's face as he looked down at the newborn child in his arms. Noticing the shawl, his warmth was replaced with agony. Taking a corner of it in his hand, he raised it to his face and breathed in the scent, closing his eyes. Opening his eyes, he gazed back down at the babe, then to Excalibur, the eyes of the dragon more luminous than ever. Forcing the numbness to return, he turned away slowly, and made for the door.

Ygraine, filled with panic, attempted to get out of bed, to run after him. But as she did, she fell to the floor.

Uther knelt down, pulling her into his arms. He glared at the Merlin's back and shouted out, "For this I will see you in hell!"

The Merlin turned around and replied firmly, "There is no hell. Only that which you create for yourself."

He opened the door and brushed passed Rodric, who, with tears in his eyes, was standing right outside, Arianrod at his side. The dog immediately laid down, and seemed to bow his head with respect.

Morgaine was coming down the corridor, and as she

reached him, she smiled up at the Merlin sweetly. He glanced down at her, his eyes revealing his affinity for her.

Then he left without a backward glance, as Ygraine and Uther wept in each other's arms.

❧ *Twenty-one* ❧

The fog was thick as the barge made its way gently across the lake to Avalon. The Merlin held the babe proudly in his arms as Viviane came into view. She was waiting on the shore wrapped in a purple velvet cloak, great joy lighting her face.

As the barge came ashore, the Merlin disembarked and stood proudly before Viviane. He carefully placed the babe in her arms, and Viviane cradled him to her with tenderness.

She gazed deeply into the babe's eyes and said, "Dearest Arthur, on this day of thy birth I most humbly hold thee to my breast, and when all is done and you have returned to Avalon, so shall I hold thee upon thy death."

And so, the Lady of the Lake and the women who shared her worship of the Goddess raised Arthur on that sacred isle. He was to remain there until the Merlin returned for him. He would then be brought forth to claim the throne, at the time of Britain's greatest need.

❧❧●❧❧

In the years to come, the lives of Arthur's parents would be in constant turmoil. However, through those years of strife, Uther and Ygraine held on to their passion for each other, vowing to never let it perish.

Just as it had been when Ygraine was born, all were told that the boy child was stillborn.

Ygraine had a desperate desire to conceive another child of Uther's, but was unable to do so.

The Saxon wars raged, and Uther was forced to divide his time between his stronghold in Avon and his new fortress at Segontium in the northern region.

Ygraine fought against the depression that so often consumed her, and was only truly happy when Uther came home to Tintagel. Unfortunately, however passionate, their time together was always brief, as Britain's High King had time for little else but battle.

Ygraine's desire to see the boy child would at times overwhelm her, and she was often tempted to use the sight to do so. But then she would decide against it, knowing that if she were to gain even a faint glimpse of him, her pain would deepen.

As the years passed, Ygraine's feelings of malice for the Merlin grew like an evil seed within her. He seemed to vanish after the birth, and she never felt the desire again to call upon him in her times of need.

Five long years passed, and Uther was beginning to wonder if he could endure the heavy burden of Britain's future.

He decided to spend Christ Mass at Tintagel, which was the first time he had done so since the boy child's birth.

It was snowing heavily when he arrived on Christ Mass eve with a fair portion of his men. As they approached, he could see torches burning in the cold night, and the sight was more than welcoming. He thought of Ygraine waiting for him, and his blood warmed in spite of the weather.

Rodric ran to greet him as Uther rode toward the stables with his men, who were all weary and hungry from their journey on this cold winter night. The men quickly began tending to their horses, eager for the feast that awaited them inside.

"It is good to see you Rodric." The tone of Uther's voice was genuine, and he smiled affectionately as he handed the reins to Rodric.

Rodric bowed respectfully, and he kept his eyes lowered as he replied warmly, "And you sire. You must be starving. There's enough food for your whole army inside. Corelia's had the cooks at it for two days straight."

Then he raised his head, looked directly into Uther's eyes and said, "We're all glad to have you home to celebrate the birth of our Lord."

As soon as the words were out of his mouth, Rodric was condemning himself for speaking them.

Uther closed his eyes, attempting to mask the pain that had suddenly arisen within them.

Rodric let out a sigh, lowered his head and said, "I'm sorry, I only meant..."

"I know what you meant," Uther interrupted, giving him a look of kindness. Then he took a deep breath, exhaling fully and said, "You would think that after five years the memory of that night would have dulled. But it seems like only yesterday that I watched my son being born, and allowed him to be taken away."

The sight of Ygraine running toward them quickly snapped Uther from his melancholy. She had no cloak about her, and her hair was unbound and covered with snowflakes.

Uther took several long strides, and had her in his arms. He held her tight for the longest time, lost in the feel of her in his embrace.

Suddenly aware of her shivering body, he removed his cloak and wrapped her in it. She looked up at him, tears dampening her lashes, and he was certain that his heart would explode with the love he felt for her.

She smiled at him, and her face was love itself as she whispered softly, "It has been too long my Lord, and I am in great need of thee."

He took her face in his hands and kissed her passionately, unaware of the stares of his men who looked on. This was an unusual sight for them, and they were enjoying the scene of this seasoned warlord, who they rarely saw even smile.

Drawing back from the kiss, Ygraine laid her head on Uther's shoulder. "I believe your men grow hungry," she murmured, noticing the attention they were drawing.

Uther turned and shouted to his men, "Go inside for the feasting." Then a grin spread across his face and he said, "I go to quench my appetite privately with my Queen."

He scooped Ygraine up in his arms and carried her into the castle, the sounds of the men's cheers following them inside.

As he carried her up the stairway he glanced around briefly, a quizzical look on his face. "Where is my shadow?"

Ygraine smiled wryly and replied, "Arianrod is in the kitchen, where he belongs this night. He will see you on the morrow."

Uther nodded in agreement as he continued up the stairs.

He did not put her down until they were inside their chamber. He set her on her feet on the hearth and pulled the dampened cloak from her, tossing it absently onto the floor.

Her cheeks were pink from the cold and her eyes sparkled with love as she looked at him.

Standing close to her, he whispered, "My words cannot express how deep the love I feel for you."

He ran his hands through her hair, then pulled her to him,

almost roughly as his passion mounted. She leaned into him, breathing in his scent as she lay her head against his chest. He cupped the side of her face, holding it to his heart as he said softly, "The days I am away from you only strengthen the bond between us. My men say that I fight with a passion they have not seen in any other man. I wonder what they would say if they knew that my woman stirs an even greater passion within me."

Ygraine looked up at him, her eyes drinking in the glorious sight of him. "Why can the wars not cease? I would give all if only I could spend the rest of my days with you."

Uther sighed heavily, then said, "I too would give all to have peace. I grow weary of the fight. I see now why my brother's fire went out. Without you, I fear mine would do the same."

He released her from his arms, and took her hand, leading her to his chair near the fireplace. He sat down and pulled her onto his lap. He gazed into the fire as he said, "If the mighty Lords of Britain would stop warring amongst themselves and band together, we would have a better chance of gaining peace."

He shook his head and shrugged his shoulders in bewilderment as he pulled his attention from the flames and looked at Ygraine. "They are fickle. From one day to the next, I know not whether they support me or challenge me." He let out a sigh. "It is hard to know who to trust."

Ygraine felt a chill go through her body, and she shuddered as the memory of Morgause came back to haunt her. She quickly brushed it from her mind and whispered, "Enough talk of war. Tonight I will make you forget your battles."

"I would be most grateful," Uther replied, a weariness in his voice and in his eyes. He rested his head against her breast and Ygraine stroked his hair.

A quiet rap on the door caused Uther to groan. He slowly lifted his head and called out, "Enter!"

The door opened and Morgaine, now eight years old, entered carrying a tray of delicacies. She glided across the floor with the grace of an antelope. She set the tray down on the table near them and smiled sweetly as she said, "Corelia bade me bring this fare to you. She did not think you would be joining in the feasting this eve."

Ygraine rose from Uther's lap, and he also stood. He leaned over and placed a gentle kiss on top of Morgaine's head, then brushed the back of his hand against her cheek lovingly, causing a huge smile to spread across her face. Then sitting back down, he looked at Morgaine curiously and asked, "When did you begin to refer to your grandmother by her given name?"

Morgaine's smile immediately faded, and she looked away, avoiding the question.

Ygraine stared at her for a moment, considering Uther's question. Then she said, "She has called her so for some time now. I too find it odd, but I never gave it much thought."

Morgaine began shifting her weight from one foot to the other, revealing her tension, and keeping her eyes averted.

Ygraine looked at Uther and said, "I believe that you are unaware of this, but Morgaine has the sight, as I do. It seems that we are both plagued with knowing that which others do not. Mayhaps she has seen something that disturbs her."

Uther gave Ygraine a puzzled look. "The sight? I knew that your hands held a gift, but I am not certain of what you speak. Do you mean you are a prophet like the Merlin?"

The mere mention of his name brought a sadness to Ygraine's eyes, but Morgaine's lit up. "Yes," Ygraine replied, a sour note in her voice. "I suppose we are much the same in that respect."

Ygraine cupped Morgaine's chin in her hand and turned

her face to hers. "Daughter, I know that the sight you possess is much stronger than my own, for I am undisciplined with it. You have spent time strengthening yours, have you not?"

Morgaine did not reply, and Ygraine continued, "I believe you honour your gift in a way that I do not. I find it an affliction at times, but I feel that you use it as a source of gaining knowledge. I have avoided questioning you in the past, for I fear you hold answers that I may wish not to know. But now, I feel compelled to beg you to answer the Pendragon's question. Why do you call your grandmother by her given name?"

Morgaine tried to turn her face away, but Ygraine held her chin firmly saying, "You will answer the question please."

A tear welled up in Morgaine's eye, and she blinked hard, forcing it to fall.

Ygraine suddenly realized that she had not seen her child cry since she was a babe. "What pains you so?" She asked tenderly, releasing her chin.

"I do not wish to cause you pain mother," Morgaine whispered. "I would choose to keep my knowledge to myself... please."

Uther, who had remained silent, offered her some words of wisdom. "Sometimes it is better to speak, even if the truth causes another pain. If it is kept within, it may turn on you, for secrets have a way of doing so."

"I have kept many secrets," Morgaine confided. Then, with an ominous tone, she said, "But if you love my mother, as I know you do, you will not bid me to share them now."

Ygraine was now feeling a desperate need to know what information Morgaine held. "I must insist you answer the question now daughter," she demanded.

Morgaine's eyes drew to Uther, and she pleaded with him silently. When he did not respond, she knew that she had to surrender. She lowered her head, as she had no desire to witness Ygraine's expression. "Corelia is not your mother."

"What!" Ygraine exclaimed, taking a step back, her shock evident. "Of course she is my mother. How could you say such a thing as that?"

Uther took Morgaine by the arm and gently pulled her to him. He looked directly into her eyes and asked, "Do you trust me child?"

Her eyes were wide as she replied sincerely, "I love you immensely, for you are my father in my heart. But I used to be jealous of you at times, for I see that my mother is only truly happy when you are here. But now that I am near grown, I feel differently. I see the way you look at her, and I have wished that some day a man would look upon me in that same way."

A bit of sadness came into her eyes, and she lowered them and said, "But that will not be the case for me. Therefore, I will seek contentment in the power of my gift."

Ygraine listened to Morgaine's words and felt as though some part of her heart were being ripped apart.

Morgaine lifted her gaze back to Uther, and her love for him was irrefutable as she said, "As for trust, you have never given me reason not to trust you, as did my father." Coldness entered her eyes, but for just a moment. "Unlike him, I have found you to be an honourable man, filled with passion."

Uther's heart melted, and he wondered at this child of such youth who spoke so much like a grown woman. He reached out and stroked her hair, then tenderly ran his fingers down the side of her face and said softly, "Then as I have both your love and your trust, you must believe me when I say, you must speak the truth to your mother now."

"I do speak the truth," she insisted. Then looking back at Ygraine, her words were filled with honesty. "Corelia is not your mother. Your mother was the former Duchess of Guent, and she died giving birth to you."

"Cease!" Ygraine shouted. Her heart was wrenching with emotion, and she turned away briefly to compose herself. Turning back, she had calmed a bit, and she reached out to caress Morgaine's shoulder as she said, "I will hear no more of this. Now please leave us."

Morgaine nodded, her sadness obvious, then turned and ran from the room.

Uther had the notion to run after her, but as he rose from his chair he noticed the tears spilling from Ygraine's eyes. She turned away from him, attempting to gather herself.

Without reason, Uther somehow knew that Morgaine's words were true. He moved to stand close behind Ygraine. Leaning into her, he rubbed her shoulders as he said softly, "I think you should speak to Corelia of this. Morgaine has no cause to speak lies."

Ygraine turned around and allowed him to pull her to him. She rested her head wearily on his chest, closing her eyes, attempting to close out her racing thoughts. Little did Uther know, the words he was about to speak would cause her more distress than he could have possibly imagined.

"If your daughter's words are true, then it seems you have a sister," he informed her.

Ygraine furrowed her brows, and he continued, "There is a Scottish Over-Lord by the name of Lot. His wife Morgause was the daughter of the Duke and Duchess of Guent."

Ygraine drew her breath in sharply, and her head jerked up. Her tears vanishing, her wide eyes held a fear that Uther misunderstood.

He attempted to soothe her by saying, "I know that Lot does not align with me, and there are tales that his wife is power hungry. But mayhaps she is not as they say, and if she were sister-in-law to me, Lot might be easily swayed."

Ygraine fought a tremendous inner battle over whether

or not to inform Uther that the tales were indeed true. Ultimately, she chose to continue to keep her past encounter with Morgause to herself, not wanting to cause Uther distress.

She laid her head back on his chest and said quietly, "I will speak to my mother. Until then, I would prefer to forget the events of this night."

"All of them?" Uther questioned, a mischievous tone in his voice and a roguish look on his face.

Ygraine could feel her blood warming, and suddenly nothing else mattered but being with her Pendragon. She looked up at him, smiled, and said lightheartedly, "Eat your supper my Lord, for I can see a great hunger in your eyes, and I fear you may devour me."

Uther raised a brow and impulsively scooped the sweet filling out of a fruit tart on the tray with his finger and smeared it on her face.

Ygraine was shocked by his action, and stood gaping at him.

He proceeded to lick the sweetness from her face, and Ygraine quickly caught on to this new way of sharing a meal. This was one feast she would never forget.

తోతు • తుత

Mass was held the next morning in the chapel at Tintagel. Uther and Ygraine attended, but spent most of the afternoon and evening in their chamber. Uther would be leaving on the morrow. Therefore, they chose to share very little of this precious time with anyone else.

During the mass, Morgaine sat between Ygraine and Uther, but spoke not a word. Ygraine's love for this child would not allow her to be unresponsive to what Morgaine was feeling. During the sermon, Ygraine reached for the child's hand and squeezed it gently. She leaned close to her and whispered, "All is well. We will speak when the Pendragon has gone. Worry not, for I will love you always, no matter what."

Uther overheard her words, and offered her a warm smile. Then he leaned over and kissed Morgaine's silken hair.

Morgaine had no verbal response, but the look in her eyes as she gazed up at her mother revealed the love she felt in return. She held onto both Ygraine and Uther's hand for the remainder of the service.

Later that day, after spending a few precious hours with Morgaine and Arianrod, Uther called all of the servants together in the main entranceway. With Corelia in attendance, he gave strict instructions that he and Ygraine were not to be disturbed. Their evening meal was to be left outside the door, and nothing short of the Saxons attacking was cause enough to be interrupted.

The servants dispersed, and Ygraine gave Corelia a hug before ascending the stairway ahead of Uther. Halfway up, she turned back around as Uther spoke his parting words to Corelia.

In a serious, informing manner, he said, "It would seem that the Queen intends to lock me away in her chamber, only to release me once I have caused her great pleasure." He raised an eyebrow, an impish look on his face. "I fear that could take hours to accomplish, for she is not easily pleased."

Uther had thought to embarrass Corelia, but her response shocked him as she said haughtily, "You should take some lessons from my Rodric then. It don't take him no time at all to give me pleasure!"

Uther laughed aloud, and he slapped Corelia on the back as if she were one of his men. Ygraine giggled, and Corelia began laughing too, but when she walked away, her laughter turned to a fit of coughing.

Ygraine made a mental note to speak to her about it, as

she had heard this coughing often lately, and it was beginning to worry her.

The day was a mixture of joy and sorrow for Uther and Ygraine. They lost themselves in each other, but the knowing that their time together was so short, distressed them.

As day changed to night, Ygraine began to feel panic over his leaving. As she lay naked in his arms, she suddenly propped herself up on an elbow and blurted out, "Let us run away together, never to be seen or heard of again."

Uther chuckled and rolled on top of her, fondling her curls. He placed several feathery kisses upon her eyelids, then said softly, "If I were any other man than High King, I would not have to run away to be with my own wife. I admit that it is a tempting thought, but I am too proud to give up this fight. I am honour bound to my country."

"Are you not bound to me?" Ygraine questioned, a sense of pleading in her voice.

Uther's eyes were aflame with his love for her as he replied, "I am bound to you in a way that goes beyond all knowledge in this world. Our souls are one, yours and mine. There is no separation between the two. So whether I be here, or on the battlefield, you are with me, and I am with you..." He brushed his lips gently against hers and whispered, "Always."

Ygraine began to weep, and he kissed her tears and they rolled down her cheeks. He cupped her face in his hands and smiled reassuringly at her, then kissed her long and deep. He made slow, tender love to her, and held her close to him through the night.

Neither of them slept. They both refused to let anything swallow up their remaining time together. As it was, dawn came all too quickly, and Uther prepared to depart.

His men were waiting on horseback as Ygraine walked beside Uther toward his mount. Rodric was securing

Excalibur in its sheath on Andromeda's side. Arianrod, very clam, was sitting straight and proud next to the horse. It was as if he knew that his master was again departing, and he accepted it.

They stopped a short distance away, and Uther questioned her of her intentions regarding Corelia.

Ygraine replied, "I have decided to let it pass. It matters not to me whether she is, or is not my blood. She is the only mother I have ever known, and I do not seek answers where she is concerned. I require no other family than that which I already have. I would ask you to also let it pass, and speak of this to no one."

Uther nodded and said, "If that is your choice, I will abide by it. I would actually prefer to have Lot show his support to me out of loyalty rather than a family tie. I would be more inclined to trust him."

Ygraine threw her arms around him and whispered, "Please be careful."

"I am safe," he assured her, grinning broadly. He pointed to the sword resting in its sheath on the saddle. "After all, I have Excalibur to watch over me."

The gems gleamed in the morning sun, and Ygraine was drawn to it. They continued toward Uther's mount, her eyes fixed on the sword.

Uther bent over and patted Arianrod on the head, receiving a lick on the back of his hand in return. He then took the reins from Rodric and swung himself onto his saddle while Ygraine touched the hilt of the sword gently. The metal should have felt cold, but it held an unnatural warmth instead. She ran her hand over it, caressing it as she said, "I have not mentioned it before, but I had a vision once of this sword when I was but a child. I was told that it would have great meaning to me some day."

She looked up at Uther and questioned, "From whom

did this sword come?"

He frowned slightly as he replied, "The Merlin. It was a gift from he. He said it would belong to our son one day."

Ygraine let out a sigh, then kissed the hilt, her lips lingering against it. Her words were directed to the sword as she whispered, "Excalibur, protect my love for me."

She looked back up at Uther, and he reached out and took her hands in his. He leaned down and kissed them, and his eyes penetrated hers as he said, "I will return soon. Wait for me."

Her eyes held his gaze as she replied, "Yes my love. For as long as it takes, I shall wait for you."

He let her hands slip away, and he waved as he spurred his mount onward. As he did, the sunlight reflecting off of his armlet flashed brightly. Ygraine did not see the tear drop from his eye as he led his men away.

෬ *Twenty-two* ඏ

Over the years Morgaine had taken an interest in learning other languages, and was now being tutored in Latin. Following her lesson after Uther's departure, she and Ygraine spoke briefly regarding their conflict on Christ Mass Eve.

While sitting on Morgaine's bed, Ygraine took her hands in hers. Looking deeply into her daughter's eyes, she said, "A love between a mother and her child is priceless. The love I feel for you is the kind of love Corelia feels for me. Tell me Morgaine, if you were to be made aware that I was not your blood, would you love me any less?"

"No, and I will always love you, just as I do the Pendragon, even though he is not my blood," Morgaine replied. "But I fear a time will come when your love for me may fade."

"How could you believe so?" Ygraine asked, unable to accept her words.

"I know not exactly why I feel so, but I do feel it," Morgaine responded. She leaned in closer to Ygraine and stated, "Love should be unconditional."

"And so it is," Ygraine affirmed, drawing Morgaine to

her and holding her close. "And so it is."

Ygraine closed her eyes, and though she prayed that
Morgaine's words would prove false, she knew in her heart
that absolutely nothing could make her lose her love for this
child. Absolutely nothing.

ৡৡ●ঔৢ

Uther was gone for four months, and Ygraine pined for
him as Arianrod used to do. Many a day it was difficult to
keep the cloak of her faith wrapped about her.

Throughout the last five years, and recently more often,
she contemplated discarding her pentacle. She did not like
the fact that it was gifted by the Merlin, but it was also the
token of Uther's devotion. Therefore, each time she thought
to take it from around her neck, the attachment she felt to it
would override her intention. Although she knew it was a
symbol of hope, she felt that there was also an even deeper
meaning attached to it. Regardless, the mere fact that it was
a memento of Uther's love was enough of a reason to keep
it.

Now with Uther gone, Ygraine thought that she would
surely go mad as the long days and nights flowed one into
the other.

The old stable-master, who had been in Gorlois' service,
had passed on and Rodric once again filled that position.
Ygraine thought he would be elated, but he had little response
and went about his business as usual.

Ygraine was truly beginning to worry about Corelia, as
she had carried her cough with her throughout the winter
months, and it seemed now that her cough was as ordinary
as breathing.

Ygraine approached her several times offering to apply
her healing gift, but Corelia always declined saying, "When

it's my time to go, I'll be ready. No sense delaying the inevitable."

When Ygraine received word that Uther was finally coming home again, her spirits soared. His message did not indicate how long he would be staying, but it did state that he would be at Tintagel within the week.

Elated, she rushed to inform Corelia of the good news, but was unable to find her.

After searching the castle, Ygraine went to the stables to question Rodric as to her whereabouts.

Rodric was grooming one of the horses, and without looking at her, he said casually, "She said she was going to gather some herbs now that the weather's calm."

Then he paused, in deep thought for a moment. Raising his head and looking at Ygraine, worry now covered his face, and he said, "But that was hours ago."

An ominous feeling suddenly came over him, and his face turned somber as he laid his hand over his heart. He immediately turned away and grabbed his coat from a peg on the stall and ran out of the stables.

Ygraine, also feeling fearful, ran after him, but she had a hard time keeping up. She called out breathlessly, "Please wait for me!"

Instead of slowing down, Rodric sped up, heading for Corelia's herb garden that was in the rear of the castle. He disappeared from Ygraine's view, and when she finally caught up with him, he was on his knees beside Corelia, who was lying unconscious in the garden. Arianrod was lying next to her, his head on her chest.

As Ygraine approached behind him, Rodric raised his fist upward and cried out, "No!" Then he put his face in his hands and began to weep.

Ygraine knelt beside Corelia and lifted her head gently to her lap. She immediately noticed that Corelia was still breathing. She reached out and grabbed Rodric's arm, jerking him from his grieving.

"She has not left us yet!" Ygraine shouted, feeling hopeful. "We must get her inside at once."

Rodric lifted Corelia into his arms and carried her to their quarters. He laid her upon the bed and sat next to her, holding her hand. His distress was tremendous, his eyes still filled with tears.

As Ygraine piled blankets on top of her, Arianrod tried to climb up on the bed, and Corelia began to stir. As soon as she opened her eyes, she began to cough.

Rodric pulled the dog back down, but he stayed close to the bed. Ygraine sat down on the other side of her and touched her wrist to Corelia's forehead. "You are on fire!" She exclaimed, shaking her head.

She rose and poured a glass of water from a pitcher on the table next to the bed and handed it out to Corelia saying, "You have a fever and we must break it."

Corelia pushed the glass away, and her voice was growing hoarse as she said, "I told you, there's no use slowing down the inevitable."

Rodric began to weep again, his heart wrenching in his chest. "Please do as Ygraine tells you. I can't bear to lose you."

"We all have to go sometime, and it's my time," Corelia whispered, before her hacking continued.

Ygraine leaned over her and said with frustration, "Why must you be so stubborn? I can help you."

"No you can't," Corelia said softly. "I don't want to be helped." A far away look came over her, and she stared into empty space. "I heard the angels calling for me child."

Corelia smiled and closed her eyes peacefully. Then suddenly, her eyes opened wide and she grabbed Ygraine's hand, her eyes revealing sadness. "There's something I have to tell you before I go," she said, her voice quivering with emotion. She began coughing, and forced herself to stop. "I've been carrying a secret around with me for a long time now, and I don't think I should take it with me." She paused for a moment, then said, "You see, I'm not really..."

Ygraine touched her fingertips to Corelia's lips to silence her and sat back down next to her. "Shhh, you be quiet now," she said lovingly. "There is nothing you need to tell me that I do not already know."

Corelia's eyes widened and they welled up with tears. She looked up at Rodric, who smiled at her through his own tears while patting her hand. Then she turned back to Ygraine. "You know?"

"What I know is that no child has ever been loved more," Ygraine whispered. "I am your daughter, and proud to call you mother."

She leaned over and kissed Corelia's cheek. When she drew away, she noticed that Corelia's breathing was barely noticeable. The coughing had stopped, and her eyes were glazed.

Ygraine rose from the bed and moved to stand at the foot of it, giving Rodric his privacy with her.

He brought Corelia's hand to his lips and kissed it. He attempted to restrain his tears as he whispered, "You've still got the most beautiful eyes I ever saw." He took a deep breath. "I love you Corelia."

Corelia did not respond, but smiled, closing her eyes as her breathing ceased. At that very moment, a golden glow appeared above Corelia. Ygraine's eyes grew wide as she stared at it.

Arianrod began wagging his tail as Rodric stood up and took a step back, also staring. He placed his hand over his heart, his mouth gaping.

The glow slowly took on the form of an angel spreading

its wings out over Corelia's body, then it instantly disappeared.

Ygraine rushed over to stand beside Rodric, and he turned to look at her, his mouth still gaping. "Did you see it?" He asked in amazement.

Ygraine nodded slowly. Then she began to weep, as her loss suddenly hit her heart heavily.

Rodric looked to be in a stupor as he walked passed Ygraine, toward the door.

"Where are you going?" She questioned, wiping away her tears.

He looked back at her, his face revealing his total confusion and replied, "To the chapel."

৯৯●৯৵

It was dusk, and the candles in the chapel had not yet been lit. The last hint of the sun shone through the stained glass windows, lending a warm splendor of colours that spilled out across the floor.

Upon entering, Rodric instantly felt wrapped up in the warmth. He slowly walked toward the statue of Mother Mary, whose welcoming arms beckoned him.

He knelt on the floor in front of her and looked up into her loving eyes as he spoke. His voice held a sense of awe as he said, "I've lost my love, and all I can think of is what I've just seen."

He paused, closing his eyes for a momentary remembrance. Opening them, he let out a sigh and said, "I saw it with my whole being, and I filled myself up with it. I never had such a feeling as this, and somehow I've got to make sure it doesn't go away."

The gold halo around Mary's head began to radiate and glow, as if she were giving him a sign of affirmation.

Rodric's eyes bulged, and he stood up, suddenly feeling as if he would explode. He raised both his hands heavenward, and he cried out with a force that had been hidden somewhere deep within him. "I call forth the power of the God in me, and from this day forward, I serve no one but myself. I am my own master!"

Ygraine stood in the doorway, and as Rodric's cry resonated through the chapel, she watched this man, her father, being transformed before her very eyes. He turned to face her, and she saw that somehow he had changed. He looked larger, but she knew it wasn't so.

She rushed to him, stopping just in front of him and whispered, "Are you all right?"

His face seemed to be chiseled from stone as he said, "The Merlin was right. There's more to this world than what meets the eyes, and I now know the true meaning of power."

He pointed to himself, touching his chest with his finger and stated, "It's right here. It's within me."

He then took Ygraine's hands and lifted them in front of his face, examining them closely. He smiled and said, "It's within all of us."

❧❧●❧❧

Rodric spent the entire night in the chapel, and when he emerged the next morning, he had made the decision to leave Tintagel straight away. He knew that his departure before Corelia's burial would appear odd, but he now had a deeper understanding of life... and death, and what other's thought no longer had meaning to him whatsoever.

He went directly to his and Corelia's room, intending to pay his last respects in his own way and gather some of his belongings. Upon reaching the door, he stopped. He shook his head and said, "There is nothing I need."

He kissed his fingertips and laid them gently against the door. Closing his eyes, he silently said his farewell.

When he was through he went directly to the stables and saddled one of Uther's stallions that he had grown particularly fond of. As he was preparing to mount, he heard someone approaching in the hay behind him. He turned to find a pale, disheveled Ygraine walking toward him.

She walked straight into him, burying her face into his shoulder, her body leaning heavily against him.

He wrapped his arms around her, willing his mind to imprint the sight and feel of her in his memory, knowing that he would not see her again in this lifetime.

She raised her eyes to his, and he was surprised to see there were no tears present. "May you find all that you seek," was all she said.

She kissed him on the cheek and slowly turned away.

As she walked away from the stables, she was aware of the horse and rider leaving, but she did not turn to observe.

The castle gate was opened, and Rodric refused to look back. He carefully made his way down the narrow path away from the castle.

In the distance he could make out the form of a lone rider. The rider reigned in, and seemed to be waiting for Rodric.

As Rodric drew nearer to the rider, he felt he knew him. There was something familiar about the eyes under the hooded cloak. As Rodric reached him, the rider pulled his hood back, and he realized he did indeed know him. There was no mistaking the Merlin. Aside from the few streaks of silver in his hair, he did not appear to have aged at all.

Rodric was not the least bit surprised at the Merlin's presence. For some odd reason, it seemed perfectly natural that he would be waiting for him.

Rodric drew his mount close to his, and the Merlin bowed his head in greeting. Rodric nodded back, and the Merlin

said, "I will take you to a place where you may find all that
you seek."

Rodric smiled warmly, and the two riders thereafter
remained silent for the duration of their journey.

Rodric was taken to the Isle of Man, where the Druids
inhabited the island. He was welcomed into the Druidic
culture of astrology, magic, the mysterious powers of plants
and animals, and the supernatural forces of nature. He would
spend the rest of his days there in complete contentment.

꽃꽃 ● 꽃꽃

Ygraine went into a deep depression, and everyone in
the castle was anxious for the King to come home. They
were genuinely concerned for their Queen, as Ygraine had
not left her chamber for days and had refused to eat.

Morgaine approached her late in the afternoon on the fifth
day of her isolated grieving, knowing that she had rarely left
the chair she was sitting in, nor had she changed her clothes.

Ygraine's face was drawn, and she was visibly exhausted.
The scent of wine permeated the air, and Morgaine knew
that her mother had consumed only that since Corelia's death.
Several empty flagons were on the table next to her, and a
tray of untouched food was on the floor.

Ygraine's eyes were closed, but Morgaine knew that she
was not in slumber. As soon as the child was near her, Ygraine
opened her eyes. She reached for Morgaine, pulling her onto
her lap. Then laying her head against the child's chest, she
fell fast asleep.

Ygraine was heavy against her, but Morgaine held her,
tenderly stroking her hair. "The Pendragon is near," she
whispered.

Ygraine slept for quite some time, and Morgaine grew
weary of holding her weight, but had not the heart to disturb

her rest. However, she was grateful as day went into night, knowing it would bring the Pendragon.

Morgaine heard his heavy footsteps in the corridor, and prepared herself for the onslaught of questions she assumed he would have.

He entered with Arianrod at his side, and the lines in his face revealed his concern. The sight of Ygraine slumped against the child made his stomach lurch.

He stopped mid-stride, his voice filled with anxiety. "What has happened? Rodric did not greet me at the stables, and Corelia is nowhere to be found. The servants all seem to have lost their tongues."

Ygraine's face was turned away from him, and when she did not respond, he gave Morgaine a questioning glance as he quickly approached.

Morgaine raised her sad eyes to his and whispered, "Corelia passed on six days ago, and Rodric has left."

Uther drew his breath in sharply, and his throat constricted with pain. As he gently ran his hand over Ygraine's hair, he swallowed hard as he attempted to digest Morgaine's words.

Morgaine sighed and said, "Mother is in a bad way. I am most grateful that you are here."

Uther gave her a half-smile, then gently drew Ygraine's body away from the child's embrace. As Morgaine rose from Ygraine's lap, he lifted Ygraine into his arms. She was limp as he carried her to the bed and placed her upon it.

"I will leave you to tend to her," Morgaine said softly.

Uther nodded, and she headed for the door, quietly calling Arianrod to come with her. The dog hesitated, but did as he was commanded. Morgaine glanced back lovingly toward Uther then left the chamber, pulling the door closed behind her.

The room was cold, so Uther immediately stoked the fire, adding several logs to quickly take the chill away.

Returning to the bedside, he lit a candle on the table nearby. As the light from the fire, and that of the candle softly illuminated the room, he saw Ygraine's face and could not believe his eyes.

She was so pale, and there were dark circles under her eyes. Her hair was tangled about her face, and she smelled like a tavern wench.

He pulled a fur cover over her, and hurried out into the corridor. One of the maids was just exiting another chamber, and upon seeing Uther, she immediately went to him. He instructed her to see to it that the bathing tub was filled with hot water straight away, then went back into their chamber, leaving the door open.

Ygraine had not stirred. He moved to the bed and laid down next to her, pulling her into his arms. She partially awoke, and she nestled into him before quickly drifting back into a deep sleep.

When several servants arrived carrying pails of hot water, Uther bid them enter, but he did not move from his place next to Ygraine. When they had finished their task of filling the tub, he requested that food be brought and left outside the door.

The servants left, and as he rose from the bed, a gentle moan escaped Ygraine's lips. He stood looking down at her, and his heart ached. She had such a strength in her, and now she appeared so fragile.

He sat next to her and carefully began to undress her. He had her almost completely unclothed before she opened her eyes, and the sadness within them cut through him like a blade.

She did not weep, and he was thankful for that. She opened her mouth to speak, then shook her head, as if the effort was too great.

He did not bother to remove the sheer cotton shift that

remained. He picked her up and carried her to the steaming tub, placing her in it.

She sighed and let her head fall back into the water, closing her eyes peacefully. Neither of them spoke, as Uther washed her hair, letting his fingers enjoy their task. Even now, he loved the feel of her beneath his touch.

Then he pulled the wet shift from her and tenderly washed her body. When he was through, he assisted her to her feet and poured a pail of clean water over her to rinse her. He then wrapped a heavy cotton sheet around her that had been warming by the fire, and lifted her from the tub into his arms.

He moved to sit in his chair by the fireplace and held her to him. She rested her head against his shoulder, and he breathed in deeply the scent of her hair.

Finally Uther broke the silence, saying quietly, "I sent for food. You should try to eat something."

Ygraine did not respond, and the sound of her deep breathing told him that she was again asleep.

He held her in the chair all through the night, knowing that she needed the security he was giving her.

Uther, however, did not sleep. He spent the night cursing the Saxons, and his ancestry. He wondered to himself why he could not have been just an ordinary man. Why must he bear this country's heavy burden, when all he truly desired was to be with his wife?

He chuckled and raised an eyebrow as he thought of Ygraine's notion to run off together, and he half-heartedly wished he had paid more attention to her suggestion.

He kissed her wet hair softly, and his smile faded as he again turned somber. He leaned his head back against the chair, whispering to himself, "I must hold on to my dream that there will be peace some day, and I hope that it will be in my lifetime."

By morning Uther was exhausted. He rose from the chair

with Ygraine in his arms, his body stiff and his muscles aching. He carried her over to the bed and gently laid her down. Then lying down next to her, he pulled her close and fell asleep. They both slept well into the afternoon.

Uther woke first, cold, and with a hunger churning in his belly. He recalled that he had not eaten since morning, the day before. He pulled the covers snugly about Ygraine, then quietly slid from the bed and stacked more logs on the fire. Afterward, he retrieved a tray of food from outside the chamber door. The food was fresh, and he smiled appreciatively as he thought of how many times the maid must have come and gone since the previous evening.

He set the tray on the bed, and moved to the other side to wake Ygraine. Her eyes held the same sadness as the night before, which disturbed him greatly.

She slowly sat up, and he propped the feather pillows up behind her so that she could lean back comfortably.

Seeing his look of concern, she reached out to caress his face. As she did, she noticed a thin scar on the right side, from his eye across his cheekbone.

Her forehead creased with worry as she said, "You were wounded. Are you well?"

He smiled warmly at her and replied, "I fear that you are in a far worse state than I." He leaned over and kissed her forehead, then said, "You must eat now. Then we will talk."

Ygraine picked at her food, while Uther devoured his. When he was finished, she pushed the tray away and reached for him. "Hold me please," she pleaded.

He immediately pulled her to him and held her close. "I am sorry that I was not here for you," he whispered next to her ear. "Oh God, I would do anything to protect you from pain... be it of the flesh, or of the heart."

"The pain is so deep," she said vehemently, drawing away slightly to look at him. "I have shed so many tears that there are none left. There is an emptiness inside of me, and you must help me to rid myself of it."

"I will help you," he assured her while tenderly brushing her curls away from her face. "I will stay with you until you are stronger. My army has held its strength, and the borders are protected for now."

Ygraine smiled, and the sadness in her eyes lightened somewhat.

She recounted to Uther everything that had happened, and when she was finished, Uther had an odd look in his eyes. He was remembering Ambrosius' death, when he could have sworn he saw a figure at the foot of his bed.

He seemed to be in deep thought as he said, "Who knows what awaits us. Mayhaps there is something better on the other side."

"I do not choose to find out yet," Ygraine said, a slight frown on her face.

Uther reached up to caress her brow as she whispered, "After all, there could be nothing better than being with my Pendragon."

She turned her head to kiss Uther's armlet before he slowly drew his hand away, and the glow from the candle caused it to shimmer.

Then looking into his eyes, she smiled warmly, and Uther saw a bit of the Ygraine he knew returning. He kissed her mouth, and she ran her tongue along his lower lip seductively. "Now I am hungry," she whispered.

"Then I shall fill you up," Uther replied, gently pushing her back against the pillows.

Ygraine sighed, as her numbed senses began to awaken, and for now she forgot her sadness and her loss. For now, she was with her Pendragon, and nothing else mattered.

❧ *Twenty-three* ❧

In the great hall in Lothian, Morgause stood by the hearth eyeing her husband thoughtfully.

Lot sat in a chair facing her, a goblet of brandy in his hand. Morgause's staring was making him uncomfortable, and he hoped to dull his nerves with the alcohol.

As he was raising the goblet to his lips, Morgause stepped forward and took it out of his hand. She lifted it to her own lips, downing the contents.

When she was through, she appeared restless, tapping her fingers against the bottom of the goblet as she said, "I believe it is time to lay a strategy to overthrow the throne. My patience grows thin, and I tire of this place."

Her mind wandered to the memory of Tintagel, and the desire for it burned inside of her.

Lot raised a brow and stood up. He walked over to the table and poured himself another brandy. He took a long swallow and turned back to her. "What have you in mind?" He questioned, unsure of whether or not he truly wanted her reply.

She began to run her finger around the rim of the goblet.

"I have decided that it is time for you to take an interest in the welfare of Britain," she informed him.

She looked away for a moment, then nodded her head, pleased with the plot forming in her mind. "Yes, I believe I have the perfect plan," she said with a sly look in her eyes.

Lot walked back over to his chair and sat down. "I would be grateful if you would share this plan," he said, a sudden interest arising in him.

Morgause smiled, pleased that she had piqued his curiosity. Her words were firm as she said, "You will align with the High King. In fact, you will become his most trusted ally, ever present at his side."

Lot was taking a sip of his brandy, and her words caused him to choke as he swallowed. He pulled out his handkerchief and dabbed at his mouth. Confused, he asked, "Why would I want to do such a thing?"

Morgause held three fingers out in front of him. "For three reasons," she replied. "First of all, you are not a warrior." She glared at him, her eyes cold as ice. "You are lazy, and need much training in the art of war. What better way than to receive that training first hand. The High King is a great warlord, and you would do well to learn from him."

She sauntered over to the table and refilled her goblet, then turned back to face Lot. "Secondly, when he is dead, who better to take his place than his right arm?"

She took a sip of the brandy and again ran her finger around the rim of the goblet as she continued. "He has no heir. The only child his Queen conceived was stillborn, and now it is said that she is barren."

She paused and smiled shrewdly, enjoying the sound of her own words. Then she said, "Which brings us to the third reason."

Lot raised his eyebrows, now thoroughly intrigued as he listened intently. She strolled back over and looked down at him. "Once you have gained his trust, and he believes you to be entirely loyal... you will slay him."

At first Lot was appalled by her words, his eyes wide with shock. But as greed, and his own desire for the throne seeped into his senses, her plan began to fascinate him.

"You are shrewd my wife," he said proudly, a wry smile on his face. "But tell me, why not plot to slay him now? Why wait? It could take some time to gain his trust."

She glared at him, curling up her lip. "You are not ready to fill his shoes," she replied matter-of-factly.

Then her eyes glazed, and she licked her lips as if she had just tasted something sweet and said, "Besides, the cut will go so much deeper than the flesh when he realizes that he has been so deceived."

The look in her eye made Lot shiver. She was so devious that he sometimes wondered why he cared for her at all. Although he had chosen to remain in Lothian, their marriage had gained him her father's lands in Guent. But it was more than that. She had such an overpowering way of manipulating him to her every want and need, but something in her was exciting to him.

Impulsively, he rose from the chair, and encircled her waist with his arm, pulling her to him roughly. He kissed her, and her lips were cold, but he was used to that. Somehow her frigidness excited him more. The challenge of breaking down her barriers enticed him.

He kissed her again, this time hungrily. She did not respond, and when he drew away, she tilted her head back and laughed aloud.

Her action made him angry and he gritted his teeth. His jaw clenched and he growled, "Why can you not allow me to warm that cold blood of yours?"

She tilted her head slightly, and her words were honeyed as she replied, "You will warm my blood when you have enough power to do so. When I am queen, my blood will boil with passion."

She rubbed his lower lip with her thumb saying, "Until then, my veins will continue to hold ice."

Then she leaned her face extremely close to his and whispered, "Make haste in gaining the High King's trust, and you may melt the ice."

She sauntered away from him, laughing as she left the room.

He was left standing alone, with nothing but his own unfulfilled desires.

He downed the rest of his brandy and set the goblet aside. Then he pulled out a small silver box from a pouch at his waist. Opening the box, he dipped his pinkie into it, withdrawing a nail full of snuff. Bringing it to his nose, he inhaled deeply. He closed the box and put it back into the pouch, then dabbed at his nose daintily with his handkerchief.

He immediately left the room to seek out one of the castle maids to attend to his personal needs.

‹⚬ *Twenty-four* ❀›

Uther had been at Tintagel for a month when he received a message from Lot that encouraged him to leave sooner than he had intended. If it was acceptable to the High King, a meeting would be arranged in Guent where Lot's cousin, Leodogranz still resided.

Although Uther was skeptical of Lot's intentions, he agreed to the meeting. He had been hoping for the support of both Lot and Leodogranz, and the possibility of gaining that support excited him.

The meeting would take place in a fortnight, and Uther planned to travel with a small army, should there be an ambush awaiting. He also sent word to Uriens requesting his presence. Uriens had proved to be Uther's most trusted and loyal ally thus far. Therefore, he wanted him at his side.

Ygraine was growing stronger, and although Uther hated to leave her, he knew that he must. This allegiance with the Scots could prove strong enough to end the Saxon wars.

He decided to wait until the evening before his departure to break the news to her. He had informed Morgaine that he would be leaving, but he did not have the heart to tell Ygraine sooner, and he dreaded the look in her eyes that he knew would be present. There had been so many farewells for the two of them, and he desperately wanted no more.

They were in their chamber the evening prior to his leaving. Uther was sitting in his chair near the fire polishing Excalibur. Arianrod was in his usual place at his feet, sleeping soundly.

Ygraine sat opposite him, watching in awe as he sensually ran a soft cloth over the hilt. The light from the fire mingled with the red gemstones in the dragon's eyes. They gleamed and seemed to come alive as the flames danced within them.

She became mesmerized at the intimate way in which he handled the sword. As she continued to watch, becoming almost spellbound, the firelight caught Uther's armlet, causing an intense flash of golden light. It made Ygraine blink hard, and she was suddenly aware of how she had been staring.

Uther smiled at her, and she was instantly overwhelmed with the desire to feel those caressing hands on her body.

She rose from the chair and stepped over to his. She attempted to take the sword from him, but was shocked, as she had no idea how heavy it was. They both laughed as she again tried to lift it, straining to move it only a short distance. She leaned it against the wall and turned to Uther, who had a questioning look on his face.

He raised a brow, and pretended to be offended, but there was amusement in his voice as he said, "You dare to interrupt the King from such an arduous task?"

Ygraine gave him a seductive look and replied, "I only thought that the King might make better use of his strength making love to his Queen, rather than his sword."

Uther laughed again while laying the cloth aside. Then he rose from his chair, and as he did, he sobered. He moved closer to her, and he gave her a serious look as he said, "That 'sword' is the reason I am able to be with you at all. If it were not for Excalibur, I fear that my life would have already come to its end."

Ygraine was immediately in his arms. "Do not speak so," she pleaded. "I cannot bear such thoughts."

Uther groaned, and Ygraine looked up at his frowning face. "Why do you show such discontent?"

He did not answer, but gave her a look that was very familiar to her. It was the same look she always received when he was preparing to deliver the news that he was leaving.

She choked back her tears as she whispered, "It is again time for us to be apart, it is not?"

"It is," he replied softly, as he tenderly stroked her hair. "But I have hopes that it will not be for long. A meeting has been arranged with Lot."

Ygraine grimaced at the mere mention of his name, but forced herself to be rational. Just because his wife was mad was no reason for her to be so suspicious of Lot.

Uther ran his fingertips gently over her worried brow. "There is a chance that the Lords of Scotland may align with me, adding great strength in driving the Saxons back for good." He laid his cheek next to hers and whispered, "When the wars are over, there will be no more farewells."

Ygraine closed her eyes and reveled in the thought. If it were true, and Uther did gain the Scottish alliance, she would have him home far more than she did now. That thought appeased her greatly, but nonetheless, she intended to seek the truth in the fire, which she had not done in a very long time.

She drew back slightly and smiled lovingly at Uther, and he was grateful that the usual tears were not present. She wrapped her arms around his neck and said, "You are wise, and I trust that you will do what is right."

A grin spread across his face, and he said graciously, "I am thankful for your support, my Lady."

He was genuinely happy that this farewell was turning out to be quite different than those in the past.

That evening, their lovemaking was lustful, and afterward they slept soundly in each other's arms.

When morning came, Uther urged Ygraine to stay in bed. He quickly dressed, and she watched, allowing her eyes to linger on his body as he did. When he was through, he stoked the fire and added several logs. He gave Arianrod, who was lying on the hearth, a loving pat on his head. Then he slowly walked toward Ygraine. He sat down on the bed and leaned over to kiss her. He groaned as he did so, and Ygraine was instantly concerned. Her eyes were wide as she asked, "What pains you?"

Uther had a mischievous look on his face as he replied, "Every part of my body pains me. I feel as though I have fought a battle."

Ygraine laughed and said, "I too have aches and pains." Then she teased him by asking, "Are you able to ride my Lord?"

Uther groaned again. The mere thought of straddling his horse made him wince.

Then he gazed into her eyes, and he became serious, for it was time to leave her. Ygraine noticed his mood change, and felt her chest tighten.

She placed her hand to her heart and whispered, "My heart truly does beat for thee. It feels as though it were being torn apart."

Uther placed his hand on his chest, and he had a look of agony on his face as he said, "We must share the same heart."

She felt as though her entire being was ready to explode, but she remained outwardly calm. She reached up and gently drew his face down to hers. He kissed her deeply, pressing his body to hers. She felt the beating of his heart against her breast, and knew that if he did not leave at once, she would never let him go.

She slowly pushed him away from her and said softly, "Your country awaits my love. Go now."

Uther hesitantly rose and moved to retrieve Excalibur from where Ygraine had placed it the night before. Arianrod was immediately on his feet following after him. When he reached the door, Ygraine called out, "I love you Pendragon."

He turned and replied, "And I you." He smiled warmly, and as Arianrod passed through the door, he pulled it shut.

Ygraine closed her eyes and listened as his footsteps faded down the corridor. When there was no more sound, she wept from the depths of her soul. Suddenly she felt so alone.

Then Morgaine entered her thoughts, and she began to feel calmer. She stopped crying and whispered aloud, "At least I still have you here, my precious daughter."

Ygraine stayed in bed most of the morning contemplating whether or not she wanted to invoke use of the fire to gain knowledge of Uther's forthcoming meeting. It had been years since she had called upon her sight, and she was not certain that she still possessed it.

The flames were dying, and she was beginning to feel chilled. She rose to tend to it, shivering as she walked toward the fireplace. Once she had added more logs and the flames burst up, they beckoned her to call upon them.

She sat on the hearth and stared into their depths, feeling the warmth envelop her. Her head felt light, and the old familiar feeling of weightlessness threatened to consume her. At first, she allowed the feeling. But suddenly the memory of her confrontation with Morgaine concerning Corelia wove its way through the haze, and she shook her head violently.

She stood up and backed away. She had never before feared what the flames would reveal, but now she was terrified. "What if I see that which I choose not to?" She questioned aloud. "I am doubtful that it may reveal answers to more than that which I seek. Besides, I must trust Uther's judgment in this matter. He will know what is truth and what is not."

She climbed back into bed, still feeling tormented. After a few moments, she took her pentacle in her hand and gazed upon it. "I must have faith that all will be well," she thought to herself. "After everything that Uther and I have sacrificed to be together, I have to believe that nothing can happen to separate us now."

She let out a deep sigh and whispered, "The power of our love will keep you safe... and the power of Excalibur in your hand."

ン・ズ・●・ズ・イ

Uther and his army made their way directly to the home of Uriens in Devon.

Uriens was waiting as they approached, and as requested, took great pride in accompanying the High King as his right-arm on such a valuable mission.

Uther and his men remained mounted as Uriens ran to greet them. Uther reached down, and there was great warmth radiating from both men as the two clasped forearms in greeting.

"We will not stop to rest," Uther said.

Uriens nodded and motioned to his stable-master to bring his horse. Uther's attention had been drawn to Morella, who was hurrying toward them, a babe in each arm and two little girls running behind her.

The sight brought a broad smile to Uther's face, but Uriens looked displeased.

As they reached him, Uther dismounted. He took

Morella's face in his hands and kissed each cheek. Then he turned to Uriens and said with dismay, "Why did you not tell me you had such a brood?"

Uriens shrugged his shoulders, and he was obviously disgruntled as he replied, "Talk of women and children does not mix with war."

Uther turned back as the two little girls came forward and curtsied. The smaller of the two lost her balance and fell down. Uther laughed heartily and bent to lift the child into his arms.

Morella said jovially, "My husband wasn't appeased with two girls. He insisted on having an heir." She glanced at each of the twins in her arms. "And now he has two."

Uther's smile faded, and a sudden pained look in his eyes made Morella realize why Uriens had insisted that she not present the children to Uther.

Uriens noticed Uther's expression of grief and gave Morella a knowing look. She bit her lower lip, wishing that she could retrieve her words, then said with compassion, "I was sorry to hear about the loss of your child."

The mention of the boy child made Uther's chest tighten even more.

Morella continued, "Ygraine sent word, but I've heard from her very little since. In fact, it's been many moons since our last communication. I've not heard from Corelia of late either. Is she well?"

Suddenly Uther realized that Morella knew nothing of the more recent events. He was unaware that Ygraine had stopped communicating with her. He regained his composure and put the little girl down. As he straightened, he said to Morella, with genuine warmth, "Your family is as beautiful as you."

Then he turned to Uriens and put his arm about his shoulders, guiding him a short distance away. In a serious voice he whispered, "I fear I have news that will upset your wife."

"What is it?" Uriens questioned softly, paying heed to the tone of Uther's voice.

Uther replied, still whispering, "Corelia passed on over a moon ago, and Rodric has gone on a spiritual quest. I do not expect him to return. Morella was very close to both of them."

Uriens closed his eyes and let out a deep sigh, dreading the task that lay before him. They both turned and walked back to Morella, who stood with a questioning look on her face.

Uther swung himself up onto his saddle, and there was a look of sympathy on his face as he said, "Be well. I will give your regards to Ygraine."

Uriens took one of the babes from Morella's arms, and with extreme kindness he said, "Come, I have news to share with you before I go."

Uther watched as they walked away, Uriens' head bent close to Morella's in conversation.

Suddenly Morella stopped, and she turned to look at Uther, her face revealing her shock and grief. Uther returned her gaze, then blew her a kiss.

She turned back to Uriens, tears filling her eyes. He gently wiped a tear from her face and leaned over to kiss her on the cheek. Morella took the babe from him, and still weeping, walked away.

Uriens quickly strode back, and taking the reins from the stable-master, he mounted his horse. He drew close to Uther and said, "She will be all right. Her grief will pass quickly. She has plenty to fill her time."

Uther nodded in affirmation, and Uriens placed his hand on Uther's forearm. He said, with deep caring, "I did not speak of the children because I am aware of how deep your pain runs. I did not want to boast about something that you have lost. For you as High King, I can only imagine your feelings over the loss of your heir."

Uther closed his eyes briefly, and when he opened them, they were filled with warmth. "You are a true friend," Uther said with assurance.

Then Uther felt compelled to plant a seed in Uriens' mind, and he leaned closer to him saying, "There will come a time my friend, after I am gone, when you will look into the eyes of one who will remind you of me. Search in your heart for the truth, and remember this day."

Uriens' eyes widened, and he quickly contemplated what Uther was insinuating. He opened his mouth to question Uther further, but Uther held up his hand to halt his speech and said firmly, "I can say no more."

Although a look of confusion remained on his face, Uriens nodded, believing that some day he would come to understand Uther's words.

"Let us go," Uther said, smiling. "We have peace to make with the Scots."

Uther raised his arm as a signal for his army, and they rode away, the dust from the horses hooves rising in the air around them as they departed.

༄ ༄ ● ༄ ༄

Uther was pleased that they had encountered nothing out of the ordinary on their journey to Guent.

It was evening when they arrived, and although nothing appeared abnormal, Uther was still suspicious. He instructed his men to remain mounted, and to be aware constantly of their surroundings. They would set up camp later, away from Guent.

Uther and Uriens dismounted and strode toward the

entrance of the castle. The torches burned brightly, outlining the figure of Lot as he awaited them. Uther's hand rested on Excalibur's hilt, the feel of it beneath his fingers giving him a sense of security.

As they approached and climbed the front steps, Lot noticed the position of Uther's hand and said pointedly, "I see that the High King does not trust easily, but I assure you that I have only the best of intentions in mind."

Uther stood in front of him and remarked, "We shall see."

Lot cleared his throat, a distinct sign of his discomfort, but said graciously, "Come, my cousin awaits inside. We are both eager to discuss how we may join together and end the wars."

Uther and Uriens exchanged a look of skepticism, both raising their eyebrows, then followed Lot inside.

They were led to a room next to the great hall, where Leodogranz sat at a large wooden table. He immediately rose and bowed low before Uther saying in earnest, "My Lord, you are most welcome in our home."

When Leodogranz straightened, Uther looked directly into his eyes, finding that he could best judge a man by what his eyes revealed. Leodogranz returned his gaze unwaveringly. In that moment, Uther knew that this was an honest man with nothing to hide.

They all sat, and when the meeting was over, Uther was indeed pleased. They had spent hours laying strategies against the Saxons, who had now moved far up the northern coast threatening both countries.

It was decided that Lot would raise an army and bring them to Uther's fortress at Segontium in the northern region. Leodogranz would bring his men to Uther's stronghold in Avon.

They would force the Saxons inland and destroy their ships. The army from Segontium would push south, whereas the army from Avon would push north, trapping the Saxons in between.

Uther slid his chair back and rose to his feet. He looked at the three men before him, who immediately stood as well, and nodded his head in approval. "It would seem that we have all finally come to realize the importance of oneness." He let out a sigh and said softly, "Ambrosius would be pleased."

Leodogranz went to stand in front of Uther, reaching for his hand. He knelt down, bowing his head as he spoke. "I have Scottish blood running through my veins, and I vowed never to swear allegiance to a Briton."

He raised his head, looking into Uther's eyes as he said, "How could a man live in this country as long as I have, and not learn to love it. This is my home now, and I beg you to accept my word that I will serve you until the day I die."

Their eyes locked. After several moments, Uther smiled slightly and said, "I accept your word." They continued to stare at each other for some time, a deep respect forming between them.

Leodogranz then kissed Uther's hand and rose to his feet. He moved aside as Lot came forward.

He also knelt and took Uther's hand, keeping his head lowered as he said, "On my honour as Scotland's Over-Lord, I swear allegiance to you. I will do everything in my power to protect both our countries."

He kissed Uther's hand, but would not look up. His avoidance in making eye contact made Uther uncomfortable. As he stood looking down at Lot's head, Uther recalled the Merlin's warning years before, and he decided that he would watch this one, and remember to never turn his back on him.

Uther pulled his hand away and Lot rose to his feet. Uther's voice was flat as he said, "I accept the alliance. I will meet you in Segontium."

Lot sat back down at the table, and Leodogranz walked out with Uther and Uriens. With daggers in his eyes, Lot glared at Uther's back as they departed.

As they were passing the great hall, Leodogranz said, "I would be honoured to house the High King and his men here tonight."

"I must decline the offer," Uther replied.

They all turned as the sound of footsteps drew their attention to a fair-haired girl descending the stairway behind them. She ran to Leodogranz and stared openly at Uther.

Leodogranz was appalled by her behavior and said ashamedly, "I apologize for my daughter sire, but she has little knowledge of how to act in the company of a King."

"I suggest you teach her," Uther said firmly, but his smile gave little value to the tone of his voice.

The girl smiled back at him, but her attention quickly shifted to Uriens, and she smiled coyly at him.

Uther thought her to be most beautiful for a child. Her hair was long, well past her waist, and her eyes were large and pale blue. Her face was angelic, but something in the way she was looking at Uriens revealed a passionate nature.

"What is your name child?" Uther questioned casually.

She looked back at him, and her voice was sweet as she replied, "Gwenhafar."

"Gwenhafar," Uther repeated softly, and as he did, a chill ran through his body.

For some unknown reason, he reached for the child's hand. Bending over, he raised it to his lips and kissed it tenderly. He looked at her smiling face, and something about her touched his soul. Then he turned away abruptly and made for the door, attempting to shake this strange sensation from himself.

Leodogranz shrugged his shoulders in dismay as Uriens followed after Uther.

Once outside, Uther stopped to breathe in the night air, filling his lungs. Both men looked up to witness two stars shooting across the sky simultaneously. Again Uther felt the chill run through him.

Uriens body also shuddered, and they looked at each other as Uriens said, "I hear that that is a sign from God that two souls are being united."

Uther raised a brow as he said, "Mayhaps it is a sign that two countries are being united.

Uriens nodded, and they proceeded toward their horses.

Uther suddenly thought of the boy child. He would be about the same age as Gwenhafar. He swung himself onto his saddle, and looked back up at the sky and thought, "Two souls, eh? What I would give to be united with my son... just once."

Uther led his army away, and Ygraine seeped into his mind. What he had done this night would please her. He smiled, thinking of how life would be when the wars were over.

"I love you," he whispered to the wind. Then he spurred his horse onward. He was weary and longed for sleep so that he could dream of his beloved.

෴ *Twenty-five* ෴

Uther spent the next two years fortifying his army. The Saxons attacked sporadically, but no major battles were fought, affording Uther the time he needed to set his strategies into motion. With the added support of the Scots, Uther was confident that Britain would soon know peace.

During that time, Lot was constantly at Uther's side. He trained hard, and Uther was impressed with his dedication. He was beginning to believe that both he and the Merlin may have been wrong about him, and deep inside he hoped that they were. He wanted so much to trust this man, who had become his shadow.

Lot was fighting a battle much stronger than any Saxon war. He fought an inner battle that tormented him to the point of total frustration. Over those two years, Lot had come to respect Uther in a way he had never thought possible. He had not witnessed such passion in any man, and he longed to be like him. He was eager to learn all that he could absorb, and the knowledge that he gained far exceeded his own aspirations. The time he spent with Uther was causing him to experience an incredible change of character.

Lot spent very little time with Morgause, who was a constant reminder of the treachery that was planned. He wished that her power over him were not so strong. But no matter what changes occurred within him, he could not seem to find any strength where she was concerned.

Lot knew that the time was growing near when their plot would need to be carried out, and it sickened him. Somehow he had to be able to do what Morgause expected of him, and he dreaded each day that passed that brought that time nearer.

Uther's visits to Tintagel were rare. He missed Ygraine terribly, but he was overwhelmed with training all of Lots and Leodogranz' men. This time was of the utmost importance, and he promised Ygraine to make every moment up to her when the wars were over.

Ygraine was miserable. She had never known such loneliness. However, she never lost sight of her and Uther's dream of peace. All these feelings of misery would be rewarded in time.

Morgaine had befriended Devon, one of the servants' boys. He was the child of the temporary nursemaid to Morgaine. They were the same age, eleven, and Ygraine was thankful that her daughter had his companionship. She also now had the faithful companionship of Arianrod who, because of Uther's extended absence, had transferred his affections to her.

In the last two years, Uther was unable to spend Christ Mass at Tintagel, and Ygraine had just received word that he would need to spend this one in Avon. She had not seen him in several months, and she could not endure the agony that their separation was causing her for much longer.

In spite of her distress, Ygraine aspired to create a festive environment in honour of Christ Mass. She instructed the cooks to prepare a magnificent feast, which would be shared by all at Tintagel who were in the High King and Queen's service.

The planning was more for Morgaine's enjoyment than anything else. She wanted so much for her daughter to be happy, and in truth, Ygraine desperately needed to concentrate on something other than Uther.

The eve of Christ Mass was full of festivities. The great hall was alive with music and joyful faces. In a corner of the room there were minstrels singing, and playing a wide variety of instruments. In another area, poetry was bring recited with fervour to a group of onlookers. The feasting table was abundantly covered with every imaginable delicacy, and the wine and ale flowed freely from the flagons that were set at one end.

Ygraine watched Morgaine with great pleasure, all the while noticing Devon at her side. He seemed to dote on Morgaine, and the attention was well received.

Devon still had his curly gold locks, and Ygraine thought something was very familiar about the look of him. Then suddenly, she thought of the boy child, and she wondered what colour hair he had. It had been eight years to the day, and still her heart longed for him.

She felt sadness overtake her, and she became overwhelmed with a dire need for solitude. She informed Morgaine that she was extremely tired, and bid her to continue celebrating without her. Morgaine seemed not to mind, as she was caught up in storytelling with Devon, Arianrod contentedly seated on the floor near her.

Ygraine graciously excused herself, and left the hall.

She barely made it to her chamber before the tears came. It seemed that nothing could fill this void inside of her. She longed for Uther, and thinking of the child only made her feel more hollow.

She paced back and forth in front of the fire, tears streaming down her face. She felt as though she were losing herself in her grief. She felt that she could not control herself, and decided that she did not want to control herself. Collapsing into a chair, she allowed her feelings to consume her, her chest aching with tremendous emotional pain. Between sobs, she cried out, "I need you Pendragon. I need you."

She reached for the flagon of wine on the table next to her, and with trembling fingers, poured herself a goblet. She raised it to her lips, but consumed none of its contents. Instead, she threw the goblet into the fire.

The alcohol intensified the flames, and they seemed to leap out at her. Her attention was immediately drawn into them. All reality was gone, and she allowed herself to fight the flames no more. She searched frantically within them, fully intending to gain sight of the boy child.

She called out to him, her voice a mere whisper, but holding a force of its own. "Come to me my son. Let me look upon your face so that it may ease this mother's broken heart."

Instantly he began to appear, and Ygraine felt a desperate desire to climb inside the fire and bring him to her. She could see his entire form, and he appeared to be in slumber. His hair, which was an incredible mixture of multiple shades of gold and red, was past his shoulders, and his face was so beautiful, but he seemed older than his present years.

She longed to touch his skin and feel the softness of his hair. She reveled in the sight of him, and closed her eyes briefly to thank God for this wonderful gift.

As she opened her eyes, she noticed another form taking shape near him. It was that of a young woman, with long, black hair, and she was leaning over him. She began to kiss his lips and he woke.

Suddenly the scene was becoming intimate, and Ygraine became confused. This was not what she desired to see, but all the same, she could not draw herself away.

She continued to watch, and the woman tilted her head to the side as he began to kiss her neck. Now Ygraine could see her face, and as she recognized it, her eyes became wide with horror. It was Morgaine.

Ygraine stood up and waved her hands in front of her as if to erase what she had seen. Her stomach churned and she felt her blood coursing through her veins. Her heart was pounding so hard that she could hear its beating.

She backed away, and her legs felt as if they would give way under her. She trembled all over, shaking her head and crying, "No, no, no."

Then all at once she was filled with rage... an uncontrollable, all consuming rage. She opened her mouth, and her words were delivered with a power she had never known. She stretched her arms up and outward, as if she were being crucified, and she tilted her head back as she cried out, "If this is truly a gift, I choose to return it!"

She glared into the flames, then turned away and rushed out onto the parapet. She raised her hands to the sky above, looking heavenward. The wind blew hard, and her hair was billowing out behind her, as she screamed with an uncanny force, "No more! I will see no more!"

In the great hall, Morgaine was still engaged in conversation with Devon. Suddenly, she blinked hard, and her entire body jolted as if she had received a severe blow. She stood up, and all colour drained from her face.

"What is it?" Devon questioned.

"It is time for me to go," Morgaine whispered numbly. She turned and slowly walked from the hall, leaving a gaping Devon staring after her. Arianrod, his head lowered dolefully, followed her out.

❧❧●❧❧

Ygraine had exhausted herself, and slept fitfully through the night. When morning came, she could not bring herself to rise. She would not be present in the chapel this Christ Mass.

Her vision was still tormenting her, and she willed herself back to sleep where she could forget. She slept until near dusk, and was only then awakened by a rap on the door.

She sat up, and her head was spinning. She eased herself out of bed and went to the door, still wearing the same gown from the night before.

Opening the door, she was astonished to find Devon standing there. She could tell that he was distraught, and asked, "What brings you?"

"She's gone," he replied, great concern in his voice.

"Who is gone?" Ygraine questioned absently, rubbing her temples with her fingertips.

"Morgaine... she's gone," he said ardently, shaking his head. "I've looked everywhere. The maid said her bed hasn't been slept in, and no one's seen her all day."

"What do you mean she is gone?" Ygraine asked in disbelief. Then her voice began to quiver with emotion as her senses became clearer. "She cannot be gone."

"Arianrod's gone too," Devon remarked.

Ygraine went without delay to Morgaine's room, and indeed, it appeared as though she had not been in her room. Ygraine scurried throughout the entire castle searching for her with Devon at her heels.

Their search was fruitless, and indeed, no one had seen Morgaine or Arianrod since the night before. Out of sheer hope Ygraine said, "Mayhaps she has gone riding."

Devon replied bluntly, "She wouldn't go riding on a day like this. It's pouring down rain and it grows dark."

Ygraine had not noticed that it was, in fact storming quite badly and near nightfall.

Now filled with panic, she rushed to the entrance door and pulled it open. The wind blew the door wide, allowing the cold rain to enter, drenching her. She ran out, calling Morgaine's name over and over.

She hurried to the stables, and while questioning the stable-master, she heard what sounded like Arianrod whimpering. He informed her that he had discovered one of the horses missing that morning. He had also discovered Arianrod tied up in one of the empty stalls. He had left him there, assuming that he was being punished.

"Punished!" Ygraine shouted. "He has never been punished in his entire life!"

Her panic was rising as she rushed into the stall and untied the fretful dog. He immediately ran out of the stables toward the gatehouse. Ygraine followed after him, the rain pelting against her. It was so cold, and she was thoroughly soaked, but it did not matter. She had to find Morgaine.

The guards caught sight of her approaching, and one of them ran to her. He pulled the cloak from his back and wrapped it around her. "What is it your highness? He questioned eagerly. "Is there trouble at the castle?"

Arianrod was jumping up at the gate, barking, trying desperately to get out.

Ygraine was near panting, and she had a hard time speaking as she replied, "My daughter... have you seen her?"

"No your highness, I've not seen her," he replied, a look of confusion on his face. Then suddenly, his eyes widened, and the look changed to one of realization.

Ygraine noticed his expression and grabbed his arm. She shook it as she shouted, "What? Tell me!"

He hesitated, then as his memory cleared, he said, "I thought it odd that one of the servants who left early last evening was on horseback, but I opened the gate for her anyway. I saw no reason to stop her. As she passed through,

I remember thinking how much she resembled the Queen's daughter, and wondered why I had not seen her before."

"Open the gate!" Ygraine screamed frantically, now becoming hysterical.

"But..." The guard began to object, but Ygraine cut him off, shouting "Open the gate at once!"

He gave a signal to one of the other guards, and the gate was immediately opened.

Ygraine proceeded to run down the narrow, muddy path away from the castle behind Arianrod, screaming Morgaine's name. Several of the guards followed after her.

She could see a rider approaching in the distance through the rain, and she thought it was Morgaine. She ran faster, her heart beating wildly.

The rider had also picked up speed and was quickly closing the distance between them. As the rider drew nearer, Arianrod ran right past him, and Ygraine realized that it was not Morgaine. He was cloaked, but she could tell by his size that it was a man.

He was off his horse before he had reached her, and only when he had her in his arms did she realize that it was Uther.

"What are you doing here!" Ygraine cried out over the sound of the wind and the rain.

He pulled her closer to him and motioned for the guards to retreat. He said with vehemence, an almost frenzied look in his eyes, "I heard you calling to me and it woke me from my sleep. I panicked and rode out alone. I knew that you needed me. For God's sake, what has happened!"

Ygraine began to cry uncontrollably as the magnitude of what had occurred hit her with full force. Uther felt her pain within himself and said anxiously, "Come, I will take you back. Then you will tell me."

He turned away from her to grab the horse's reins, and Ygraine fell to her hands and knees in the mud.

As he turned back, she raised her eyes to the sky, the rain falling heavily on her face as she screamed, "Why God? Why have you done this to me!"

Uther had changed horses on his way to Tintagel, and obviously this one was unaccustomed to loud noises. The shrill sound of Ygraine's voice caused the horse to bolt toward the castle.

Uther pulled Ygraine to her feet, but her legs would not hold her. He lifted her into his arms and carried her back.

Devon was still standing inside the entrance when Uther burst in carrying Ygraine. The boy was shaking and his face was pale.

Uther looked around at several of the other servants, who had gathered inside and shouted, "Will someone tell me what the hell is going on here!"

Ygraine touched his face with trembling fingers and said, "Please take me upstairs. Then I will tell you."

He quickly carried her up the stairway and into their chamber. When he set her to her feet, she had calmed somewhat, but still trembled.

She wiped her muddy hands on her dress, then began wringing them together nervously. Uther took them in his own, and as he could wait no longer for an explanation, he said intensely, "Please, Ygraine."

She pulled her hands away and covered her face with them as she cried, "Morgaine is gone."

"What do you mean she is gone?" Uther asked incredulously, taking her hands away from her face.

"Just listen to me," she pleaded. "Morgaine is gone and she will not be returning. I do not know where she has gone, and I fear I shall never know."

He stared at her in bewilderment, and Ygraine turned toward the fire and said, "You see my love, this 'sight' that my daughter and I share has torn us apart."

She turned back to Uther, who stood with confusion covering his face. She attempted to explain. "I had a vision last evening, and in that vision I saw what appeared to be an immoral act. I saw Morgaine with our boy child, and they were loving each other in a way that siblings do not do."

Uther sat down heavily in his chair, shaking his head and running his fingers through his hair.

He looked up at her, and he was obviously puzzled as he said, "I have lived with you long enough to know that what you speak is truth. I do not question your words, but I am confused. We do not even know where the boy child is. How could Morgaine have been with him?"

Ygraine attempted to explain further. "What I saw was in a future time. They both appeared older than their present years. I assume that a time will come when their paths will cross."

"Mayhaps that is so," Uther agreed, trying to reason with her words. "But I do not understand why Morgaine has gone away."

"I do," she murmured. "Three years ago after our conflict over my parentage, Morgaine told me that she feared a time would come when my love for her would fade. I do not believe she even knew what the circumstances would be, but she felt it all the same. She said to me that love should be unconditional, and I assured her that it is."

Ygraine moved closer to Uther and knelt beside the chair. She took his hand between both of hers, her disillusion apparent as she said, "She did not believe me or she would not have left. Somehow she knew that my vision came to me, for we are bonded. I do not think that she knows what it was I saw, but she felt my violent reaction, and she acted on it."

Ygraine's eyes again filled with tears, anger now bubbling to the surface as she said, "If she only knew that I spoke the truth. My love for her could never fade, but my love for the almighty God is surely being tested!"

Uther's eyes revealed his own inner pain as he said, "How much more are we to lose?"

"All I have left is you," Ygraine whispered. Then with certainty, she stated, "And I will not give you up." She paused, forcing her emotions to subside, then said, "Suddenly, I feel I have found strength in what I have suffered, and I will fight against any force that tries to take you from me. My daughter has strength, and she will survive."

Her tears flowed from her eyes and she lowered her head saying, "But it breaks my heart to know that she believes I have lost my love for her."

Uther pulled her onto his lap and wrapped his arms around her. She was chilled to the bone and longed to be out of her wet, muddy clothes, but she could not leave the comfort of his embrace.

She wept as he held her. Then, as her tears began to subside, he gently lifted her chin, gazing at her. She noticed that his eyes held as much pain as she was feeling.

She caressed the side of his face, and their eyes beheld each other's as she whispered, "End the wars and come home to me."

Uther nodded and whispered back, "I shall."

߷ *Twenty-six* ߷

Morgaine went directly to Avalon where Viviane, wearing her purple, velvet cloak, awaited her arrival just as she had when Arthur had been brought to her.

Viviane held her hand out to the child as she stepped away from the barge, but no words were spoken. They shared such a deep understanding that words were unnecessary.

Viviane took the child's face in her hands and gazed lovingly into her sad eyes. Then she embraced her, holding her tightly to her breast.

After a few moments, Viviane again gazed into Morgaine's eyes. This time the sadness had faded, and Morgaine offered her a sweet smile.

Viviane returned her smile, then extended one side of her cloak to encompass Morgaine in it. Holding the child close to her, with her cloak wrapped around them both, Viviane guided her away from the shore.

She took Morgaine to a room that was next to her own. She had planned to keep the child very near to her, as Morgaine was destined to be the recipient of all of Viviane's knowledge and wisdom.

Arthur was to have no interaction with Morgaine, but they had caught a glimpse of each other on the day of Morgaine's arrival, and upon first sight had developed a tremendous bond. Thereafter, they met secretly whenever possible.

Arthur would remain on Avalon for more than six additional years, and during that time their relationship would be greatly nurtured.

Morgaine was indeed aware of Arthur's identity, but hers, on the other hand, was not revealed to him.

Morgaine and Arthur came to love one another deeply, which would ultimately prove to be disastrous for Arthur and the kingdom that he would give birth to.

❧❧●❧❧

Uther was only able to remain at Tintagel for two days, which was longer than he could actually afford. He had given the element of time no thought at all when he first rode out, and despite his desire to extend his stay, it simply was not possible.

During that time both he and Ygraine had gone into mourning. Their feelings of desolation were so deep that it was as if Morgaine had not only made her departure from Tintagel, but from life itself. To Ygraine, knowing that she would not see her daughter again, there was no difference.

The dismal weather lingered, the gloominess equivalent to what they were feeling in their hearts. It continued to rain the entire two days that they remained in their chamber.

Uther had sent guards to comb the countryside for Morgaine, but she was not found. He also organized a search for Arianrod, but he was not found either. He did, however return the morning of Uther's departure.

The rain had subsided, but the day was cold and bleak.

Uther, wrapped in his cloak, said his farewell at the entrance door. He did not want Ygraine to catch a chill, and even though she pleaded to come outside, he would not hear of it.

He took her into his arms in the open doorway and held her tight for several moments. Then he pulled away slightly, as he felt her begin to tremble from the cold air rushing in. "I must go," he said hesitantly.

She sighed heavily and nodded. Even though she was not weeping, her sadness was still quite apparent as she gazed up at him with red, swollen eyes.

Uther took her face in his hands and whispered, "I adore you."

Her tears immediately threatened to bubble to the surface, and he quickly stepped away. He was unable to witness her grief any longer, continuing to hold his own emotions in check, which he had done to the best of his ability for two days. Many times he felt as though he would break down, but he needed to be strong for Ygraine.

He briskly walked to where the stable master held the reins of his horse, his heart breaking over leaving her in this way. He quickly mounted, blew her a kiss, and headed for the gate. As it opened, he began to ride through, but stopped suddenly.

Arianrod was lying in the mud just outside the entrance. He was still alive, but obviously quite ill.

Uther was instantly off his horse. He tore the cloak from his back and wrapped Arianrod in it. The guards immediately came to offer their assistance, but Uther shook his head as he lifted him and carried him toward the castle himself.

Ygraine was still standing in the open doorway watching, and her heartstrings tore open as Uther approached.

"Oh God, no," she cried out.

There were tears spilling from Uther's eyes as he entered

the castle with Arianrod in his arms.

Ygraine followed close behind, as he carried him to their chamber and placed him upon the soft furs on the bed.

Ygraine covered him with a heavy, wool blanket as Uther turned toward the fire. She began to tenderly stroke Arianrod's head, and while gazing into his eyes, she heard Uther sobbing.

She went to him at once. Standing behind him, she wrapped her arms around him, laying her head against his back. He continued to sob, unable to control his emotions any longer.

After several moments, he attempted to regain control of himself. He slowly turned around, and with pleading eyes asked, "Can you heal him?"

Ygraine let out a deep sigh, dreading the words that she would utter. "No, I cannot."

Uther questioned her with his eyes, then said, "But I've seen the power you possess."

"Yes," Ygraine responded. "But Arianrod does not wish to live any longer."

"How do you know that?" Uther questioned, tears glistening his eyes.

"I just do," Ygraine replied. "I can see it in his eyes. There is an emptiness there... the same emptiness that I feel in my heart."

Understanding completely, Uther nodded slowly, then went to kneel at the bedside. He laid his head on Arianrod's side while stroking him tenderly.

"You go boy," Uther whispered. "It's all right."

Arianrod could only muster enough strength to raise his head momentarily to gaze at his master one more time. Then he surrendered, resting his head back down on the bed, closing his eyes.

Uther felt the animal stop breathing beneath him, and he

again wept openly.

Ygraine knelt down beside him, and for the first time, it was up to her to be strong. He turned toward her, and she held him in her arms, comforting him, as he had done for her so many times before.

Soon Uther pulled himself together, and when he raised his head, his eyes were full of fire. "Enough," was all he said.

It was all he needed to say, for that one word held all the meaning in the world for both of them. It truly was enough.

With that fire burning inside of him, it took Uther only a year to accomplish what he had promised Ygraine... to end the wars. His army had been successful in driving the Saxons inland, and many of their ships had been destroyed. Herne however, had been fortunate enough to escape on one of the ships that remained secure. It was assumed that he had fled back to Germany, and that he no longer would be a threat to Britain.

The northern border was totally protected, and the Saxons had been successfully driven to Dyfed, between Segontium and Avon. The Saxons that survived the battles there had fled south. Uther continued to push them further and further south, and only when he had driven them passed Bodmin, south of Tintagel, did he decide to rest briefly. He felt an overwhelming need to see Ygraine before preparing for what he had planned to be the final battle.

In that year, through the bloody battles that raged, Uther never lost sight of his vision. Now that the Saxons were losing their strength, he began to feel the reality of it.

Garrisons had been set up along the coastline, and there were troops at each one keeping watch for any Saxon stragglers and any new ships arrival.

Leodogranz had been sent back to Avon with a fair portion of the army. Uriens, also with a sizeable number of men, had been sent to Segontium. The troops that remained with Uther had set up camp in the village below Tintagel with Lot. They were given one day to rest, as Uther planned to attack the next evening.

Uther had not seen Ygraine in over a year, and as he rode up the path to the castle with a small troop of his men, he felt as he did that night in the cave when he thought of being with Ygraine for the first time. The anticipation of being with her now made his insides quiver.

When he arrived, Ygraine was in the chapel where she spent every evening praying for him.

She heard the sound of horses approaching, and the flame igniting within her heart center told her that it was Uther. Taking her pentacle in her hand, she held on tightly to it. She remained kneeling in front of the altar, knowing that he would find her.

She held her breath as she heard the creaking sound of the door opening. She waited until she heard the door close before rising and slowly turning around.

They stood staring at each other, neither of them able to move. Ygraine was visibly labouring to regulate her breathing as her emotions flooded to the surface.

Uther was feeling lost in the sight of her. As he gazed upon her face, the fever raging within his chest intensified with his every breath.

Ygraine extended her arms, silently beckoning him to her.

He walked toward her, but ever so slowly. He stopped just short of her outstretched arms, and there was a fiery passion in his eyes that reflected Ygraine's as he said, "I cannot allow myself to touch you here in this place. For if I do, I will surely take you right here in God's house, and He will be forced to bear witness."

Ygraine waved her hand in reference to all of the sacred,

stone figures that seemed to be watching and said, "Let them all bear witness to our love, for I desire you here... and now."

Uther's lips were immediately upon hers, his arms crushing her to him. His hands moved to cup her face, as he continued to devour her mouth. Then still holding her face in his hands, he gently kissed her closed eyelids, stopping to taste the tears that were falling from them.

He ran his fingers through her hair, drawing a handful to his face and breathing in deeply of its fragrance. Releasing it, he pulled her tighter against him, his hands caressing her back as he again sought the sweetness of her lips.

She was breathless as she pulled away slightly, whispering with yearning, "I have waited so long. I cannot believe that you are here with me."

Uther smiled warmly, and he whispered back with assurance, "It will not be long before I am able to be with you permanently. The wars are near over."

Ygraine drew in her breath sharply, and Uther's words radiated through her entire being. "Oh God, how I have longed for this," she cried softly, laying her cheek next to his.

"I too have longed for it... and you," Uther murmured next to her ear.

Ygraine drew her head back and gazed intently into his eyes as she said hastily, "Make love to me... right now."

Uther paused a moment, then pulled her to him and kissed her passionately.

The door to the chapel creaked opened and Lot abruptly rushed inside. Uther spun around and had his sword drawn before Ygraine realized what had happened.

There was a grave tone in Lot's voice as he said, "I apologize for the intrusion sire, but I have urgent news."

"What is it!" Uther barked, completely agitated at being disturbed.

Lot replied, "Saxon ships were sighted off the coast of Penzance. They've laid anchor and are headed this way. They can't be too far behind the scouts."

Uther closed his eyes, took in a deep breath, and released it loudly as he opened his eyes. "Wait for me outside," he said flatly, re-sheathing his sword.

Lot nodded and immediately left, leaving the door to the chapel slightly ajar. Ygraine could hear the urgency in the voices of Uther's men outside as they prepared to depart, and her heart sank.

Uther turned to her, and his own eyes were filled with unshed tears.

Ygraine had gone pale, and a knot was forming in the pit of her stomach. She stared at him, and as he opened his mouth to speak, she put her hands over her ears and pleaded, "Do not speak the words. I know you must go, so please... just go."

Uther reached for her hands and drew her close to him. Their faces almost touched as he brought her hands to his lips, his kiss lingering upon them. They were both aware of the tear dropping onto her hand from his eye as her tear also fell and mingled with it.

With his thumb, Uther gently touched the spot on her hand where the tears had fallen and whispered, "We have shed many tears you and I." He paused, then said with finality, "No more."

He let her hands fall, and their eyes were locked as he slowly backed away.

As he neared the door, she covered her heart with her hands and called out softly, "I love you Pendragon."

He nodded, then turned away from her, and was gone.

ଓ *Twenty-seven* ଓ

The Saxons had quickly made their way north, meeting Uther's army only a short distance from Tintagel. Herne was leading them.

Lot kept a keen eye on Uther, for as much as he dreaded it, he knew that the time had come to fulfill his treacherous plot. He had been hoping that Uther would fall at the hands of a Saxon, but Uther's strength and fortitude on the battlefield was unmatched.

The moon was but a sliver, shedding little light on the ensuing battle. The loud clanging of metal against metal rang out, as did the death cries of many.

Uther wielded Excalibur with a tremendous force, feeling an incredible exuberance at being on the final stair leading to his vision of peace.

Uther's army was exuding its powerful strength, and it was obvious that the Saxons had no chance of winning this battle. Most of them were on foot, whereas the majority of Uther's men were on horseback, seeming to give them great advantage.

Uther made out the form of Herne as he came into view.

He bore a definite resemblance to his father Hengist, as he sat astride his war-horse. He was not as massive in size as Hengist, but the long, golden braid hanging from his head gave way to his identity.

Uther urged his own mount, the same spirited giant that had belonged to Hengist, in Herne's direction.

Out of the darkness, one of the Saxons charged toward Uther on foot from the side, impaling Andromeda with his spear. The horse reared, throwing Uther from his back, before falling heavily to the ground.

Uther rose, stunned, the wind knocked out of him.

Lot quickly dismounted his own horse and rushed to Uther. From behind, Lot grabbed Uther's shoulder, and as Uther turned, still dazed, Lot knew that this was his moment of choice.

Lot had his dagger in hand, and as Uther caught sight of it, Lot realized that he had made his choice.

Uther looked up from the blade into Lot's eyes, and in that split instant of time, Uther knew what Lot's intentions were.

With one hand still on Uther's shoulder, Lot immediately drove the blade into Uther's left side.

Uther went to his knees, his eyes wide with shock and horror as he continued to stare at Lot.

Lot dropped the dagger, and gaped at the King's blood on his own hand. He looked back at Uther, who was still staring at him in disbelief, and he shook his head in sorrow as he backed away.

Herne had caught sight of Uther as he fell from his horse, and was fiercely attempting to draw nearer to him. Now, from a short distance away, he saw Uther on his knees, and let out a resounding war cry.

Lot turned away from Uther, and grabbed his horse's reins. He swung himself onto his saddle, and quickly left the battlefield.

Now several of Uther's men saw him kneeling, and knew that the King had been wounded. Without hesitation, they rushed to his aid.

Excalibur was lying on the ground near Uther, and he reached his hand out toward it. One of his men lifted the sword and handed it to him. He held onto it as his men carried him from the battlefield, the tip dragging through the dirt.

He was taken to a small clearing amidst a heavily wooded area where they awaited some sign of the outcome of the battle. They did not have to wait long before several other men joined them with the news that the Saxons had retreated.

Uther lay on the ground perfectly still, staring straight up as his mind frantically tried to interpret what had happened. After all this, to be felled by his ally was inconceivable.

Somewhere in the back of his mind he heard the cry of Herne, and he knew that even though the Saxons had retreated, they would be back. Mayhaps not in the near future, but they would return. Uther knew that he was dying, and when the Saxons received the news that Britain's High King was dead, they would return with a vengeance.

Uther's men quickly lifted him onto a litter, placing Excalibur next to him, and carried him back to Tintagel. One of Uther's men rode ahead of them to give warning.

Ygraine was still in the chapel when the soldier arrived. She heard the rider approach, and thought it to be Uther. She rushed out of the chapel just in time to partially hear the exchange of conversation between the soldier and the guards.

She ran to the soldier, reached up, and grabbed his arm, pulling him from the saddle. "What are you saying!" She screamed.

The soldier was taken off-guard, and he stumbled as his feet hit the ground. As he regained his composure, he looked at the frantic expression on Ygraine's face, and found that he could not tell her the news.

She grabbed his shoulders and shook him violently as she screamed, "Tell me, tell me!"

He stepped back from her and said remorsefully, "I'm sorry your highness. But the King has been grievously wounded. They bring him home."

Ygraine's heart jolted, and she stared at him, her mouth agape. Taking in a deep breath, she attempted to calm herself, but her voice quivered as she commanded, "You wait here. When they arrive, the King is to be brought immediately to his chamber. Do you hear me?"

He bowed his head respectfully. "Yes your highness," he replied, his voice revealing the sorrow he felt.

A distant roll of thunder was heard as Ygraine ran across the grounds and into the castle. She was besieged with a panic she had never known.

She hurried to their chamber, and when she entered, she knew not what to do with herself. She was frantic beyond belief. She felt as if her head would explode as the blood rushed through it. Another distant roll of thunder seemed to mirror what she was feeling inside. She paced the length of the room, all the while her panic rising.

Then suddenly a thought entered her mind, and all was well. She stopped her pacing and looked down at her hands. A smile slowly spread across her face as she realized there was naught to worry about.

"I can heal him," she whispered confidently. "It matters not how deep his wound. Gorlois' wound was fatal, and I saved him."

She become flooded with a sense of serenity, and as it washed over her, she sat down, staring at her hands. She kissed each palm saying, "Thank you." Then she rested her head back against the chair and waited.

Her wait seemed endless, but when she heard voices and the loud clamor of armored feet in the corridor, she rose from the chair confident, her gaze on the open doorway. However, the sight of Uther being carried on a litter nearly brought her to her knees. They began wobbling, and she wanted to cry out in agony, but she forced herself to remain composed.

She pointed to the bed, and the men gently lifted Uther and laid him upon it. He was still staring straight up, deep in shock. Excalibur was placed next to him. The litter was left on the floor near the bed.

As each man passed Ygraine, they stopped in front of her before leaving, bowing their heads briefly, showing their respect.

Ygraine laid her hand on the arm of the last man and said softly, "I cannot remove his mail. Will you help me?"

"Yes, of course your highness," he replied, eager to be of assistance. He immediately did as he was bid, which was not an easy task.

Ygraine did not watch. She kept her back to them the entire time. Once he had completed what was requested of him, Uther was left lying in his under-tunic, which was blood soaked.

After giving his King one last sorrowful look, the soldier made for the door, but Ygraine's voice halted him. He turned back around as she said firmly, "Notify all in the castle that I have left strict orders not to be disturbed. There will be consequences to pay should anyone disobey me."

"Yes your highness," he replied. Then he bowed slightly and left the room, closing the door behind him.

Distant thunder again rumbled as Ygraine turned around. The sight of Uther lying on the bed bleeding was more than she could bear. She rushed to his side, and leaning over, took his face in her hands. She turned his head slightly toward her so that she could look upon him fully.

His eyes were wide with a look of disbelief in them, and his voice was strained with emotion as he said, "Now I understand why the Merlin took our child."

Ygraine fell to her knees, tears coming to her questioning eyes as Uther said, "If this could happen to me, then God only knows what might have happened to the child."

His eyes glazed with tears, and he slowly shook his head saying, "What has become of man's honour? I fear he knows not the meaning of the word."

"I do not understand," Ygraine cried.

"I stand for peace and truth," Uther stated, his voice still strained. Then he looked deep into Ygraine's eyes, trying to grasp some kind of understanding in what his next words meant as he said, "Lot did this. My ally... my Judas."

Ygraine was aghast. She gasped, and her hand covered her heart as she cried, "No, it cannot be!"

Uther closed his eyes briefly, and when he opened them, he said with great sincerity, "What I would give to look into the Merlin's eyes as I am looking at you now, and beg his forgiveness."

"You will be able to do so," Ygraine whispered assuredly.

Calming down, she rose from her knees and sat next to him. She held her hands out before him and said, "There was a time when you said to me that these hands might heal you some day." She smiled and said confidently, "And so they shall."

Uther's eyes suddenly held hope as he looked at her. He laboured to breathe, then said, "Yes, I remember that time."

Ygraine placed her hands over the gaping wound in Uther's side, but the blood continued to seep through her fingers. She kept her hands there for several moments, but the blood did not cease to flow.

The thunder was again heard, this time louder, and the sky lit up with a blaze of lightening.

Ygraine's heart skipped a beat as she removed her hands and stared down at her bloodied palms in disbelief. Then she began to weep, for she realized that she had effectively, and completely relinquished her power the night of her last vision.

Uther reached for her hands, and his voice was growing weaker as he said softly, "I fear my love, that it is my time to cross over. But oh, what I would give to borrow only a little more."

"You cannot go," Ygraine cried out, her heart wrenching in her chest.

Uther sighed and whispered weakly, "I shall miss you so."

Desperation was rising within her. She grabbed onto Uther's arms, her entire being pleading as she cried, "I want to go with you."

"It is not yet your time," Uther replied, his voice much weaker now. "But know that I shall wait for you."

Tears streamed down Ygraine's face as she released her hold on him and asked, "How will I find you?"

Uther whispered assuredly, "I will find you." He attempted to smile as he reached up to touch one of her tears. "It matters not how long it takes. I shall wait... and I will find you."

His hand dropped from her face, and his eyes were losing their focus. He let out a deep sigh and slowly reached for Ygraine's pentacle. He held it as she leaned over, her lips quivering as she kissed his lips tenderly. Then she whispered, "I love you."

Uther's voice was barely heard as he replied, "I love you... Pendragon."

The pentacle slipped from his hand, and his eyes closed as his breathing ceased.

Ygraine stared at him, unable to believe or accept that

her beloved was gone. It felt as though a lance had pierced her heart. She rose, and her primal scream, "No...!" could be heard throughout the castle.

Uther's men were in the great hall. A crack of thunder seemed to shake the room, and a bolt of lightening lit the sky as rain began to pour from the heavens. They all dropped to one knee on the floor in silent prayer for their King, for they knew that he had passed.

ဢ&●&ౖ

The soft glow of two candles burning shone on the faces of Viviane and Morgaine as they stood behind the stone altar in the chapel at Avalon.

Morgaine paid close attention to Viviane, who was pointing to a diagram inside a large, leather-bound book. Then, looking up to the sky through the opening above the altar, Morgaine followed Viviane's gaze as she pointed to several distant stars.

Suddenly, one of the candles sputtered and went out. Morgaine's attention was instantly drawn to it, and she stared intently at the smoke drifting away from the wick. Then she gasped and took a step back. Her face filled with extreme sorrow as she looked at Viviane, who sighed and placed her hand over her heart, closing her eyes.

Unable to remain standing, Morgaine dropped to her knees. She began to weep deeply, her mournful wailing echoing through the chapel.

Viviane knelt and drew Morgaine into her arms. Morgaine crumpled into her embrace, her body wracked with sobs.

As Viviane continued to console Morgaine, her own tears flowed, and her heart wrenched as she felt the pain of both mother and daughter.

∽❧•❧∼

Ygraine was to remain with Uther in their chamber for three days.

The thunderstorm had passed, but the rain continued to pour as if the sky itself were weeping. The room was dark except for the fire that burned, it's golden radiance cascading over the bed where Uther lay.

Ygraine eased him from the bed and onto the litter that she had placed a fur coverlet on. Then kneeling down on the floor next to him, she removed what was left of his clothing.

Afterward, she moved to a nearby table and filled a basin with clean water. Carrying it and a soft, white cloth, she returned to Uther's side.

Kneeling back down on the floor, she proceeded to carry out her own sacred ceremony for her beloved.

Her face was drawn as she dipped the cloth into the water and began to tenderly wash his body. She took her time, stopping to caress and kiss each and every scar. She whispered words of love to him as she cherished and adored every bit of his flesh.

Quite some time had passed, and the fire began to die, the smoldering embers shedding very little light, or warmth into the room.

Her sacrament nearly complete, she put the cloth back into the basin, and ran her fingers lovingly over the armlet on Uther's wrist. She bent to kiss it, her lips lingering against the gold as silent tears fell from her eyes.

Raising up and leaning over him, she gently brushed the hair away from his forehead with her fingertips, then slowly ran her thumb along the scar on his cheek and said, "My love for you reaches far beyond all depths and breadths of this world."

She held his face between her hands and kissed him gently

on his lips, then laid her cheek upon his. Withdrawing slightly, she placed one hand over his heart, the other over her own. She closed her eyes and shook her head sorrowfully and whispered, "My fire has gone out. The blood no longer flows through your heart. Therefore, my own heart can beat no longer."

She opened her eyes, and as she gazed at Uther's face, a tear welled up in her eye and fell. She said softly, "Do not stray far my love, for I shall soon join you."

Noticing the room was now nearly dark, she rose to retrieve a tallow candle from the bedside table, and placed it on the floor next to Uther. She covered him with another fur blanket, then lifted Excalibur from the bed. She sat on the floor near him, holding the sword across her lap. The dragon's eyes were dull and lifeless.

She remained in their chamber with Uther the entire three days, as if standing guard. On the third day, she performed her own rite of passage for him, knowing full well the honour that was now being bestowed upon her. She was assisting in the ascension of her beloved King.

The servants were extremely worried, and curious as to what would keep their Queen confined in such a way. Several of them went to the chamber door, but were afraid to knock. However, they did take turns sitting outside the door, should they be needed.

At the end of the third day, Ygraine emerged from the chamber, dragging Excalibur behind her.

The maid sitting there jumped to her feet and bowed low. She could feel the cold air from inside the chamber as it filtered into the warm hall, and she shivered.

Ygraine's face was expressionless, and her voice was void of all emotion as she said, "My King has been prepared. He is to be carried to the chapel on the litter in which he rests."

The maid simply nodded, not knowing what to make of

the situation.

Then Ygraine said, "I will cut the hand off of anyone who attempts to touch him."

The maid's eyes grew wide at her statement, and she hesitated before again bowing low, then hurried off to summon several servants to do the Queen's bidding.

Her eyes empty, and as cold as the room within, Ygraine remained at the chamber door, waiting.

When the servants arrived, she admitted them into the chamber and watched intently as they lifted the litter. She followed close behind, still dragging Excalibur, as the servants moved Uther's body to the chapel.

ೞ *Twenty-eight* ಞ

Uther's body had been laid upon the altar on the litter. Pine boughs surrounded his form, the scent meant to replace the smell of death in the air from his long confinement in their chamber.

No one came to pay their respects to this King, who had given his all for his quest to bring peace to Britain. The British Lords and petty kings were already warring amongst themselves for the throne, and Uther's army had disbanded, having no leader to follow. Out of the fear of being unprotected, many of the servants had left also, and those that had stayed out of loyalty to the Queen were now preparing to depart as well.

The chapel was dark, except for a single candle that burned near Uther's head. It sent out an eerie glow around him and the solitary griever who knelt beside him.

Ygraine rested her cheek on his forearm, her head swimming with exhaustion as her fingers caressed the gold band on Uther's wrist. Excalibur rested on the floor next to her.

Something moved slightly in the darkness near Uther's

feet, and through the haze that had seemed to overtake Ygraine, she caught the movement out of the corner of her eye. "Who is there," she questioned numbly, raising her head slowly.

There was no reply, and as her eyes adjusted to the darkness, the figure became clear. Upon recognition of him, she felt a flame ignite deep within her, suddenly her drained body filling with a fiery rage that threatened to consume her.

Trembling, she raised herself up slowly to stand on wobbly legs. As she regained her strength, she lunged at him with the force of a warrior.

She threw herself at him, pummeling his chest with her clenched fists. "How dare you come here now!" She screamed. "You have not come here as a Merlin, but as a vulture to feed off of my sorrow! Have I not given enough? Do you desire more? Well I have no more to give. There is no more life force to feed off of!"

The Merlin remained still, allowing her to vent her rage against him, knowing all too well her feelings of anguish.

She was seething as she shouted, "I have lost all, and for what? Destiny!"

She stepped back, and breaking the chain, she pulled the pentacle from her neck and threw it at him. Then she began to tremble again as the rage drained from her, and she crumpled into a sobbing heap upon the cold floor.

The Merlin bent to pick up the pentacle lying at his feet, and he gazed at it a moment before tucking it safely away inside his cloak. Then he knelt in front of her, grasping her shoulders firmly. "Look at me Ygraine!" He commanded.

She raised her head slowly, her breath coming in short gasps, feelings of nausea rising in the pit of her stomach.

He released her and looked deep into her eyes as he said with certainty, "I know what it feels like to lose all and have nothing, all for the sake of destiny. I have walked the same path as you Ygraine, and I have suffered and felt your suffering. Fate has a heavy hand, and we have both felt the weight of it."

Ygraine looked at him, her eyes pleading as she spoke. "Why have you chosen me as your pawn? Why? I do not understand."

Her pained expression deepened as she said, "I have done what you have asked of me. I have given birth to a child that is to be a great king... a child I could not once hold in my arms." She crossed her empty arms over her breast. "I have lost all that have loved me, and that I have loved. I have witnessed such dishonour and deceit. My own daughter will deceive my son." She shook her head, tears spilling from her eyes. "And now I have lost my precious, precious King. I have nothing left."

She paused, gasping for breath, then cried, "I can take no more, and all I want to know is why. Why me?"

He looked into her pleading eyes, feelings that he had suppressed rising like bile in his throat, as Evanona's face cut through his vision like a blade.

He replied matter-of-factly, "It could be no other."

She tilted her head to the side, questioning, and he continued to gaze deeply into her eyes as he said, "I held you in my arms Ygraine, and I gazed into the windows of your soul after cutting you free from your mother's womb. Upon her deathbed, you and I made a pact, and you have fulfilled your destiny... out of your own free will."

Ygraine looked at him intently, tears again spilling forth as the truth penetrated her heart.

The Merlin took her face gently in his hands and raised it close to his own. His voice was barely a whisper as he said, "I am your seed father Ygraine."

She immediately began to sob and fell against his chest. He put his arms around her and said softly. "I loved your mother more than mere mortal words can describe, and I have loved no other since. You think I am hard and unfeeling." He let out a sigh and said, "I am not. I have pain that runs as deeply as your own. In the years that have passed, I have felt your pain also."

He pulled away slightly and lifted her chin. "And I feel your pain now... daughter."

Her tears flowed, and he wiped them away gently. "We have lost much, but there is more to live for," he assured her. "There is Arthur, your son, and he shall need us. We must be there for him."

His gaze intensified, as well as the tone in his voice as he said, "You must believe that there is a higher purpose, otherwise all has been for naught."

"Arthur," she whispered with love in her voice. Great warmth had come to her eyes, and she said softly, "I live to hold him, but once."

"And so you shall," the Merlin stated.

Ygraine could only gather enough strength to nod her head in affirmation before collapsing against him.

The Merlin held her close, and as he felt the beating of her heart, a tear threatened to escape his eye. He fought it back with all the strength within him to honour his vow to never shed another, as he envisioned Evanona's blood on his hands mixed with his own tears.

৩৯০●৯৫৶

Ygraine could not return to her and Uther's chamber. Instead, she went to Morgaine's.

She slowly dragged Excalibur into the room. She laid the sword next to the bed and fell onto the soft fur blankets, quickly drifting into a deep slumber.

When she awoke the next morning, the rain had stopped,

and bright sunlight filled the room. A warm fire blazed, and she had been covered with soft blankets. The Merlin was sitting in a chair next to the bed, where he had been watching her sleep. She was so drained of feeling, that his kindness, nor his presence, had any affect on her at all.

She sat up slowly, and her head started to throb. Her hand went to her stomach as it began to gnaw, and she vaguely remembered eating three or four days before. She wearily lay back down and stared at the canopy above her.

The look in the Merlin's eyes reflected his empathy as he said, "I know that you are weakened Ygraine, but we must speak."

She did not respond, and he continued, "Do you choose to remain here at Tintagel? If so, arrangements must be made for your protection."

She spoke very slowly and quietly as she replied, "This place holds no love. It is but an empty shell, as I am. My passion has died with the Pendragon. It will not be long before I follow, for there is no more flame in my heart."

She paused, then looked over at him. "I choose to return to the sanctuary."

He nodded, and she looked back up at the canopy. She shook her head and took a deep breath, exhaling fully before saying, "Is it not ironic how we are sometimes called back to a place that we never could have imagined?"

The Merlin sighed then said, "You have chosen wisely Ygraine. The boy Devon has left, but he will return in the years to come to claim Tintagel for his own."

Ygraine immediately turned to look at him, her brows furrowed and her eyes questioning.

The Merlin answered her unspoken question. "He is Gorlois' bastard son."

Ygraine chuckled to herself, as she recalled how unusual it was that the maid had lingered at Gorlois' funeral, and also the familiarity she saw in Devon. "Of course he is," she said dryly.

The Merlin nodded and said, "His mother has made him aware of his parentage, now that Uther has passed. Since Gorlois left no heir, Devon will not be denied his ancestral home. Had you chosen to remain here, you would have had to fight for what is yours."

"Fight?" Ygraine asked incredulously. "I think not." She shook her head and said, "Life's battles for me are over. I concede"

"Are you sure of your decision to return to the sanctuary?" The Merlin questioned. "There is another alternative. Uriens has received word of Uther. He will come for you."

Certain of her choice, Ygraine nodded.

As the Merlin looked into her eyes, he saw there the same emptiness that he felt in his own heart. He rose, unable to witness her torment any longer and said hastily, "Make ready then. I will escort you back."

She was quick to reply, "I am ready now. Excalibur is the only possession that I shall be taking with me."

"As you wish," he replied.

Ygraine eased herself from the bed, keeping her hand on the bedpost to steady herself.

"Wait here," the Merlin instructed. "I will make preparations for the journey."

As he headed for the door, Ygraine called out, "But we must prepare the funeral pyre."

The Merlin turned to her, and there was a look on his face that she had never seen before. It was fleeting, but she was certain that it was a look of complete and utter bliss.

He let out a deep breath and said, "Come with me Ygraine."

She hesitated a moment, then bent to lift Excalibur. The Merlin was immediately at her side, taking the sword from her grasp. "Allow me," he whispered.

Ygraine nodded graciously, and she and the Merlin left the chamber.

＊＊●＊＊

As they entered the chapel, the sun spilled through the open doorway, flooding golden light onto the altar.

Ygraine made her way slowly forward with the Merlin following very close behind. She squinted, attempting to gain sight of Uther through the blinding light. The brightness was far beyond normal and seemed to be more of a supernatural nature than a natural one. She felt the hair on the back of her neck stand on end, and it wasn't until she was directly in front of the altar that she realized that Uther's body was gone.

Confused, she dropped to her knees, and she ran her hands slowly over the stone.

The Merlin knelt beside her, laying Excalibur on the floor nearby. The look of bliss returned to his face momentarily as he said, "The King has ascended, taking his body with him."

She looked at him in awe, then her attention was immediately drawn to the statue of Mother Mary. As she turned her head and gazed up adoringly at Mary's loving face, whose eyes seemed to be looking directly at her, she whispered, "Just as the saviour did."

The Merlin nodded slowly and replied, "Indeed."

She drew her gaze away from the statue and looked back at the Merlin. Her eyes filled with joy and a euphoric smile lit her face. Then Ygraine rose to her feet, and she effortlessly picked Excalibur up from the floor. With newfound strength, she proudly carried it from the chapel.

＊＊●＊＊

Mother Marta had aged considerably, but her eyes still held the same loving warmth that Ygraine had remembered.

The cottage however, was not the same. It was empty except for the small bed that she and Morella had shared, a low, wooden table next to it with a single candle burning, and the rocking chair.

She was glad for the changes, for she did not want any memories surrounding this life of solitude that she had now chosen.

She asked the Merlin to place Excalibur on the bed and said, "I will sleep with what I have left of my King."

He closed his eyes briefly and sighed before saying, "I shall return in five years. When I do, I will be taking Excalibur with me." Then he gently placed the sword on the bed.

Ygraine sat on the edge of the bed and laid her hand on the sword protectively. "Why?" She questioned.

He replied, "It will be a necessary tool in proving Arthur's identity, and it will then belong to him."

He paused, then said with assurance, "Uther would have preferred that Excalibur be wielded. It is not ready for eternal rest."

She nodded, then said wearily, "But I am ready for eternal rest. Five years is a long time to wait." Then she sighed heavily and concluded with, "But I shall. I cannot leave until I have laid my eyes upon Arthur."

The Merlin's eyes lightened and he had a look of pride on his face as he said, "Arthur will give justice to the Pendragon name. He will fulfill his father's vision of peace." He looked into her eyes and whispered, "I promise you."

He allowed his eyes to roam over her exquisite face, and he had a fleeting desire to embrace her, but something inside of him would not allow it. Hesitantly, he stepped away from her and made for the door.

As he departed, Ygraine sat on the bed, her weariness consuming her. She touched the dragon's eyes on Excalibur with her fingertip and said warmly, "Rest for now. Then you shall protect my beloved son, as you did my beloved King."

༄∽☙●❧∾༄

Uriens immediately left Segontium and rode to Tintagel upon receiving word of Uther's death. His journey was very long, and it felt as though it were the lengthiest of his entire life. He could not believe that his dear friend was gone, and only when he rode up the path to the castle did the reality of it begin to seep into his senses.

There were no guards at the gate and it was wide open. As he rode through, his heart began to beat wildly in his chest, for there was no one in sight.

He dismounted and walked quickly to the entrance of the castle. The door was slightly ajar, and he pushed it open slowly with his boot. He stood in the doorway, and suddenly he felt as empty as that which he now gazed upon. There was nothing left. Marauders had taken everything.

He stood there for several moments breathing heavily, then his emotions ran wild, and he sprinted up the main stairway, taking several steps at a time. Instinctively, he made his was to Uther and Ygraine's chamber. He threw the door open, and stood staring at the empty room. Then he walked slowly to the center and shouted, "Where are you?"

All at once, he felt as if the room was spinning around him, and he fell to his knees and began to weep. "Where are you?" He cried as he put his face in his hands.

"He is home." The voice of the Merlin temporarily shocked him from his grieving.

Uriens' head jerked up, but he did not rise from his knees.

He began to weep again as he gazed up at the Merlin, who was standing in front of him. Uriens' pain was quite evident on his face as he clutched at his chest with both hands and cried out, "My heart is breaking!"

The Merlin knelt, looked deep into Uriens' eyes and said softly, "I know."

Uriens fell against the Merlin's chest, and he held him as Uriens wept.

Then suddenly, Uriens pulled away and rose to his feet. His voice revealed great concern as he questioned, "What of the Queen? I must look after her. He would have wanted me to protect her."

"She has made another choice," the Merlin replied, also rising to his feet.

Then he noticed the look of sympathy for Ygraine in Uriens' eyes, and he said, "Uther's body may be gone, but he is with his beloved in spirit."

Tears again came to Uriens' eyes, and the Merlin said with compassion, "Know this, gentle knight... a time will come when you will again help to fulfill Uther's vision of peace."

Uriens nodded slowly, then whispered, "I loved him."

The Merlin released a sigh and replied, "I too loved him."

Uriens turned away, attempting to suppress his anguish. Through his tears, he said, "I shall never forget him."

The Merlin raised a brow and said, "It is important that you do not. Keep the look of his eyes within your soul."

Uriens turned back around and looked at the Merlin with questioning eyes, but asked nothing. He knew somewhere deep within him that a day would come when he would fully understand the Merlin's words. He envisioned Uther, and suddenly his misery subsided. He smiled warmly and said, "How could anyone forget the eyes of the Pendragon."

⊂ℬ *Twenty-nine* ℰ⊃

Lot had immediately made his way home to Lothian, where Morgause anxiously awaited his arrival. She had already received word of Uther's demise, and could not wait to hear the details.

She was in the great hall sipping a fine wine in solitary celebration when one of the servants informed her that Lot was approaching. She quickly set the goblet aside and hurried out to greet him.

It was a blustery day, the wind whipping outside in gusts.

As he reigned in, she pulled her cloak tightly about her, and with great anticipation, rushed toward him. He slid from his saddle, and ignoring Morgause, went directly to his chamber.

She was stunned by his action, and stood outside for several moments before regaining her composure.

Then suddenly, she threw her hands up in the air and said, "Of course, he suffers from a case of remorse. I forget how spineless he truly is." She turned on her heel and went inside.

When she entered the chamber, Lot was kneeling at the

bedside, his forehead resting on his clasped hands.

Her hair was extremely wind-blown, her usual neatly coifed bun hanging limply to the side of her head. Loose strands hung lifelessly about her face giving her the look of a crazed woman as she laughed and said smugly, "How touching. He prays for forgiveness."

She sauntered across the room, and went to stand behind him. Lot had not moved a muscle.

She gave him a few moments, tapping her foot impatiently. Then she put her hand to her mouth in a mock yawn and said, "Could this 'praying' wait for another time?"

Lot did not respond, and she asked, disgruntled, "You were not fool enough to allow anyone to witness the act, I assume?"

His head remained lowered and his voice was strained with emotion as he replied, "God bore witness to my treacherous deed, and now I am forever damned!"

Morgause sighed, then said in a demanding tone, "Enough of your simpering. I grow impatient for the news."

Lot slowly raised his head, staring straight ahead, but he remained kneeling. He asked sarcastically, "What news would you like to hear? Would you care to know how much he bled? Or mayhaps you would like to know how much he suffered." He let out a deep breath. "What exact picture would you like me to paint for you?"

"I would like for you to describe the look on his face," Morgause replied, hatred in her voice, and in her eyes.

Lot's body began to tremble, as the haunting vision of Uther staring up at him in disbelief flashed across his mind. His inner torment was tearing him apart, and it was revealed in his voice as he said, "I cannot forget the look in his eyes."

"You truly have been affected by this," Morgause said, amused.

She laid her hand on his shoulder, and she spoke as if to

a child. "It will pass, and you will soon forget."

Lot spun around as he rose to his feet. He grabbed her wrist roughly, squeezing it tight.

Morgause's eyes were wide with shock, and Lot's glistened with unshed tears. He said through clenched teeth, his voice quivering with the intensity of what he was feeling, "I will not forget. It is branded in my soul."

He paused briefly, glaring at her, then said, "As my penance, I shall take that look to my bed every night for the rest of my life, and thereafter."

He pushed Morgause away from him forcefully, and she stumbled backward into the wall. She rubbed her wrist, staring at him, dumbfounded. She attempted to collect herself, but the look of shock already on her face intensified with Lot's next words. He seemed to spit them out at her as he said, "In truth my dear wife, I would prefer taking that to my bed than you."

He continued to glare at her for several moments, the sight of her revolting to him. Then he shouted, "Get out!"

Morgause made no move. Her mind was confused. "What of Tintagel?" She questioned.

"Tintagel?" Lot repeated, finding it hard to believe she could speak the words. "Tintagel will never be yours!" He growled. "Now get out of my sight!"

Morgause did not know whether to try his patience or not. She had never seen this side of him. She decided to push a little further, and in a sugary, meek tone asked, "But, what about the throne? Should we not attempt to..."

She stopped mid-sentence, the look of fiery rage in Lot's eyes unnerving her. She cautiously stepped past him and headed for the door.

He waited until he heard the sound of the door opening, then turned around and said coldly, "You will no longer be sharing this chamber. Choose another. But make sure there is enough distance between us that I never have to look upon you."

Morgause stood in the doorway, staring at him in bewilderment. The thought crossed her mind to try to sway him, but as she opened her mouth to speak, she reconsidered. Instead, she swallowed hard, stepped back and pulled the door shut.

Lot stood staring at the closed door for several moments, then dropped to his knees as Uther again appeared in his vision. He cried out, "Dear God, please help me to forget!" Then he put his face in his hands and wept.

❧ Thirty ❧

Five long years passed before the Merlin returned to wake Excalibur from its place of rest.

Ygraine was kneeling at her bedside in prayer when he silently entered the cottage. Her eyes were closed, and her back was to him, but she felt his presence.

Her hand was trembling as she reached out to touch the sword with her fingertips. She softly ran them over the hilt, then up and over the dragon's head, amorously caressing the eyes. After a moment, she drew her hand away and let out a deep sigh.

She was dressed in a long, white, woolen gown, and her hair was unbound, her long curls hanging to her waist. Her eyes were tear-filled as she rose and turned to face the Merlin, who stood just inside the doorway.

The room was dark, except for the glow of a single candle burning next to the bed. It sent out an ethereal, golden radiance that surrounded her, and for an instant it appeared to the Merlin to be Evanona who stood before him. His heart leapt momentarily at the sight, then quickly calmed, as he realized that it was indeed Ygraine.

He whispered, with a sense of appreciation, "Your years have brought the look of your mother to you."

A tear slipped down her cheek and she lowered her eyes saying, "I should have liked to have known her."

"Mayhaps in another time you shall," he said kindly.

"Mayhaps," she responded, as she raised her glistening eyes to his.

She smiled, but her eyes did not, and she turned away from him and sat on the bed. Again, she began to caress Excalibur, running her fingers gently up and down the length of it.

From behind her, in the dim light, the Merlin saw her tears as they fell onto the blade. He moved forward, and placed his hand on her shoulder. He could feel her sorrow beneath his touch, and he quickly pulled his hand away.

He took a couple of steps back, and there was a hint of emotion in his voice as he said, "I must take Excalibur... but I shall soon return." He paused, then said, "I will be accompanied by your son."

She rose and turned again to face him. She nodded, and her voice was strained as she whispered, "Please hurry, for the Pendragon awaits me."

Empathy filled his eyes, and with compassion he said, "For your heart, I tell you Ygraine, that Uther completely fulfilled his destiny. Though fate played a role in his life, it did not rule him. He never felt sorry for himself. Deep within, he accepted the outcome of his choices, and he lived his life with a passion that can only be justly rewarded."

The Merlin felt a gentle breeze brush past him, and the candle flame began to flicker. His eyes scanned the room quickly, and he said with confidence, "He does await his beloved."

Ygraine closed her eyes momentarily, lost in a feeling of tranquility as a feathery sensation flowed over her face. She smiled, and after a few moments, she opened her eyes. Her tears were no longer present. "What of Arthur?" She questioned.

A slight smile tugged at the corners of the Merlin's mouth, and he filled with pride as he replied, "As I once told you, Arthur will give justice to the Pendragon name. Because of his reign, Britain shall know peace for the first time. He will give the people something to believe in other than war by bringing spirituality to their hearts. He will give birth to a kingdom that only Heaven can match, where all will reside in oneness." He paused, his eyes lighting up. "That kingdom shall be called Camelot."

Ygraine closed her eyes, attempting to envision such a place. She smiled blissfully then opened her eyes and said, "I pray that you are right. I have a need to know that our suffering will give reward to others."

"And so it shall," the Merlin whispered, nodding as he gazed into her eyes. "And so it shall."

She held his gaze for a moment, then watched his every move as he walked to the other side of the bed and lifted Excalibur. Her chest tightened, and her throat constricted with pain as the sword left its resting place.

As he was moving passed her, she laid her hand gently on his arm to halt him. He stopped, and she bent to kiss the dragon's head. When she straightened there were tears spilling from her eyes, but her face was expressionless.

The Merlin took her hand and brought it to his lips. He kissed it tenderly, and said with genuine affection, "I honour you in a way that goes beyond words."

A sob escaped her lips, but her outer appearance remained unchanged. His eyes met hers briefly as he let her hand slip away from his. Her pain was still so evident, as was his own.

He drew in a deep breath and exhaled loudly, then said,

"I must go now. Britain grows eager for its new high king."

Ygraine nodded, and he took a couple of steps backward while staring at her. Then he turned and left.

She sat on the bed and stared at the empty space where Excalibur had been. She ran her hand slowly over the imprint that remained. The breeze again blew through, the candle flickering.

She smiled warmly and raised her eyes upward as she said lovingly, "It will not be long now."

ল *Thirty-one* ১

The Merlin had summoned all of the British Lords, petty kings, and the Scottish Lords Lot and Leodogranz to the Salisbury Plain near Amesbury. In his message to each of them, it was indicated that the rightful heir to the throne would be presented.

They would gather as requested, but the majority of them would do so out of nothing more than curiosity.

In five years time, Britain had become totally divided. The Lords and petty kings could not agree to follow anyone as high king. Therefore, they were forced to protect their own lands separately. Because of this, Britain was quickly losing its battle against a complete Saxon take over.

Arthur's noble identity had never been revealed to him. Although Viviane had taken the role of his Aunt, nothing more was ever disclosed. He had questioned her many times about his heritage, but was always given the same response. "You shall know all that is needed when the time is right."

Morgaine's wisdom and power had grown tremendously. She was being prepared to take Viviane's place as High Priestess of Avalon. However, many more years of training were necessary before Viviane would make the choice to cross over. She had to be absolutely certain that Morgaine was completely ready to fulfill her destiny.

Shortly before the Merlin's arrival on Avalon, Viviane spoke with Arthur privately in the chapel.

He had never before been permitted inside, and he entered cautiously. His eyes were wide with anticipation, as if expecting some cataclysmic event to take place.

Viviane was standing behind the altar, and she smiled, witnessing the expression on his face. She beckoned him forward with a gesture of her hand, and looking all around, he slowly made his way to her.

"Are you uncomfortable Arthur," she questioned softly.

His eyes were still wide as he replied, "No, not uncomfortable... but honoured."

"Ah," Viviane said proudly. "Spoken like a true king."

Arthur's head tilted to the side, his eyes questioning her remark.

She responded, "You have asked for many years who you are Arthur." She smiled warmly saying, "The time has come for you to know all."

The look of anticipation in Arthur's eyes intensified.

"Come Arthur," she urged, moving toward a stone bench against the wall to the side of the altar.

Arthur followed her, and as Viviane sat, he stood staring at the carved angel in the wall above her. A smile spread across his face and he also sat, but very near to her, as if her closeness was needed.

Viviane took his hands in hers and said, "I am the one that is honoured, for I have been blessed with a task that has brought great joy to my life."

She touched the side of his face with her cupped hand lovingly and whispered, "I have grown to love you dearly."

Arthur's eyes returned her sentiment, but he remained

silent.

Her hand returned to his, and her eyes held such warmth as she said, "Your father was a king, Arthur... a very proud and noble king. The last high king that Britain has known.

Arthur's mouth dropped open slightly, for he was in awe of what he was hearing, but also, something within him resonated with her words.

She noticed his demeanor and smiled, squeezing his hands. Then she said, "You are his heir Arthur."

His eyes widened, then he closed them for a moment. As he opened them, Viviane could see his acceptance of her words and continued on. "You were brought here to me for protection, and to be raised in such a way that you would acknowledge your spirituality."

Arthur's forehead creased, and he tilted his head. "Why did I need to be protected?"

Viviane sighed and released his hands, resting hers in her lap as she replied, "Because of the ways of mankind. There were those that would have sought to destroy you Arthur." She shook her head pitifully and said, "Deception runs rampant through the hearts of those who are power hungry."

His eyes again grew wide, and Viviane reached out to caress his cheek before saying, "Also Arthur, there are those that would have called you bastard, and would not have acknowledged you as the High King's heir."

"Why," he questioned innocently.

She replied, "Your mother was wed to another at the time of your conception. The Duke that I speak of was killed in battle the same night. Your parents were wed shortly after."

Arthur's brows drew together as he attempted to absorb what was being said.

"Some would think it wrong, what took place," Viviane explained. "But it was not wrong," she stated firmly.

"Destiny called to them, and they answered the call."

He lowered his head, in deep thought. Viviane lifted his chin gently with her fingertips and gazed into his eyes, her own filling with sorrow as she said, "Your parents loved one another deeply, and they suffered a great deal over the loss of you."

Arthur brought his hand to his chest, and it was as if he felt the grieving himself.

"Arthur." Viviane's direct tone gained his full attention. "It has been five years since your father's death, and no one has been accepted to succeed him. Britain is in dire need of a leader." She paused, taking in a deep breath and exhaling slowly. "They will accept you now."

Arthur swallowed hard and said, "I am not yet a man. How am I to be a king?"

"You will be well supported," Viviane reassured him. "There is a man that is wise beyond all imagination, and he will be ever present with you."

His eyes filled with wonder. "Who is this man?"

"He is called... the Merlin," Viviane replied, her face radiating warmth as she spoke his name. "He is bound to you by loyalty to both God, and blood. He is part of a great divine plan to bring about peace, and also Arthur, he is your grandfather."

Arthur took a deep breath and closed his eyes. He said softly, "I do not doubt any of your words, for something inside of me tells me they are truth."

He opened his eyes, and suddenly they showed amusement as he said, "I pray that both my grandfather and my country have patience, for I know not the first thing to do as High King."

Viviane smiled broadly, and she gently brushed his hair away from his forehead. "Ah, but you will Arthur. You have been chosen to fulfill the Merlin's prophecy and bring peace to these lands. The knowledge of how to do it will come easily and naturally. You will see." She paused, gazing into his beautiful blue eyes. "After all, the Pendragon blood runs through your veins. Therefore, you are already filled with your father's passion, and it will soon be awakened. It matters not that you are only fourteen years in age."

"Pendragon?" Arthur questioned.

"Yes Arthur," Viviane replied. "Your father's name was Uther Pendragon."

"Uther Pendragon," he repeated proudly, straightening his spine and holding his head high. Then suddenly a realization came to him. "My father has passed, but what of my mother?"

Viviane's entire being filled with warmth, and Arthur felt it in her words as she said, "Your mother is Ygraine. She is the daughter of the Merlin and Evanona, my dear, deceased twin sister. After your father's death, your mother returned to a sanctuary, where she spent her youthful years." She took Arthur by the shoulders, and her voice quivered slightly. "She waits for you Arthur, with great longing in her heart."

Arthur jumped to his feet, and he said with earnest desire, "I must see her."

Viviane rose, and she laid her hand gently on his arm. "You shall see her Arthur. But first you must ready yourself to leave. The Merlin arrives soon, and you must take this time now to meditate and prepare for the next stage of your journey that you are about to embark upon."

Arthur nodded slowly, and he turned away to leave. Impulsively, he spun around and embraced Viviane. There were tears in his eyes as he rested his head against the side of her face and said, "I love you, and I shall miss you ever so much."

"I love you, beloved Arthur," she whispered with great sincerity. "And when the time has come for you to cross over, I will be waiting for you."

He withdrew slightly, gazing into her eyes as she said, "You shall find respite in my arms, here in Avalon."

Arthur smiled and backed away from her, his eyes never leaving hers.

He left the chapel, and Viviane's heart truly ached. Not so much for herself, but for Ygraine. She shook her head in sorrow and whispered, "Your suffering is near over dear one. But first you shall embrace your son and fill him with all the love you have for him."

She sat back down on the bench, and Evanona entered her thoughts. She lowered herself to her knees, and she began to pray for all that had suffered for the sake of fulfilling destiny.

※※●※※

Arthur was waiting on the shore alone when the Merlin arrived on the barge. The Merlin did not disembark. In fact, he turned and faced the opposite shore. Arthur quietly joined him, and both remained silent as they crossed the lake from Avalon. They appeared as statues on the barge, standing erect, facing the shore ahead.

Arthur was in deep thought, feeling a bit forlorn as they drifted farther from the island. He was also somewhat baffled as he recalled his secret farewell to Morgaine in the woods. She had little reaction to the information he shared with her concerning his identity, which he found to be quite odd. She had simply said that she had always known that he was destined for greatness.

Then, as he bid her farewell, he bent and kissed her hand gallantly. As he rose, she smiled warmly at him, but soon took him completely by surprise. She stepped closer, and before Arthur knew what was happening, she kissed him passionately. Confused, he pushed her away from him.

Something inside of Arthur revolted at this show of affection that was so unlike Morgaine. He had deep feelings for her as well, but not in the way of lovers. Something within him also felt that, even though they parted with Arthur being mystified, he would see her again.

As the barge drew nearer to the shoreline, Arthur noticed two horses tethered to a post, and he knew that they were for himself and the Merlin. Arthur cleared his throat, and his body tensed.

The Merlin felt his reaction, and without looking at him said, "To be king you must first learn to bond with the spirited beasts that will hold your weight in battle."

Arthur replied candidly, "Bonding is no great feat... but riding may be."

The Merlin raised his eyebrows and said, "Hmmm, I had not thought about your lack of discipline in that area. I cannot present you to the nobility of Britain with you hanging onto the mane of your mount in fear."

Arthur pictured in his mind what the Merlin's words suggested, and the thought of it made him laugh aloud. As he did so, the Merlin looked at Arthur in dismay. Instantly, the Merlin received the same vision in his own mind and a deep, throaty sound emanated from his mouth that Arthur perceived to be laughter.

The Merlin immediately stiffened, his eyes taking on a look of bewilderment, as if the sound that came from his own mouth was foreign to him.

Arthur noticed the Merlin's reaction, and raised a brow, revealing Uther's identical mannerism. Then he laughed again, heartily. This time, the Merlin did not respond, but met Arthur's gaze, and for the first time in a very long time, the Merlin felt a spark of life in his heart.

The bonding that began on that day grew stronger with each passing day for the rest of Arthur's life.

ڡ ڡ • ڡ ڡ

By the time the Merlin and Arthur arrived in Amesbury, Arthur had, to the Merlin's astonishment, comfortably mastered the animal beneath him.

It was early dawn, and though it was midsummer, the wind blew in gusts as they rode across the plain. The skyline was tinted with shades of gold and orange, and in the faint light of the rising sun, Arthur could see in the distance a large mass of enormous stones. As they drew nearer, he noticed, to his amazement, that the stones were erect, as if standing, forming a circle.

Arthur's eyes were wide with wonder, and the Merlin smiled at his reaction and said, "The mighty nobles will not be easily convinced that you are the Pendragon's heir. They will need to see power beyond all conception." The Merlin nodded his head, a sense of satisfaction filling him. "We will show them what their mortal minds crave."

Reaching the stones, they dismounted and the Merlin proceeded to retrieve Excalibur from where it was strapped to his saddle. Arthur watched casually, but as the Merlin removed the cloth surrounding it, his eyes bulged as the sword's magnificence was revealed.

The Merlin walked into the center of the ring of stones and drove the sword into the ground. He beckoned Arthur to join him, and as he did, Arthur felt pressure in his chest, as if something were trying to free itself. He gazed upon the sword, and fell to his knees in front of it.

The Merlin raised his head high and said, "Arthur, meet Excalibur."

"Excalibur," Arthur whispered, a sense of wonderment and respect filling him as he visually drank in its majesty.

"This was your father's protector, and now it is yours," the Merlin explained. "He wielded it in the name of peace and truth, and you shall do the same."

Arthur put one hand around the hilt, the other around the pommel, embracing the dragon's head. The feel of it beneath his touch opened up a dam within his heart center. He wept deeply as the sword awakened, the energy within it entering his fingertips, and coursing through his body. He felt as though his heart was expanding in his chest, and although it was quite painful, he reveled in the pain.

The Merlin bowed his head, patiently waiting as the Pendragon vibration within Excalibur merged with Arthur's.

The sun continued to rise, the earth basking in its golden splendour.

After several moments, the Merlin broke the silence, saying in a resounding voice, "Rise Arthur."

Arthur slowly rose to his feet, his body trembling with the tremendous life force that he felt surging within him. He did not remove his gaze, nor his hands from the sword.

The Merlin commanded, "Raise Excalibur and make it one with you."

With one hand, Arthur pulled the sword from the earth's grasp.

The Merlin continued, his voice reverberating in a loud, deep tone. "You now walk this Earth as both Master and King. Show your power Arthur! Own it!"

With the strength of a man, Arthur raised the sword high into the air. He opened his mouth, and the sound that escaped came from the depths of his soul as he screamed, "I Am!"

The sun had fully risen, and its rays reached out to touch the sword, starting at the tip of the blade, and moving down its entire length. The metal shone brightly as it reflected the golden radiance from above, and the eyes of the dragon were again gleaming.

ৡৡ●ৡৡ

It was after noon when the nobles began to arrive. Arthur
sat astride his horse a short distance from the stones with
Excalibur in his hand. The power that he exuded was
tremendous, his entire being radiating the confidence that
he felt within. The Merlin stood proudly next to Arthur,
holding the reins.

One-by-one the noblemen dismounted. As they did, they
stood gaping in awe of what was before them. They began
to speak amongst themselves as to the impossibility of what
they were witnessing.

The Merlin and Arthur remained silent until the last of
the nobles, Uriens, arrived. His attention was drawn more
to Arthur than to the stones, and he reined in near Arthur. He
did not speak, but traced every part of his face with his eyes.
The corners of Uriens' mouth revealed a slight smile as he
gazed into Arthur's penetrating, blue eyes, which reflected a
memory of Uther. Uriens recalled Uther's words that were
spoken years before: "There will come a time when you
will look into the eyes of one who will remind you of me."
Uriens' smile broadened, and he looked at the Merlin,
nodding his head as he said, "Indeed."

The Merlin returned his smile, then led Arthur's horse to
stand in front of the stones, as the others were all closing in
quickly.

Arthur received many sets of glaring eyes at once, but he
kept his composure, his body erect in the saddle.

One of the Lords stepped forward and said in a sarcastic
tone, "So, this is supposed to be the son of the Pendragon,
eh?"

"This is the son of the Pendragon," the Merlin stated
firmly.

Leodogranz then came forth, and pointing at the stones

said, "I believe I speak for us all when I say that I cannot comprehend how these stones have appeared. But I am sure that you, Merlin the prophet, can explain."

The Merlin nodded and said with reverence, "It is a gift from the Universe... a symbol of unity. Look well upon them, for they represent each and every one of you."

They were all temporarily speechless, for the Merlin's words held great meaning for them all. They gazed upon the stones, then at each other.

Then Leodogranz spoke again. "What about the boy? You say that he is of the Pendragon. Do you have proof?"

The Merlin replied, "If I give you proof, will you follow him?"

Leodogranz shrugged. "I will follow him," he affirmed, then looked around at the faces of the others.

Hesitantly, they all nodded, but it was quite obvious that they did not believe that proof would actually be given.

The Merlin turned and winked at Arthur, then gave him a nod. Arthur slid from his saddle and carried Excalibur to the center of the stones with the Merlin following. The others all gathered around the outside of the stones, gazing in.

The Merlin's voice carried out to all as he took Excalibur from Arthur and said, "This was the Pendragon's sword, Excalibur. I am certain that you all recognize it."

Sounds of affirmation came from the crowd, and the Merlin continued. "It holds the Pendragon vibration within it from being wielded only by Uther. Only one who shares that vibration is destined to wield it again."

Leodogranz said, "I believe I understand your words, but how can you prove that this boy is such?"

"Watch closely," the Merlin said intently. Standing very straight and tall, he held the sword out in front of him and plunged it deeply into the ground.

Several of the nobles began to laugh, as it appeared that

the Merlin had just performed some great feat of strength, when to them, he obviously had not.

The Merlin raised a brow and gazed at them saying, "You would think that it would be quite effortless to retrieve this sword from where it stands, would you not?"

Some of them nodded, some shrugged, and many of them still chuckled.

With a tone of daring in his voice, the Merlin said, "Then you would not mind attempting to do so?"

One of the petty kings became annoyed and growled, "What kind of game is this you play?"

The Merlin replied in earnest, "I assure you sir, this is no game. Mother Earth will not release her hold on Excalibur unless the Pendragon vibration is within the hand of the man retrieving it." He paused, then said, "She is stronger than all of you put together. Would you like to test your strength against hers?"

His words were taunting, but the nobles were still unbelieving, and many of them were anxious to be done with this foolishness and be on their way. However, Leodogranz came forth and said, "I see no reason not to make this attempt. If what you say is true, then I will not be able to retrieve the sword. But if I do retrieve it, what then?"

"You will not retrieve it," the Merlin stated with conviction.

Leodogranz stepped into the center of the stones and positioned himself in front of the sword with a great show of arrogance. He grasped the hilt and pulled hard. The sword did not budge. The look on his face revealed to all watching, his confusion. He tried again, pulling with all his might, but his attempt was fruitless. A third try left him completely breathless.

He stepped back and stared at the sword in bewilderment. Now the others were more than eager to have their try, and one-by-one they did so, but to no avail.

All the while Arthur remained at the Merlin's side, standing in silence, his gaze fixed upon Excalibur.

Uriens was the last to come forward. He gazed upon the sword, but did not attempt to retrieve it. He turned to Arthur instead, and there was deep sentiment in his voice as he said, "You have the eyes of the Pendragon. I do not doubt your worthiness. Therefore, I do not need to test it."

The others looked on in amazement as Uriens knelt before Arthur, bowing his head and saying, "I swore fealty to your father, and my dear friend. I now swear my loyalty to you, his son." He gazed up into Arthur's eyes and asked, "What name have you been given?"

Arthur lifted his chin high and replied, "My given name is Arthur, and I choose to honour my father's surname of Pendragon."

Uriens took Arthur's hand and placed a gentle kiss upon it. Then he again gazed up into Arthur's eyes and nodded appreciatively.

The voice of Leodogranz forced them to break eye contact. "You may be sure of this boy's identity Uriens, but I am not. He needs to retrieve the sword."

Uriens smiled as he rose, and he moved aside so that Arthur could have his chance.

Arthur stepped forward, taking hold of the hilt firmly in his hand. The sword was easily lifted from Mother Earth's grasp, and Arthur held it high, his presence emanating the pride that he felt.

"I want to try again!" One of the Lords cried out.

"You may all try again," the Merlin replied lightly, but his expression revealed his knowledge that it was but a waste of time.

He took the sword from Arthur and again plunged it into the Earth.

Each tried again, but none could retrieve it. When they had all practically exhausted themselves in their attempts, Arthur again came forth and freed it with no effort at all.

The Merlin slowly scanned the faces of all present, then said, "This boy is your only hope."

Uriens had tears in his eyes as he again dropped to his knees in front of Arthur.

The others remained indecisive. After what they had witnessed, there was no doubt that Arthur was the rightful heir to the throne. However, none of them possessed the fortitude to step forth and follow Uriens' lead.

Lot was present, but had remained mounted and distanced somewhat from the rest. He had not taken his eyes from Arthur since his arrival, and now he made his way forward. Without hesitation, he dismounted and entered the ring of stones. His eyes were tear-glazed as he dropped to his knees next to Uriens and extended his hand out to him.

Uriens clasped Lot's hand firmly and held it, as all of the nobles, without further delay, came forth simultaneously. Kneeling one next to the other, they clasped hands until there was a complete circle around Arthur and the Merlin.

ℭꝶ Thirty-two ℰꝺ

Arthur would take his father's home in Viroconium for now. But before any arrangements would be made, he felt the urgent need to visit his mother.

The Merlin and Arthur journeyed to the sanctuary immediately following Arthur's acceptance to the throne at the sight of the enigmatic stones.

They arrived near dusk, and the Merlin awaited Arthur in the receiving room, giving mother and son the privacy that he knew was needed.

The red glow from the setting sun spilled in through the window of the cottage, cascading across the room to the doorway. Its gentle rays settled on Ygraine as she lay resting on her bed.

A light rap on the door caused her to sit upright. She swung her legs over the side of the bed, and facing the door, she called out softly, "Please enter."

The door opened, and Ygraine's breath caught in her throat. She held it, and her eyes welled up with tears while drinking in the sweet sight of her beautiful child, the suns ruby rays illuminating his presence.

She let out her breath, and her chest felt as though it was being crushed. Her hand covered her rapidly beating heart, and a tear slipped down her cheek.

They just stared at each other for several moments, as they were both beset with their emotions.

Ygraine took a deep breath, and her voice quivered as she said, "I have waited so long to look upon you my son."

She paused, attempting to normalize her breathing. "I never even held you in my arms," she cried, raising her empty arms in reference.

Arthur felt her love pouring into him from across the room, and his voice also trembled as he said, "You may hold me now mother." He grinned, and his uncanny resemblance to Uther was clearly discernible.

Noticing the extreme likeness, Ygraine sucked in her breath sharply and brought her hand to her mouth.

Arthur rushed to her. He dropped to his knees and she embraced him, holding his head to her breast and rocking him gently. Tears poured from her eyes as she felt the warm breath of her beloved son close to her heart.

He remained in her arms for quite some time. Neither of them wanted to release the other, both enmeshed in the bonding that was taking place.

Finally, Ygraine reached down and cupped his chin in her hand, drawing his face up so that she could look at him fully. She smiled and kissed his cheek tenderly, then gazed into his phenomenal eyes. "You have your father's eyes," she cried.

"And my mother's heart," Arthur whispered.

Her weeping increased, for the words he spoke touched her more deeply than he could have imagined.

She stroked the side of his face, and through her tears, she said, "I am proud of you. You will give justice to the Pendragon name and accomplish what your father tried so desperately to do."

A sudden chill surrounded them, and a gentle breeze brushed passed her. Ygraine let out a dreamy sigh, then smiled and said, "He is with us now, and although you may not feel it, he embraces you."

Arthur shivered and replied, "I do feel him, for his presence is strong, as he was."

"Yes," Ygraine whispered, closing her eyes and envisioning her beloved King. When she opened her eyes, the Merlin was standing in the open doorway. She smiled at him and mouthed the words "Thank you."

The Merlin nodded and came forward. He stood behind Arthur, who was still kneeling in front of Ygraine and said, "Arthur will be well... I promise you."

Arthur rose and took Ygraine's hands in his. He smiled warmly and said, "I will come often to see you, and when I have ended all the wars, you shall come and live with me in my kingdom."

Ygraine nodded, but her tears flowed, for she knew in her heart that she would not see her son again in this incarnation.

She kissed him on the cheek again, desperately trying to hold back her tears, and Arthur slowly backed away.

The Merlin leaned close to Ygraine and whispered, "I shall return when the Pendragon comes for you."

She smiled, and the Merlin's arm encircled Arthur's shoulders as he guided him toward the door. When they reached it, Arthur pulled away and ran back to Ygraine.

She stood and drew him into her arms. She ran her fingers through his hair, and breathed in the scent of it. As he pulled back slightly, she slowly ran her fingertips over his face, then kissed his forehead, each cheek, and then gently upon his lips.

As he looked at her, his eyes of the Pendragon penetrated

her soul as he said with all his heart, "I love you mother."

She brushed the hair away from his forehead and whispered, "And I you, Arthur the Pendragon."

He beamed, filling with an even stronger sense of pride at the sound of his full name being spoken for the first time.

Then stepping back, he unsheathed Excalibur, holding it out before her. His stature and his voice revealed his pride as he said, "I would be most honoured if the Queen of Britain would acknowledge me formally as heir to the High King's throne."

Ygraine's chest once again constricted as her emotions came rushing to the surface.

Arthur knelt before her, bowing his head reverently as he continued to hold the sword out before him with both hands.

Ygraine swallowed hard, took a deep breath, and reached for the sword. The Merlin watched in awe, as Ygraine took the hilt between both her hands and silently called upon all her strength before raising Excalibur above Arthur's head.

Her voice held the tone of one who was bred to royalty as she spoke. "I call upon all Gods and Goddesses as my witness, for they are all One. As Queen of Britain, I hereby grant succession of the High King's throne to the one, and only heir of the Pendragon."

Her arms were shaking from holding the weight of the sword as she touched the tip to each of Arthur's shoulders.

Then she lowered the tip slowly to the floor, and Arthur raised his eyes to meet hers as she said proudly, "Long live King Arthur."

Arthur rose, and their eyes locked in a loving gaze as he said, "Long live the Queen."

Ygraine smiled and leaned over to place a gentle kiss upon the dragon's head of Excalibur before Arthur slid it back into its sheath.

Arthur returned her smile, and his eyes adored her as he slowly backed away.

The Merlin gazed at her from across the room, and their eyes met. His words were penetrating, and they held such depth of meaning to her as he said, "Know that you are loved."

She smiled as she placed her hand over her heart, releasing a deep sigh.

The Merlin stood gazing at her for several moments, then he and Arthur departed.

Ygraine stared at the closed door, and when she was certain that they were gone, she laid back down on the bed. The candle began to flicker as the breeze blew gently across her. She closed her eyes, enjoying the peaceful feeling washing over her. She sighed and whispered contentedly, "Now I am ready."

❦ *Thirty-three* ❧

Ygraine passed within the month, and as the Merlin had said, he came to her.

The single candle burned next to the bed, and the full moons' light shone brightly through the window, illuminating the otherwise darkened room.

Mother Marta, still abbess, although quite aged, sat in a chair near Ygraine praying quietly.

The Merlin entered silently, and he stood in the doorway gazing across the room at Ygraine's peaceful face as she lay dying in her bed. Her eyes were closed and she appeared to be sleeping soundly. He could feel a lump beginning to form in his throat, but he remained outwardly calm as he walked toward the bed.

Mother Marta smiled warmly and rose to her feet to greet him. She extended her hand and he took it between both of his, squeezing it gently. With great affection he brought it to his lips and placed a soft kiss upon it. She had been loyal from beginning to end, and his respect for her ran deep.

He released her hand, and with compassion, she patted him on the shoulder, revealing her affinity for him in return.

Then she moved past him toward the door.

As soon as she was gone, the Merlin knelt on the floor at the bedside. He rested his clasped hands on the blanket near Ygraine's hand.

Ygraine was extremely weak, her breathing very shallow. Although she had no physical illness, and it would seem as though she were dying of a broken heart, the Merlin knew that she had simply chosen to leave her body.

His eyes roamed over her face and he had an overwhelming desire to place a kiss upon her forehead. Surrendering, he began to lean forward slowly, and Ygraine opened her eyes. Immediately he withdrew, but the warmth remained in his eyes as he gazed into hers.

She was pleased to see him. She smiled, then ran her tongue slowly over her parched lips.

Instantly, he retrieved the glass of water from the bedside table, and helped her to partake of it.

She smiled again, her eyes revealing her gratitude, then wasted no time questioning him. In her last hour of life her children were foremost in her mind. "Is Arthur well?" She inquired.

"Arthur is quite well," he assured her, placing the glass back on the table.

"Is Morgaine well?" She asked, knowing that he would possess that knowledge.

"She is well also," he affirmed. "But Morgaine may not fulfill her destiny."

Ygraine sighed sorrowfully, and there was a hint of disappointment in her voice as she said, "I feared as much."

"I have not given up hope however," the Merlin stated, taking her hand in his to offer her comfort. "Her soul is very powerful."

Ygraine sighed again and said, "I had a vision once of she and Arthur together. I felt that she would deceive Arthur one day."

The Merlin nodded slowly. "It will be deception... but the deception will occur out of her love for Arthur."

Ygraine closed her eyes, his statement causing her to momentarily revisit her last vision. It was as if the Merlin had gone back with her, for his next words were spoken as if he were seeing the intimacy that was witnessed years before as well. "Morgaine will bear Arthur's child... a boy child."

Ygraine opened her eyes as he continued, "Because of him, Arthur's life will turn to turmoil. But not until after he has done all that he has chosen to do."

Ygraine took a long, weary breath, sorrow coming to her eyes. "Camelot will fall, will it not?"

The Merlin also let out a sigh and replied, "Yes. But there will be peace for a time."

Tears welled up in Ygraine's eyes. "Why?" She asked pleadingly. She took another deep, laboured breath. "After all that we have been through... why?"

The Merlin answered frankly, "Mankind is not ready for Camelot. They may end the wars, but their battles within themselves will continue to rage."

He shook his head sorrowfully and said, "Man suffers from greed. If there were but one seedling left on this Earth, they would fight for possession of it, rather than nurture it so that it may grow and be shared."

He paused, then said, "Greed was Uther's fatal slayer."

Ygraine's heart wrenched and she closed her eyes again briefly, a tear slipping down her cheek.

As she opened them, the Merlin gently wiped the tear away and said, "Unfortunately, Arthur's time here will end for the same reason. His own son will seek to possess the kingdom, and in so doing, will destroy it."

Then his gaze penetrated her soul as he said, "And so it will be Ygraine, that Camelot was born of betrayal, and so shall it fall."

Her eyes overflowed with tears, and they spilled forth as she grew weaker. "If I had only waited," she whispered.

The Merlin felt her remorse and squeezed her hand as he said compassionately, "Have no regret. It serves no one."

His words were soothing, and she let out a sigh of relief. Her tears subsided and she closed her weary eyes.

There was a sudden heaviness in the air, and the Merlin felt a chilling presence lingering. Ygraine smiled blissfully, as she felt the presence also. She began to let go, feeling as if she were drifting away.

The Merlin quickly leaned in closer, squeezed her hand again, and whispered her name. Hesitantly, she opened her eyes. Leaning very close, he gazed directly into their depths, speaking with an urgency. "At your birth, you and I made a pact Ygraine... and now on your deathbed, I ask you to make another."

"Yes?" She questioned weakly.

He replied, "When mankind is ready, you and I will return. We will do it all again, and Camelot shall be reborn."

Ygraine's heart exploded with love for this man, whom she once loathed. A loving smile slowly spread across her face and she whispered, "Yes father, we shall do it all again."

The Merlin released her hand and quickly retrieved the pentacle from inside his cloak. He leaned over her and clasped the now unbroken chain around her neck. "This is the Star of Prophecy," he whispered, holding back his own raging emotions. "It belonged to your mother. It will return with you."

Ygraine wrapped her fingers around it tight, and she again smiled affectionately at him as the eternal breath of life seeped from her body.

Suddenly the shadowy form of Evanona appeared behind the Merlin. She spoke, but her words were not heard. "I know how it feels, my precious daughter, to wait so long to hold your child in your arms, as I wait to hold you now."

Just then, Ygraine closed her eyes, and the Merlin leaned forward, placing a tender kiss upon her brow.

Evanona laid her hand gently on the Merlin's shoulder, and he stiffened as he felt her presence. Then as he withdrew, Ygraine's head fell limply to the side.

He immediately gathered her up into his arms, and he wept openly as all the years of sorrow that had been locked inside of him, poured forth.

An intense gold flash of light appeared near Ygraine's hand, Uther's armlet visible for only a split second.

"It matters not how long it takes, I shall wait... and I will find you."   Just as he had promised, her Pendragon was indeed waiting for her.

Epilogue

THE REIGN OF KING ARTHUR SPANNED MANY YEARS. HE FULFILLED THE MERLIN'S PROPHECY, AND HIS DESTINY, AND BROUGHT PEACE TO BRITAIN.

ARTHUR BUILT HIS KINGDOM OF CAMELOT WHERE HE LIVED WITH HIS QUEEN, GWENHAFAR.

MORGAINE LEFT AVALON, AND YGRAINE'S VISION EVENTUALLY BECAME A REALITY.

MORGAINE BORE ARTHUR'S SON, MORDREAD. WHEN HE WAS GROWN, HE SOUGHT TO CLAIM CAMELOT. AS A RESULT, CAMELOT FELL.

ARTHUR PASSED IN THE ARMS OF VIVIANE, THE LADY OF THE LAKE. HE RESTS IN AVALON WITH EXCALIBUR... UNTIL IT IS HIS TIME TO COME AGAIN.

To contact the author call or write the publisher at

Ms. Lacey Hawk
4440 Vicobello Ave.
Las Vegas, NV 89141-4254

1-702-407-1718